SHARD

by

James R. Benn

SHARD

ISBN: 978-1-7379472-0-2   Print Paperback
ISBN: 978-1-7379472-1-9   E-Book EPUB

Book Interior and E-book Design by Amit Dey | amitdey2528@gmail.com

Also by the author

Dedication

For my wife, Deborah Mandel.

*Hear my soul speak. Of the very instant that
I saw you, Did my heart fly at your service.*

The Tempest – Act 3, Scene 1

Chapter 1

"Let's take a walk."

Ethan Shard beckoned Skitter to follow him, his head inclined toward the rice-paper door of their hut. They rose half-way, their bodies hunched in deference to the sloping roof, barely five feet high at the edges. They didn't bother straightening at the center pole, since the hut was circular, and the flimsy door was only five feet high as well. Heads bowed, they stepped over the supine bodies of their hut mates, who groaned and cursed quietly, so quietly that their passions and pains hardly broke the surface, tamped down under plumes of frosted breath.

Skitter danced across the twelve-foot room, his feet finding the small, bare spaces between bodies, avoiding the straw mats that marked the tiny boundary of each man's territory. He was quick, small, and wiry enough to move with a certain grace even in this dark, cramped, and cold place. He reached the door two steps ahead of Shard and slid the rickety wooden frame open, drawing it shut behind them before the men inside could summon up a complaint about the sharp blast of wind laced with gritty dust.

"Where we going?"

"Anywhere," Shard said, and they both gave a harsh snort of laughter, settling into a determined stride on the well trod path along the wire, toward the high ground and the crumbling cliff face where refuse was dumped. Skitter knew he would follow Shard without hesitation. It was a habit born out of greed and glory, solidified in terror and survival. They stood, looking out over what little was left of the garbage pile. After being picked clean by guards and prisoners, then scavenged by civilians who trudged up the hill from the village below, it wasn't much. Huts only marginally better than those housing the Americans were scattered along the valley floor, surrounded by fields where busy families worked the ground to prepare for planting.

"Hardly the Ginza, Skitter."

"It ain't hardly anything, Shard. This whole damn country ain't worth shit," Skitter said, sitting on a rock, intently watching one of the villagers below. A young woman, obvious even at this distance. Skitter's eyes lapped her up, not out of lust, but in hopes of keeping the memory of lustful things alive. Shard sat next to him, lifting his head to the sky, willing the clouds to part and grace his face with warm sunshine. It was springtime, but early spring in North Korea was nothing but the cold grayness of a lingering winter's harshness. "Now Japan, that's something else. We were kings there, remember?"

"Yeah," said Shard. "I remember." It was what he said every time. Conversation was all the living had left, and by now there was little hope of saying anything new. They spoke their lines like actors, playing their parts and wondering if the play would ever end.

March 1950
Tokyo, Japan

They met on the Ginza. Not met, collided, right in front of the Hattori department store, which served as the main PX for GIs in Tokyo. Shard was standing on the sidewalk, lighting a cigarette and wondering how to spend his evening. He was tall and lanky, which made it easy for him to see over the heads of the crowd and spot the ripple of trouble headed his way. A little American sprinted out of a side alley, nearly losing his balance as he turned and ran into the crowd, head down as if to bury himself in the mass of pedestrians. Shard watched the commotion, eyeing the three Japanese who followed, arms pumping, pushing aside everyone, even GIs in uniform. Not the usual Japanese behavior, not these days at least. Shard lost sight of the American, and as he watched the Japanese, the little guy burst out from between two sailors and took Shard down like a linebacker.

"Sorry, buddy," the speedster said, helping Shard stand while placing himself behind the bigger man. "There's some guys after me." Shard watched the crowd part as the Japanese men came toward them. Two glowered with such vehemence that even other Americans, these lords of occupied Japan, faded away. The man in the center, wearing a leather jacket and a scar along his jawbone, stood close to Shard but kept his dark eyes zeroed in on the little GI.

"You cheat," he said. "You owe."

"Akira, please understand, I'm the one who's been cheated. I had no idea those boxes were stuffed with newspaper. But this isn't the place to discuss business, is it? My associate here has a line on five hundred pounds of sugar. We were just about to check it out." The nervous GI, still a half step behind the bigger man, put his hand on Shard's shoulder.

"You owe," Akira said in a low growl, giving Shard a quick glance. "Five hundred?"

"Yeah, yeah. I'll call you tomorrow and we'll straighten this out. Okay?" Skitter grinned, as if he were doing Akira a big favor. He inclined his head, as if to look deeper into Akira's mind. His dark eyes darted back and forth, surveying the landscape of the thug's face, his feet shuffling back an inch or so, ready to bolt if need be.

"You pay," Akira said. "Tomorrow." He vanished into the crowd as it surged along the sidewalk.

Shard shook the hand off his shoulder. "First, I don't have five hundred pounds of anything. Second, what the hell was that about?"

Before he answered, the GI glanced around, checking the faces in the crowd, wary of more toughs or maybe the MPs. "Akira's with the Ozu Gang. Heard of them?"

"Yeah, sure," Shard said, eyeing the other fellow more closely. "They run the black market in Shinjuku. Hey, don't I know you?"

"Maybe. I seen you around the base," the guy said, his eyes narrowing as he took in Shard's casual, knowing reference to the gang. And his broad shoulders. A strong one, tall, trim and in shape, not pudgy like a lot of the young men who gorged on army chow while pulling easy occupation duty. "I'm with the Quartermaster Company. Head clerk."

"Yeah, that's where I saw you," Shard said, remembering the private he'd given a stack of requisitions to the week before. Could have been for five hundred pounds of sugar for all he knew. "Well, good luck with that Akira fellow. And the sugar."

"Hey, let me buy you a drink. Least I can do." Shard knew what he meant. Although he hadn't lifted a finger, he'd stood toe to toe with Akira, who looked like he could make tough guys edge away with little more than a glance. Shard shrugged. He hadn't made up his mind about the evening, so why not?

"Sure. Name's Ethan Shard."

"Elliott Skinner. But they call me Skitter. Come on, I know a place."

"I bet you do," Shard said.

It was a pachinko parlor, a gambling dive lined with pachinko hardware, the Japanese version of slot machines. These were smaller than the American ones and used tiny chrome balls that zipped through a maze and made a crackling metallic sound that filled the dim smoke-filled rooms. Two US Army privates in their khaki uniforms were out of place. They attracted curious glances from the few customers who weren't gazing into their pachinko. Skitter entered a back room, dimly lit and empty of the noisy machines. He was welcomed with bows, handshakes, and laughter. Skitter spoke a few words of Japanese and gave a low bow himself, and Shard was impressed. The kid knew how to behave, even if it was only good business. They were shown to a table and cold beers appeared. American beers, like at the PX.

"How'd you get the nickname, Skitter?" Shard asked, wiping the foam from his lips.

"On account of how I move, I guess. I can get in and out of places real easy, always could."

"Ever get caught?" Shard asked.

"Only once. Which is why I'm here today," Skitter said, opening his arms to take in the pachinko parlor, Tokyo, and all of Japan. "I got nailed coming out of a grocery store with a side of beef. Damn thing was bigger than I was. The judge said the army or prison. Wasn't a hard choice. How 'bout you? What are you doing in the army?"

"I didn't have a good reason to do anything else," Shard said, his eyes drifting away, closing that line of questioning.

"I love the goddamn army," Skitter said. "It brought me to the land of opportunity. Business is good, know what I mean?"

"Like at the PX today?"

"That was a little mix-up. Someone got greedy and lifted a dozen cartons of smokes from a shipment. I'd never stiff the Ozu Gang. No percentage in that. I'll make it up to Akira."

"How? Steal some army sugar?"

"Yeah," Skitter said. "You got any problems with that?"

"You mean scruples?"

"Scruples? What the hell are scruples?"

"Never mind," Shard said, a fraction of a smile playing on his lips. "No, I don't mind a little breakage here and there. Uncle Sam's got plenty, the way I see it. Hell, every officer I know sells his liquor on the black market. They make a fortune doing it."

"No kidding," Skitter said. "No reason we shouldn't get ours, is there? What's your job on base?"

"Motor pool," Shard said. "I drive a deuce-and-a-half."

"Man, this is your lucky day, truck driver," Skitter said, his grin growing wide. "I'm branching out, and I need a partner. Someone your size and smarts, with wheels. Feel like making some money?"

Shard felt like it. Most guys in the Occupation Army did, but it was mostly small potatoes. He was looking to make the big score, and so was Skitter. A partnership was born in that pachinko parlor, sealed with a handshake and the clink of sweating beer bottles.

It didn't take them long to prosper. Using bribes, phony orders, falsified requisitions, and pure bluff, Shard and Skitter moved pallets of salt, sugar, chocolate, soap, beer, C-Rations, and a couple of hundred mattresses for a whorehouse out in Roppongi. All from army warehouses, delivered on army trucks, to the Kanto Ozu Gumi gang. Even scar-faced Akira smiled when he saw Shard and Skitter coming.

Their officers were oblivious. This army wasn't the one that had won the war back in '45. Except for a few career soldiers, the veterans were all back home with jobs, wives, and kids. This was the Occupation Army of 1950, a few hundred thousand young men with a compliant population, riches packed in warehouses, a desire for adventure, and time on their hands. The Japanese people welcomed the black market and the goods it provided. The gangs, with the politicians in their back pockets, ran it all and didn't do a half bad job of providing food and other necessities for the populace.

In the first month of their partnership, Shard and Skitter did well. By the end of the second month, they'd gotten rich. They weren't the only ones. The army reported in *Stars and Stripes* that the monthly remittances back to the States exceeded the entire monthly payroll of the US Army in Japan. Everyone was in on the scam, either turning a blind eye or too dim-witted to join in.

One day Skitter and Shard ended up in Funabashi, out in eastern Tokyo. They'd delivered five cases of Scotch to a Yakuza brothel, a mammoth operation that served hundreds of GIs every day. It ran like an assembly line, so smooth that a soldier would take off his shoes at one end and pick them up, cleaned and shined, at the other when he left. They were offered some of their pay in services but declined and took the cash. The offer had put them both in the mood, and they agreed it was time for a party.

They found a couple of *pan pan* girls and took them for dinner and drinks to start off the evening. *Pan pan* girls weren't professional prostitutes and were less likely to carry any of the venereal diseases that made the Yakuza brothel a crapshoot. These were young girls, mostly from rural areas outside Tokyo, who liked to dress in western clothes, go out on the town with Americans, and earn some yen in exchange for sex. No pimps, no gangsters involved. Shard liked the American-style clothes the girls wore; it reminded him of home without breaking his heart.

It was a pleasant June evening, and they were soon drinking saké at a table outside a busy restaurant, laughing with the girls as they tried to communicate with bits and pieces of each other's language. Skitter was teaching them dirty words, and each time he whispered one they'd giggle.

A couple of GIs took a table next to them. They were the only other Americans in the place, and one of them leaned in their direction as he signaled for a waiter. "Hey, you guys hear the news?"

"What news?" Shard asked.

"The North Koreans. They attacked over the demilitarized zone. Thousands of 'em. Got the ROKs on the run." The

Republic of Korea troops—ROKs—were South Koreans, ill-equipped compared with the Russian-supplied North Koreans.

"Aw, we'll bomb the hell out of the goddamn Reds," Skitter said. "Maybe MacArthur'll drop the atomic bomb on the bastards. Worked last time around. Don't worry, they'll never make it to Japan. Not our problem."

The sergeant shrugged and ordered two beers. Shard drank his saké and wondered if Skitter wasn't a better thief than strategist. He tried to sound nonchalant about the prospect of war, but he couldn't carry it off the same way Skitter did. At the end of the evening, he gave his *pan pan* girl more money than was reasonable and left wondering what had possessed him to do that. Skitter was nowhere to be seen, but he knew how to take care of himself. Shard drove the truck back to the base with the overzealous caution of a man who'd had too much to drink and even more to worry about.

Reveille sounded at dawn. Not the distant reveille of a single bugle call, a good hour or so after the sun rose, which had been the lazy custom on the post for as long as either man had been there. This was reveille over the loudspeakers, harsh and insistent as the long shadows of sunrise crept over the parade ground. Noncoms with clipboards patrolled the barracks, calling out names and ordering men to fall out and get in formation. Shard was up and dressed in fatigues by the time his name was called, having known with a cynic's certainty it would be. He watched as one GI approached a sergeant and said with all sincerity that he hadn't had his coffee yet. Promptly ordered to drop and do fifty pushups, his arms quivered at twenty, he cried at thirty, and vomited at thirty-three.

"Jesus H. Christ," the sergeant said, shaking his head as his eyes settled on Shard. "Don't stand there like an imbecile, Private. Get these men into formation, now." Shard shepherded the bewildered men onto the field, watching as lines of GIs filed out of the other barracks. He spotted Skitter, who grinned like this was a great joke, and they'd all get hot joe and donuts when it was over. Prodded by the noncoms, the men formed up in sloppy lines as if they never had drill instruction. Most hadn't since basic training, and it showed.

"I am First Sergeant Hector Kelso," a voice boomed out from in front. First Sergeant Kelso, with six stripes on each sleeve of his crisply starched khaki shirt, stood with his hands on his hips and surveyed the mob of bleary-eyed men. "You men are being formed into a provisional infantry company to be shipped to Korea to fight the Reds. Your units have declared you nonessential, which means that you are either troublemakers, incompetents, or damned unlucky. I have been given one week to get you in shape, and I plan to make the most of it so you don't disgrace yourselves in combat." He did an abrupt about face and the buck sergeants organized the men into squads for physical training.

"Jesus," huffed Skitter as they ran along the airfield road, transport planes taking off in a constant stream, airlifting men and supplies to Korea. "This guy's likely to get us killed, Shard."

"I believe his idea is to keep the North Koreans from killing us, Skitter. Sounds sensible to me." Shard slowed his stride to stay with Skitter. The name notwithstanding, Skitter was built for sudden bursts of illicit speed, not this constant grueling pace around the huge runway. Sweat soaked his fatigues, tinged with the odor of saké and dissipation.

"Best way to stop that is to stay far away from Korea," Skitter spat out, then heaved in a lungful of air. "I know a guy."

"You always know a guy," Shard said, his arms pumping evenly.

"This is a guy with pull, but not the kind of pull I ever needed before. And I know he's hungry to make some dough. You know we got too much yen on our hands," Skitter said, gasping as he ran. "We can't send it all home, and even if we exchange on the black market, we'd have to smuggle the dollars out. And it won't do us much good if we're dead."

"We can put it in a Tokyo bank," Shard said. "Let it earn interest and get it when the fighting's over. They're only calling it a police action, not a war." Dust swirled at their feet. Skitter's arms flailed wildly as he struggled to keep in formation.

"Lemme talk to my guy. He's in G1."

"Personnel?" Shard asked, shouting above the sound of an incoming aircraft.

"Yeah. He can make things happen. It'll cost, though. Maybe Germany, how 'bout that? We'll find some nice blond girls over there for a change. Whaddya say, Shard?" They both looked up as a twin-engine C-47 came in for a landing. There were holes in the fuselage and part of the tail section was shot away. Ambulances raced along the tarmac to meet the aircraft at the far end of the runway, their flashing lights splashing the red painted crosses with the bright crimson color of fresh blood.

"Talk to him," Shard said.

The days ticked by. Calisthenics in the morning, followed by runs around the airfield. Weapons instruction, then the firing range. More running. By the third day Skitter managed to keep pace. He'd go off at night, negotiating with his pal in G1. The price they settled on was one thousand American dollars cash for each of them. That wasn't a problem.

On the fourth day, they were given bazookas at the firing range. They divided into two-man teams, one man to carry and fire the bazooka, the other to carry ammo and load. Shard and Skitter did well; they already knew each other, trusted the movements of their pal. Skitter would load the bazooka from the rear, tap Shard on his helmet and move away from the rocket blast, picking up another round as he did so. They became adept at hitting plywood targets out to one hundred yards.

"You boys are good," their instructor said, kneeling next to them as they waited for the targets to be set up again. "But watch yourselves out there. These bazookas are from the last war; those Russian tanks have damned thick armor. Go for a rear shot if you have to."

"Sarge," Skitter said, with a healthy regard for his own survival, "if we take a rear shot, that means the tanks have gone by us. We'll be surrounded."

"I'm just telling you," he said, "that the 2.36 inch bazookas are outdated. The new 3.5 inch model should be able to handle the Russian tanks just fine."

"When are we getting those?" Shard asked.

"Soon," was all he said. That night Shard read in the newspaper that the Defense Department had cut the new bazooka out of their budget before the war and was now scrambling to get the 3.5 model into production. Meaning it would be forever before they saw them in Korea.

On the fifth day, First Sergeant Kelso held small group instruction in hand-to-hand combat.

"Now this stuff will be useful anywhere," Skitter whispered to Shard as they sat cross-legged on the ground. He was attentive and even raised his hand when Kelso asked for a volunteer.

"To take out an enemy sentry silently," Kelso said, coming up behind Skitter, "approach his back and swing your left forearm against his throat, pressing hard on the Adam's apple." He took two steps and had Skitter in his grip. "Dig your right elbow into his right shoulder and place your right palm on the back of his head. Grasp your right biceps with your left hand and apply pressure. This will strangle him." Skitter's eyes widened as Kelso put the move on him. He was close to passing out, and his arms searched for a grip to get away from the first sergeant's embrace.

"If he still resists," Kelso said calmly, "move your right hand so that the edge of your hand presses on the back of his head. One quick sharp push and the pressure will break his neck." He placed the edge of his hand on Skitter's head, turning him so the group could see.

He let Skitter go and gave him a pat on the back. "Good job, son."

On the sixth day, Skitter handed over two thousand dollars to his G1 contact. Their transfers would come through the next day. They spent the night in their barracks, cleaning weapons under the watchful eyes of their sergeants. Each man had stashed rolls of cash in his gear, their nest egg for setting up operations in Germany or wherever their transfer took them.

Shard oiled his M1 rifle and sharpened his bayonet. He'd miss Japan, the easy duty and cheap prices, friendly civilians and their odd food. It had been an adventure. He knew in his gut that things would never again be so free and easy. He couldn't say why, but he couldn't shake the notion that something would go badly wrong. He checked his blade with his thumb, and blood welled up as the steel split his skin.

Chapter 2

April 18, 1953
Camp Eleven, North Korea

"That was almost three years ago," Skitter said, following Shard as he walked away from the overlook. "And I still hate that sonuvabitch with a passion."

"Took our two thousand and gave himself a transfer," Shard said, echoing the same complaint that Skitter trotted out nearly every day, his vehemence as strong as the morning they found out.

"I shoulda seen it coming," Skitter said, his head bowed in thought, as if this was the first time it had occurred to him. "He could have been sent to the front himself, so of course he'd look out for number one. It wouldn't make any sense to take a chance on our transfers; he might endanger his own paperwork. So he takes our money, and ships out that same morning. Except he's headed to the Panama Canal while we're on our way to Pusan."

"He gets the tropical paradise," Shard began.

"And we get the shaft," Skitter finished. It was a well-worn routine. "Where we headed?"

"Let's check the sergeants' compound, see if we can pick up any scuttlebutt."

"Those guys don't know anything," Skitter said dismissively. "No one does."

"Why don't you ask your buddy Comrade Yuan what's happening?" Shard said, his face going hard as he spoke the name.

"He's not my buddy, damn it! I wish you'd stop saying that."

"You should have never gone to those classes," Shard said, taking Skitter by the arm and turning him forcibly to face him. "It's not worth it."

"Sure it is," Skitter said, peeling Shard's hand off his arm. "The room's heated and we get rice with meat for lunch. Probably dog, but who cares? It's real meat. I wouldn't take it from the goddamn North Koreans, but the Chinese aren't as bad. Right?"

"Not as bad isn't the same as good," Shard said. He let go of Skitter's arm, smoothing down the fabric of the blue quilted cotton jacket, a gift from the peace-loving Chinese people, as they'd been told. They had passed the first winter dressed in the clothes in which they'd been captured, minus anything that the North Koreans had stripped off them. The quilted jacket and pants were warm, it was true. The food had improved slightly. But there was a reason for that, a sinister reason. Nothing happened in Camp 11 that didn't serve the interest of their captors. "Come on, let's see if we can find Shirt."

"Okay," Skitter said, casting a glance around at the other POWs who were starting to emerge from their huts. He quickstepped to keep up with Shard, hustling to stay within his shadow.

"You still hanging around that birdie, Shard?" Vic Callahan said, blinking away the darkness as he emerged from his hut.

"It's a free country, Callahan," Shard said, and they both smiled in spite of the question. Skitter turned away but didn't stray far from Shard's side. They stopped at the kitchen where Shard gave Horseface—a Chinese guard who got his name due to his equine features—a couple of cigarettes. Big ears, a long nose, eyes set far apart, and Horseface it was.

"What's for lunch, Horseface?" Shard asked, miming the motions of eating. Horseface spoke no English, or at least didn't let on that he did. The cigarettes were the price of admission: two American smokes for a ten-second walk through the kitchen, in the back door and out a side door. The rules had long ago been solidified. Don't take anything obvious, don't get caught. All the cigarettes in the world wouldn't save a POW who got spotted stealing food. And Horseface would beat you senseless while smoking your cigarette to cover up his own corruption.

Shard walked quickly, the Korean women who cooked their food keeping their eyes averted. They must steal, too, Shard thought, not blaming them, but wishing the guards would let the POWs cook their own food to minimize the pilferage. By the time he left through the side door, Horseface was lighting up with the other guard, a new kid who could be pliable and friendly one minute and cruel the next. This was a good minute.

"Jesus, you make me nervous every time you do that," Skitter said. "They see you and it's the turnip hole for you." Skitter jammed his hands in his pockets, jumping up and down to keep warm and work off his nervous energy.

"Come on," Shard said, picking up his pace and walking behind the woodshed, a three-sided structure where firewood for the cook stoves was kept. They squatted on the far side, shielded from the guards, the wind, and most of the wandering POWs. Shard produced a rice ball from his pocket. It was smaller than a tennis ball, a mixture of rice, millet seed, and an unidentifiable vegetable, and probably a twig or insect as well.

The two men huddled together, and Shard pulled the rice ball apart, a half cupped in the palm of each hand. Skitter held out his hands and Shard dropped half in, without losing a grain of the gelatinous ball. They ate in silence, focused on taking in each morsel, their heads bowed as if in prayer, their hands lifted as if to God.

"Thanks," Skitter said when he was done licking the palms of his hands.

"No need to thank me," Shard said. "I owe you."

"Wasn't nothing," Skitter said, looking away. It made him uneasy to think about Shard being in his debt. "You still think the sergeants got any scuttlebutt?"

"Shirt always knows what's going on. Always has, hasn't he?"

"You got that right," Skitter said, straightening up to catch the meager rays of sun that were beginning to break over the compound. "He knew that first day on the ship." He sighed at the memory.

July 1950
Transport ship, Sea of Japan

"We're in for it, boys," First Sergeant Kelso said, leaning against the rail of the transport ship and watching Japan fade into the distance. The sky was clear blue, the chow decent, the seas calm, but worry lined his face. A couple of

GIs walked away, not wanting to hear bad news, or maybe not wanting to think a man they'd come to trust had doubts about their survival.

Skitter edged away, but Shard grabbed him by the shoulder and moved closer to Kelso and the half-dozen men still gathered around. "Why, Sarge?"

"Plenty of reasons," Kelso said, spitting into the water. "We got no heavy weapons. They got T-34 tanks. They've massed forces for this attack, we're sending in units piecemeal. Task Force Smith went in to fight a delaying action south of Seoul and got themselves overrun with heavy casualties."

"What are we gonna do?" Skitter asked, his voice a hoarse whisper.

"Fight. There's one thing you got to remember out there," he said, turning to face the men. "You'll feel like running. Don't. It'll get you killed, and then your buddies will be killed. Don't give your back to the enemy. If you get an order to withdraw, do it in good order. If you don't, fight. Remember that." Kelso turned away, hands gripping the railing, his knuckles white. Shard heard him mumble something under his breath, curses maybe, or a prayer. Either possibility troubled him.

Shard didn't think much of prayers. He'd prayed as a kid. A lot. Nothing ever came of it but disappointment. Curses, he'd learned before he was ten, were a sign of pain to come.

They docked at Pusan, marching down gangplanks and onto waiting trucks. South Korean soldiers milled about, some with weapons, others without helmets or gear. They stared at the transport as if willing themselves aboard and away from the oncoming North Korean forces, fear etched into their faces. Small, neat buildings lined the road away from the waterfront. Walking wounded limped past them, making for the ships in the harbor. There was no organization, no military police directing traffic. Gaunt, hollow-eyed GIs with bloodstained bandages and filthy uniforms went in one direction, while First Sergeant Kelso's company with their freshly shaved faces and clean fatigues went in the other. Someone said they were going to a place called Sangju, to stop the North Koreans. Shard figured Sangju might be right, but not the part about them stopping anyone.

Trucks ground their low gears climbing hills, leaving the summer greenery of the coast behind. Hills turned to mountains and morning to dusk as the convoy labored through passes and switchbacks, the terrain growing increasingly barren, as if Korea grew rocks as a cash crop. After fifty or so miles, they passed through Taegu, a city with military vehicles parked everywhere. Artillery batteries were dug in behind ridges, and supplies were stockpiled under camouflage netting. Officers stood at a crossroads, watching the vehicles heading into the hills.

"Why ain't we stoppin' here?" Skitter asked, looking around as if someone might have a reasonable answer.

"Because there aren't any North Koreans here," Shard finally said, breaking the apprehensive silence. If officers were standing around out in the open, this was a safe place. And safe was not their destination. The trucks rolled on, picking up speed on a road along the river valley, then climbing again into the ever-present mountains. Numbed by fear of the enemy, the unknown, and the hard wooden benches, most men nodded off, holding their M1s tightly to their chests.

Skitter fidgeted, keeping Shard awake with his movements and constant questions.

"Think they'll have hot chow?"

"Where the hell are we, anyway?"

"I wish I was back in Tokyo."

"I can't wait to get to the front, I really can't. Maybe if I get a medal, they'll send me home."

Finally, Shard had had enough. "Yeah, they'll send you home in a box. Get some rest, it might be your last chance for a while."

"Funny," Skitter said, glad for any kind of response as darkness settled over the countryside.

The trucks lurched to a halt on a dirt road that had thinned out to nothing more than a cow track. Engines switched off, and in the moment of stillness before the men disembarked, low rumbles were heard echoing in the hills ahead.

"Shit, is that thunder?" Vic Callahan griped.

"Artillery," his buddy Mike Hanson said. "I'd rather get wet."

"Maybe it's ours," Callahan said. Nobody argued with that vain hope.

They formed up by the trucks, waiting for orders in the darkness. Listening to the rippling booms in the distance, each man wondered what it was like at the front where the shells were landing. Up there, the sound would not be as soft and yielding. No one would mistake it for a summer storm.

"Listen up," Sergeant Cooper said as he gathered the twenty men from their truck into a semicircle. Cooper was a buck sergeant, newly promoted. He'd been firm and in charge during their training. Now he looked anxious and had trouble clearing his throat. "First Sergeant Kelso is scouting out the path ahead. We're taking over a position up that hill." He stopped to cough and spit. "You men move ahead by twos and pick up bazookas from the truck in front of us."

"What hill, Sarge?" Callahan asked. "I can't see a damn thing out here."

"Get your bazooka, Callahan," Cooper said. "Let me worry about the hill." He looked worried enough for them all. It was pitch black, faint moonlight hidden behind thick clouds. Shard took a bazooka, and Skitter hefted two canvas rocket bags, each with three rockets. Shard went to grab another, but the corporal handing them out waved him off.

"Six rounds per team, that's all we got."

"What if we run out?" Skitter asked.

"You fire off six rounds at those T-34s and you're still alive, then run like hell," he said. "Come on, move it."

"Bastard," muttered Skitter as they followed Cooper up a rocky path, the bags heavy on his shoulders, along with his M1, ammo, field pack, and assorted gear. As eyes adjusted to the night, the man ahead became a dark form hunched over with the weight of weapons and weariness. Callahan stumbled, and Hanson nearly tripped over him, unleashing a string of curses.

"Shut the fuck up," Cooper hissed. "For all I know Kelso is dead and the NKs are waiting for us. Jesus Christ, don't you get it? This is the real thing. No second chances, godammit!"

"We know, Coop," Shard said in a low voice. "Won't happen again. Show us the way, okay?"

Cooper turned away from Shard's calm words, his foot slipping on loose gravel. Shard steadied him, his hand patting Coop's shoulder before letting go. Skitter wondered how he managed it, here in the middle of nowhere, in the pitch black, with the enemy waiting somewhere out there to kill them. He wanted to know how Shard could think of anything else but the fear he felt churning in his gut. Skitter gulped and felt the dryness in his mouth, almost choking on it. He'd never admitted it to himself before, but that was what had drawn him to Shard that day on the Ginza. He'd been scared of what Akira might do, but he'd done his best to hide it. When he slammed into Shard, it had been like hitting a rock in the middle of the road. Shard didn't move, didn't step back when Akira approached with his well-practiced look of menace. Skitter knew it wasn't an act. Shard took his measure of Akira and decided he wasn't worth as much as a flinch. It was like that now, the reassuring tone, the pat on the back. How did he do it? Skitter's legs shook, fear trembling them, daring them to be true to his nickname and take off, away from the danger and the strange enemy ahead.

They climbed farther up the winding trail, slipping and falling on stones and roots, their gear and curses creating a cacophony of sound, metal against flesh against rock. The night air turned cold as they sweated under their burdens, their lungs laboring in the thin air.

"Hustle, hustle," came the urgent whisper from Sergeant Kelso as he worked his way down the line, pulling the men forward, manhandling them up the steep incline. "Almost there."

It wasn't much of a destination. A ridgeline filled with foxholes and shell craters. Debris littered the ground ahead, a clearing of rocks and dirt that plateaued before beginning its descent. Figures sat in the darkness, visible by the once-white bandages many of them wore. Maybe fifty or so. Not far away, rows of feet stuck out from ponchos, as if a whole platoon had laid down in formation.

The dead.

"You four, with me," Kelso said, pointing at Shard and Skitter along with the other bazooka team, Callahan and Hanson.

"Is that the company we're relieving?" Shard asked as they waited for Hanson. "They look like they took a beating."

"Two companies," Kelso said. "Or what's left of them." Kelso led the four of them to a road that snaked beneath the ridge. It was a switchback, and curved around the side of hill, probably the same road behind the lines where the trucks had left them off. He pointed out a foxhole to Shard and Skitter, then took Callahan and Hanson about twenty yards further out.

"Christ," Skitter said, falling into the hole. "This thing ain't deep enough." It wasn't half the depth it should have been. Skitter and Shard dropped their gear and went to work with their entrenching shovels. The soil was loose, as if the hole had been filled in.

"Artillery," Shard said as he surveyed the ground and tossed dirt out of the foxhole. "Must have hit close and filled in it." His shovel hit something that wouldn't give, and he tried to dig around it. He scraped loose dirt away and finally made out what it was. An arm. Skitter gasped and backed up, trying to get out of the hole, but his boots scrambled against loose dirt, and he fell forward, stifling a scream.

"Help me," Shard whispered. "Let's get this poor bastard out and then we can finish. We need to dig out at the rear too. Don't want you falling back in when the North Koreans come for a visit."

"Yeah, okay," Skitter said. He didn't care how Shard stayed so calm. He liked it and that was enough. They worked on digging the body out, placing it well to the rear. Then they dug a narrow trench so they could get out quickly when they needed to.

"You boys all set?" Kelso said, appearing out of nowhere.

"Yeah," Shard said. "Found a body in here. Hope we make out better."

"Pay attention and you'll have a chance," Kelso said. "If the NKs come again, it will be straight down that road. The attacks today were all infantry, and our guys beat them back. But that was probably an advance force. When they return, it'll be with tanks. You'll have a clear shot, but wait as long as you can, okay?"

"Sure, Sarge," Shard said. "But we only got six rockets."

"I know. Like I told the other team, fire two, then move out and take up another position. You stay in this hole too long and you'll die here, like that poor slob."

"We just have to fire two?" Skitter said, faint hope catching in his throat.

"From this position," Kelso said. "Move up the ridge and fire two more. Then come into our positions. Hopefully, you can stop a couple of them before they get too close."

"And then?" Skitter asked.

"Well, we'll see," Kelso said. "There's a ROK unit on our left flank. They're attached to the 24th Regiment like we are. The rest of the 24th is on our right flank, on the next hill. So we're not alone out here, boys," Kelso said. "One of you keep watch at all times, understood?" They understood.

"I don't think I'd be able to sleep much anyway," Skitter said as Kelso faded into the darkness. They arranged their weapons, cut some branches from the spindly brush behind them to try and hide the freshly turned earth, and settled in to watch the road. Noises from the ridge had died down, a sign that the company had finished digging in and was waiting for dawn, an attack, or maybe a miracle.

"Think Kelso knows what he's doing?" Skitter said, after a few minutes of silence.

"Yeah," Shard said. "He fought the Japs in the last war. The only problem is the rest of us don't know much about combat."

"Hell, I only know how to get out of a fight," Skitter said.

"We follow orders," Shard said. "Remember what Sarge said about running. It gets people killed."

"Sure, sure," Skitter said. "All I'm saying is, once we fire off these rockets, we can move out, right? If all hell breaks loose, we can probably take that road right in front of us."

"Don't you think there's a reason why we came up that trail and not the road?" Shard asked.

"Oh yeah. Why?"

"Because it's probably mined," Shard said. "Why don't you get some shut-eye? You can spell me in an hour."

"Okay," Skitter said, scrunching himself down into the earth like a burrowing animal. He closed his eyes, but fear rose up from his belly, and he knew he had to stay connected to Shard, a guy he could count on. "So where you from, anyway? I never thought to ask."

"Tokyo, and I wouldn't mind being back there now," Shard answered in a low voice.

"Naw, you know where I mean. Where are your folks from?"

"Ohio," Shard said.

"The guy in Personnel was from Ashtabula," Skitter said. "You know the place?"

"No," Shard said, with a faint smile invisible in the night. "That's up by Lake Erie. We're from down south. Little place called Blue Rock. Not even a real town, only some farms near the river and a gas station."

"You got family there?" Skitter asked. He had never asked Shard about his past before. They'd had too much future to look forward to. Tonight, things looked a little different.

"Not so it matters. How about you?"

"Michigan. Place called Lewiston, way north of Flint. Lots of big trees, that's about it. Hey, what was that?" They aimed their M1s down the road. It sounded like stones rolling down a hill, the same kind of noise they'd made on the gravel trail. It was there, then it wasn't.

"Animal?" Skitter whispered.

"Callahan or Hanson, maybe?"

"What the hell would they be doing out of their hole?" Skitter asked. "We might shoot 'em."

Before Shard could answer, they were distracted by the deep boom of artillery, followed by the screeching of shells in flight, the high-pitched noise ending in terrific explosions, as if boulders were being hurled down from the heavens. The ground shook and the air filled with smoke and grit. The hits seemed to be on the ridgeline behind them, and Shard looked up in time to see rocks and debris cascade down the road, coming to rest yards in front of them.

"Christ," Skitter said. "Think anyone's alive up there?"

"Yeah, if they dug in good," Shard said. The shelling stopped as soon as it had begun. "Wasn't that much."

"It was enough for me. Maybe we should go up there, see what happened?"

"No. We stay put, like Kelso said." Shard gripped his M1, feeling the reassuring smoothness of the wood, the weight of the weapon, the symmetry and balance of it. It calmed him enough to say the words again, even though he hardly believed them. "We stay put."

Skitter slept. Shard stood watch, the bazooka handy. He thought he heard movement, maybe somebody crawling. Or Callahan taking a piss. Or a rabbit. Did they have rabbits in Korea? The sound faded into silence as he watched the sun begin to rise far to the east. There were too many hills to see the dawn, but the first slivers of light were beginning to show low on the horizon.

A trail of phosphorescence arced across the sky, first one, then another, blossoming into stark white brilliance, hanging in the sky as if two new suns had been born. Shard knew they were parachute flares but was powerless to think about what that meant. He drew his eyes away, blinking against the harsh glare that lit the ground like pavement along the Ginza on a Saturday night.

"Omigod," Skitter whispered, shaking Shard's arm. "Look."

Dark specters were advancing, backlit by the flares, their shadows long and menacing. Coming up the slope and crossing the road in front of them, hundreds of North Koreans, bayonets at the ready. A grinding sound rose beyond them, creaking metal on metal like mechanical monsters rising up from the bowels of earth.

Tanks. Big T-34 Russian tanks, heading straight for them. Machine guns barked from the ridge above, cutting into the ranks of the infantry. The North Koreans fired back, charging the slope as hand grenades were tossed into their midst, leaving a trail of writhing bodies behind. Shard was mesmerized, as if he were in a movie theater watching a newsreel. Dark images played out in the flickering light of dying flares and muzzle flashes, black and white images on the silver screen. Men and machines moved in slow motion, the sounds of battle loud, a cacophony cresting against his chest as his ears rang and his body vibrated. More flares burst overhead, their parachutes swinging lazily in the breeze, the lights hypnotic as they swung back and forth, casting wobbly shadows over the terrain. He had trouble picking up the bazooka, as if he were moving through a thick haze, every effort demanding all his energy and focus. He had none to give, every ounce of strength sapped by the bright light, the sudden impact of the attack, the terror of night turned day, the quiet turned to chaos.

"Shard, we gotta go," Skitter said, tugging Shard's sleeve, ready to run but afraid to go alone.

"Load me," Shard said, hoisting the bazooka onto his shoulder.

"They'll see us," Skitter cried, as he took the rocket from the bag and loaded it, tapping Shard on the helmet as he leaned away, burying his head against the earth.

Shard exhaled, letting the sight settle onto the target. The tank was rumbling slowly their way, its turret swiveling toward the ridge. Figures darted in front of the sight, blurred visions of North Koreans running from the bullets and grenades pouring down on them. He and Skitter were still undiscovered, hunkered down, the camouflage of branches screening them from the enemy. But not for long.

Shard pressed the trigger, and the rocket took off straight and true, heading for the spot where the turret joined the body of the massive tank. He saw a spark and a puff of smoke, but the T-34 kept coming on, the turret now swiveling toward the threat, searching for them, waiting for the next round. The first rocket had bounced off like a firecracker hitting a stone wall and done as little damage. But Shard was ready, oblivious to the danger, his whole universe focused down the sight, ready to take his next shot as soon as Skitter loaded. Skitter was still there, surprising him as he tapped his helmet and leaned into his side.

Shard fired. Lower this time, hoping to hit a tread. He missed, this rocket exploding harmlessly a few yards in front of the tank. Bullets began to dig up the ground around them and zing overhead as enemy soldiers fired in their direction. He ducked and followed Skitter out of the foxhole, as an explosion hit off to their right, showering them with dirt and branches. They scrambled up the hill as machine gun fire chewed up the landscape, the tank working its coaxial gun, searching for them in the dim light of dawn. They climbed an outcropping of rock that hung above the road.

"Here," Shard said, taking cover behind a boulder. Skitter slid back, sending rocks rolling down the hill. Shard took a grenade from his pocket, ready to pull the pin. But no one shot at them, no foreign words were shouted, only the constant fire from the road below assaulted their ears.

"Load me."

He rested the bazooka in a natural cleft between two boulders. From this height, he could fire down onto the top of the tank, where the armor was weaker. If no one spotted them, he'd have a perfect shot when the T-34 rounded the corner to head up the hill and finish off the company. He waited, the bazooka lined up on the spot where the tank had to turn, listening to the deep, throaty sound of the engine, the clanking of the treads, shots being fired, explosions, shouts, and cries until it all melded into one sound, the terrible crescendo of battle. Finally, with a great grinding of gears, the tank rolled into his sights. He waited for two seconds until the front and turret passed, then fired. The rocket hit. Instead of bouncing off, it penetrated the thinner armor, sending a blast of black smoke skyward. The tank shook with a powerful and terrible internal explosion, grinding to a halt, yellow flames seeking escape from the cauldron within.

"Christ," muttered Skitter. "We did that?"

"Damn right we did. Load." Skitter loaded him, but the next tank in line revved its engine and reversed. He had no target. "Let's move."

They eased away from their hiding place, unsure of where to go. Shard looked back to see two grenades sailing through the air, dropping close to the rocks where they'd been. Twin explosions spurred them on, up the hill, seeking shelter from their pursuers. Rifle fire sounded from every direction, confusing them, sending them scurrying one way, then the other.

"This way, to the road," Skitter urged, after they'd hidden in a gully. "I think it's down there." His voice was choked and frantic, his eyes darting everywhere, looking for safety and certainty, finding only desolation.

"No, they'll be all over the road," Shard said, trying to clear his head, to think it through. It was impossible. Bullets flew, the sharp *crack* overhead sounding closer and closer. Muffled explosions echoed in the hills. "We have to get back to the ridge. We're dead out here alone."

"We'll be dead there too," Skitter said. "The whole damn company might be dead already." Gunfire rippled, the harsh sounds echoing off the hills, making it impossible to tell where it was coming from. Death was everywhere, in every direction, lurking in every choice they made. As long as they were separated from their unit, the new light of day lessened their chances of survival.

"We can't stay in this gulley," Shard said, grabbing Skitter by the shoulder and peering into his eyes. "And we can't run. We can't leave the others. Besides, it's a chump's move. The two of us don't stand a chance wandering around alone. Right?"

"Sure," Skitter said, calming himself. He was relieved when Shard took charge. He had a way of explaining things that made sense. Except nothing made sense out here, nothing except running as fast as he could, throwing away his weapons, helmet, all the heavy gear hanging off his web belt. He was fast, but not faster than bullets, so he knew Shard was right. Shard understood the odds. Shard knew the last thing Skitter wanted was to be a chump. Or dead.

"Okay. We'll find Kelso and see what his plan is. Okay?" Shard said.

Skitter agreed. He gave in, afraid to be left out here alone. He knew his limitations. If he couldn't run away, he'd find a crevice in the rocks, curl up, and shake in his boots until the North Koreans found him. He didn't want to think further than that. He focused on Shard leading the way, taking him to safety, protecting him like he did that first day on the Ginza. He followed, lugging the remaining bag of three rockets, cursing his luck, cursing that bastard in Personnel, cursing Shard for following orders, wishing he were back in those Michigan woods he couldn't wait to get out of as soon as he'd turned eighteen.

They made it to a crest near the top of a hill, struggling through brush and staying off the narrow path. Shard pointed and Skitter saw a section of road through the undergrowth. North Korean soldiers trotted along it, their rifles with long bayonets held high, their pale sand-colored uniforms matching the dust they kicked up.

"They're going around," Shard said. "To hit the company from behind."

"What should we do?" Skitter asked. "There's only two of us."

"Let's get closer," Shard said. They left the bazooka and rockets behind. They were too heavy and cumbersome to carry, and Shard doubted they'd see those tanks again. Infantry was something else; they'd see plenty more North Koreans.

"Where are the ROKs?" Skitter asked. "They should be on this hill, shouldn't they?"

"Yeah," Shard said. "Unless we got turned around, this should be our left flank." They slowed, moving warily, not wanting to stumble into a position and get killed by the wrong Koreans. Near the top, they encountered the telltale signs of a dug-in position. Sandbags, discarded ration containers, the smell of a newly-dug latrine trench, cigarette butts. The foxholes were empty. The South Korean soldiers were gone.

"They took off," Skitter said. "The bastards."

"I don't know," Shard said, checking the position. "There's nothing left behind, no signs of a fight. Maybe they got orders to pull out."

"Look," Skitter said, moving behind a rock. "The road." The North Koreans were spreading out, moving slowly, scanning the hill for signs of resistance.

"They think the ROKs are still here," Shard whispered. "We gotta move fast."

"Damn right we do," Skitter said. "Kelso probably got his orders too. We're the last goddamn GIs out here."

They eased back, staying low, until the crest of the hill was between them and the advancing North Koreans. Then they ran. Jumping rocks, sliding down rough paths, they bolted as fast as their aching legs and heavy gear would allow. As soon as the NKs found the ROK position abandoned, they'd move fast and come up behind Kelso, if he were still there. The terrain began to look familiar, and Shard held up his hand, signaling a halt.

"This is the path we took last night," Shard said. "We're almost to Kelso's position." Rifle fire picked up, as did the sound of muffled explosions, grenades maybe, echoing off the hillside. Again, no way to tell which direction the sounds came from. Behind them or above them, it was impossible to know.

"We gotta get to those trucks," Skitter said. "That way." He pointed downhill.

"No. We go up. We have to warn Kelso and the others."

"They could be gone already," Skitter said, a nasal whine of fear making him sound as though he were on the verge of tears. He looked away, not wanting Shard to think he was a coward, knowing he was so much less than a hero.

"We don't know that. Go down the path if you want. I don't know if the trucks are still there, or if the NKs are. Me, I'm going up." Shard turned and darted up the path, easily navigating the stone outcroppings that had been so difficult in the darkness. He heard Skitter behind him. Shard knew he'd come. Skitter hated being alone.

Shard took a long step over a rock and fell, his boot catching on something slippery. Blood. On the side of the path were two dead ROK soldiers, their bodies riddled with bullets. Shard stood, dazed by the hard fall, trying to clear his head and take in what it meant.

Skitter knew. He pulled Shard back, grabbing him by his web belt and taking him to the ground as burp guns fired and chewed up the vegetation, right where Shard had been standing.

"Ambush," Skitter said. "The Reds got those two. They were probably on their way to tell Kelso to pull out."

"Could be," Shard said, curling up behind a rock, trying to make himself small. Bullets pinged and ricocheted around them as the North Koreans sprayed the area. "Maybe their radio is out, and they never got the order."

"Has to be," Skitter said. "Otherwise, the Reds wouldn't block this path." Skitter understood the angles. Every situation had angles to be played. This one was easy. "And they won't care if we head back."

"We could try going around," Shard said, not thinking much of the idea.

"There's a reason this path is here," Skitter said. "It's just a jumble of rocks out there. No cover. We'd be spotted in minutes, either by the Reds with the burp guns or the ones coming up behind us. There's only one play, Shard."

Skitter was right. They'd tried, but there was no way to get back to Kelso. They didn't have much time to get off this hill before it was surrounded. "Okay, let's go."

They crawled backwards down the path, keeping their heads low, hoping the North Koreans only had a few men stationed at the ambush point; enough to block the path, but not so many they could send out a patrol to find them.

Shard felt shame coursing through his body. He'd left the company behind. He hardly knew them, but it was wrong. You shouldn't leave anyone behind. It was something he'd told himself since he was a kid, ever since he'd failed at that very thing. He had never wanted those feelings gnawing at his gut again. He wished he could melt into the earth and vanish. But all he could do was crawl. It would have to do.

"Our guys," Skitter said, a few minutes later. They were nearing the road, and he began to scan the landscape, hoping to find the trucks warmed up and waiting to take them away. He spotted the road, saw green fatigues marching along it, and stood, waving his arms. "Hey, wait up."

Shard saw them too, the familiar green fatigues. But there was something wrong. First, they were South Koreans, not American GIs. Second, they had no weapons. They were prisoners. A column of ROK soldiers, probably the ones from the hill, defeated, their faces downcast.

Skitter saw it, too, but not in time. The smile was still on his face when three North Korean soldiers charged the path, bayonets aimed at his belly. He dropped his rifle and lifted his hands high. Shard rolled over, his hands up as well. There was a lot of yelling, and one of the NKs smashed his rifle butt into Skitter's gut. He doubled over, his hands gripping his midsection, and that only made the NKs angrier. They hit him again and again, until he had both hands showing.

Their captors prodded the two men down the path toward the road. The line of prisoners was long, a couple of hundred silent and sullen men. South Koreans mainly. A few Americans.

At the road they were searched. A North Korean with rancid breath went through their pockets, tossing wads of cash onto the ground. The wind blew the greenbacks into the road, and one GI stooped to pick up a twenty. Guards swarmed him, thrashing him with rifle butts, yelling incomprehensible orders. He staggered on for a few steps, then fell by the side of the road, holding his hands to his bloodied face. A North Korean kicked him, placed his foot on his gut, and drove his bayonet into his chest. The GI screamed, and the soldier drove his rifle in again, twisting the bayonet savagely.

The screams went silent.

The North Korean searching Shard and Skitter laughed, speaking to them as he went through their belongings, his tone mocking but his meaning clear. They were nothing now. He took their cigarettes and rations, their wristwatches and lighters. He pointed to the line of prisoners, still talking as if they might understand. It wasn't hard to get the point.

Shard and Skitter joined the procession, stripped of their helmets, web belts, and gear. Their clothes hung loosely on their bodies, as if everything had been held together by what the Reds had taken away. The captured men looked like ragamuffins, dusty and grimy, all lethal intent vanquished, irrevocably replaced by vacant stares and the sudden shock of capture.

They were prisoners of war.

Chapter 3

April 18, 1953
Camp Eleven, North Korea

"Firewood," Shard said to the Chinese guard. He nodded, letting the two men pass. They were allowed to forage for fuel, in pairs. For the enlisted men, this camp had no walls, no barbed wire. North Korea was all barbed wire, the whole damned country.

The road took them by the sergeants' camp. Officers and sergeants were fenced in. There were fewer of them, but the wire wasn't so much to keep them penned in as to keep them away from the enlisted men. Divide and conquer.

"Hey, birdie," one of the sergeants yelled, walking parallel with them on his side of the wire. "Why don't you come in here and sing your song?"

"Ignore him, Skitter," Shard said. "He's new. Parker, I think. Came in last week."

"Yeah, what's he know?" Skitter said, keeping his eyes to the ground.

"Where's Shirt?" Shard asked, slowing his pace. Once, contact had been forbidden and punished. Now, the guards didn't bother you as long as you kept walking.

"Beriberi's got him down," Parker said. Unlike most prisoners, Sergeant Parker still had cheeks that had not gone gaunt. Shard envied him.

"Any news on your side?"

"Nothing. I'm still the newest guy. You?"

"We got a new prisoner yesterday. Warren, from the 7th Division. Captured at Pork Chop Hill, wherever the hell that is."

"He had no idea?"

"Somewhere on the MLR," Shard said, coming to the end of the fence. "Where else? Tell Shirt." The Main Line of Resistance—where life, death, capture, terror, and pain played out for months at a time as each side settled into trench warfare and battles were fought for a ridge or hilltop that looked exactly like the next one.

"OK. See you, birdie," Parker said in a singsong voice. Skitter kept Shard between himself and the wire. He was scared of the sergeants' cage and the reactionaries in there. Not as scared as he was of the Chinese, but a close second.

"I wish these new guys would pay more attention to the news," Skitter said. "Warren didn't have a clue where he'd been or what's happening."

"Yeah, inconsiderate of him to get captured before he read the paper," Shard said. Along the MLR, staying warm and alive were a GI's priorities. Few ever knew where they were in terms of places on a map. They were up front, waiting for the Chinese to attack, or waiting to launch their own attack. The next hill was as far as geography extended. Or six feet deep.

They walked for ten minutes before they began to look for firewood. The area had been denuded last year, but after the winter snows, there were dead branches to be found if you went far enough into the gullies and ravines. They brought out fallen limbs and snapped them with their feet, stacking them at the side of the road.

"The war could almost be over," Skitter said, picking up the conversation while they rested.

"The peace talks?" Shard said. "I'm not sure I believe that's happening. How long do they need? It's been going on for months, if you believe the Chinese."

"I read it in the newspaper we got last month."

"The People's Daily Worker doesn't count," Shard said.

"There's got to be some truth to it," Skitter insisted. He leaned his head toward Shard, lowering his voice even though they were alone with their bundle of sticks. "Are the names still safe?"

"There's a good one," Shard said, turning away from Skitter. He pointed to a weathered branch, the bark hanging off in clumps. It was dense and thick, good firewood, better than anything they'd found. Too hard to break by stomping on it, they took it to a grove of saplings and wedged it between two trees, pushing until the hard wood broke under pressure. They fell as the last piece cracked, pitching forward as the wood splintered. The exercise had exhausted them, and both men stayed where they fell, heaving in gasps of the cool air. Skitter got up first, excited at the prospect of a decent fire, no more questions about the war or names. As Shard watched him pick up the pieces, a wave of sorrow overcame him, tears nearly bursting from his eyes.

Broken. Everything had its breaking point, everything could end up in pieces. Like strong wood could be snapped by pressure applied in exactly the right place. There was no denying it; no denying the consequences either.

"You okay, Shard?" Skitter asked. He was loaded up, and Shard was still on the ground, his eyes blinking furiously, focused on something far away. That wasn't like Shard; he didn't drift off like so many of the guys. That wasn't Shard's style; he was always *here*, wherever here happened to be. It worried Skitter.

"Winded, that's all," Shard lied. He picked up the last length of wood and followed Skitter to the road. It was a road like most in Korea. Gravel, mud, ruts. Like the road that led them here, three long and desperate years ago.

July 1950
Outside of Sangju, South Korea

They marched all day. No water, no rest, no food. The terrain was barren, rocks and scrub brush the best it had to offer. No cover, no escape. At midday, the column was halted, briefly, to separate the South Koreans from the Americans. Their guards pushed the fifty or so American prisoners toward a side road; the South Koreans were headed somewhere else. When the guards tried to get the South Koreans moving down the other road, the ROKs panicked. Some of them screamed, others begged, and a few fought each other with fists, for no reason Shard or Skitter could figure.

"They think they're going to be killed," Skitter said, and as soon as he did, three ROK prisoners took off at a run, sprinting across the rocky ground, making for a clump of trees about one hundred yards out.

Half a dozen guards shouldered their rifles, taking their time aiming. They fired, and puffs of dust exploded from the backs of the fleeing men, the bullets cleansing them of the dirt caked on them by battle and struggle. Bodies tumbled forward, a jumble of limbs crashing into the earth. Shard was reminded of a deer he'd shot, and as he watched the guards it was like watching his hunting buddies, smiles and nods, congratulations all the way around. They slung their long Russian rifles over their shoulders and returned to the column. It was docile now, the South Koreans glad only to be alive and breathing. Sudden death can improve on most any reality.

The Americans walked on. Their guards were dismissive of any attempt to communicate. Skitter mimed drinking, giving a little Japanese style bow to show he meant no disrespect, but all he received was a menacing look.

"What's gonna happen, Shard?" Skitter asked. "Where do you think they're taking us?"

"No idea," Shard said. Two guards waved their rifles back and forth, grimacing as they did. No talking. Fair enough, thought Shard. We got nothing to say anyway. He shuffled along, feeling the dryness at the back of his throat. Road dust stung his eyes, and he ached to rub them, but his hands were grimy from digging in. When was that? Last night?

He moved one foot in front of the other, trying not to think. He'd been good at that as a kid. When things got tough, when the cursing flowed, he would go away. Out in the backyard or by the chicken coops, but that wasn't where he really was. He would go nowhere, a place where people couldn't touch him. He hadn't needed to go there for a long, long, time. But right now, it felt like home.

It was almost dark when Skitter grabbed his arm. Guards were shouting, rifle butts working to move the prisoners off the road. An ancient truck rumbled up and stopped by a broken down mud hut. Bits of the rice straw roof hung on, most of it caved into the interior.

"A truck," Skitter whispered. "Now we can ride."

"There's fifty of us," Shard said, watching the vehicle. Two soldiers rolled out a drum of communications wire. US Army wire. They began cutting lengths of it as two other North Koreans took buckets off the truck bed and set them down in the dusty yard by the ruined shed. One of them turned to the prisoners gathered at the side of the road.

"Take boots off. Then eat." He pointed to the feet of the GI closest to him and then to the buckets. The GI sat down and unlaced his boots, removed both, and stood holding them, waiting to be told he could eat. The others followed suit. "Leave boots," the North Korean said. "Leave boots." Two guards with bayonets leveled stood by the buckets, watching to be sure the prisoners left their boots by the road.

Shard looked around for an officer or a sergeant. He saw a corporal who looked like he was still in high school, fear fierce in his eyes. Not seeing anyone take charge, Shard stepped forward in his stocking feet and told the men to split into two groups, one for each bucket.

"We don't have to listen to you, pal," one big GI said, brushing past Shard. "I'm hungry." Men hurried to get their share, but Shard turned and grabbed the huge GI by the collar, hard enough that his feet went out from under him. POWs slammed into each other, and the guards holding their rifles stepped back nervously, knuckles white as they clenched their weapons.

"Simmer down, fellas," Shard said, stepping around the crowd and in front of one of the buckets. "Everyone's getting a fair share. Anyone got a problem with that?"

"I got a problem with you, you sonuvabitch," the GI said, getting up and dusting himself off. "We'll settle it some other time."

"Okay by me, Tiny," Shard said. Some of the men laughed, and the tension lessened. The guards relaxed too, sensing a riot had been averted. "Like I said, divvy up and we'll see what's for dinner." The GI he called Tiny glared at him, then pushed his way in front of the group by the other bucket. A rough line formed for Shard's bucket, men sensing the other would be emptied quickly.

"What the hell is it?" Skitter asked.

"Corn," Shard said, looking at the contents of the wooden bucket. "Uncooked. Soaked in water."

"We got nothing to eat it with," Skitter said. At the other bucket, Tiny scooped up two handfuls and stuffed his face.

"Here's what we do," Shard said. "First thing is a drink. Everyone gets one drink from the bucket. Then the line goes around again, and each man gets one handful, until it's gone. Then we drink any water that's left. Fair?" Heads nodded, and Shard held the bucket as each man in turn tipped it gingerly to drink in the water. Skitter moved in, but Shard told him to wait. They'd go last.

"It ain't fair, Shard," Skitter complained, but he went along with it. By the time they took their gulps, most of the water was gone. The corn kernels were next. Each man took one handful, moving away to eat their share, watching their bucket, judging how much would be left.

Shard watched the North Korean who seemed to be in charge. His eyes flitted between Tiny and Shard, as if he was assessing their strengths. Then he gave a signal, and his men picked up the POWs' boots and threw them into the truck.

"Hey!" One of the GIs yelled, and then hid his face, afraid of retribution.

Shard walked a few paces toward the North Korean, then stopped. He didn't speak. He didn't want to commit an offense, and he knew the rules were bound to be capricious. He had experience with that.

"You sleep here tonight," the North Korean finally said. "No boots."

"Here?" Shard said, pointing to the dilapidated hut.

"No," the Korean said. "On ground. No boots. Eat."

Shard returned to the bucket. After a couple of dozen men had put their filthy hands into the corn, what was left was a mixture of mud, mashed kernels and bits of cob. It was barely a handful. Skitter tipped the bucket so the remains flowed out into Shard's cupped hands. An insect wiggled out of the mess, and Skitter plucked it, squished it between his fingers.

Shard ate. The hunger had been bad, but the mixture filling his stomach was worse. The hunger remained, along with a sharp ache, the dirt and uncooked corn conspiring against him, the pain staying with him, not letting go.

"Stand!" The Korean barked, drawing his pistol. An officer, Shard thought, struggling to his feet.

"They gonna shoot us?" Skitter asked, eyeing the pistol. Other guards leveled their rifles, advancing with bayonets to within feet of the prisoners.

"They wouldn't have fed us first," Shard said. Then he remembered the communications wire being cut into pieces. "They're going to tie us up. So we don't escape."

He was right. Guards moved in, holding lengths of wire. They bound the POWs' hands behind their backs, then shoved them onto the ground. Shard anticipated the tight knots and flexed his arm muscles as the wire went around his wrists. He relaxed, and was rewarded by a slight looseness, enough so the blood flow wouldn't be cut off during the night.

"Sleep," the Korean officer ordered. "You move, we shoot."

"No boots, trussed up like pigs, where does he think we'd go?" Skitter said. "Bastard," he added in a whisper. Skitter had been kicked around a lot before he joined the army and found a home fit for a petty thief. He was used to strong-arm tactics and could call upon a reservoir of familiar resentment whenever an officer, cop, judge, or crook—it didn't matter which—did him wrong. It didn't make him any more comfortable lying on the ground, hungry and miserable, but it did validate what he knew of human nature. He wasn't surprised to find himself here.

Shard was fueled by a different anger. He watched the officer drink from a bottle and light up a cigarette as he ordered his men about. It looked like they were cleaning out the hut. He averted his eyes when the Korean turned his gaze on the POWs. Shard knew he'd already attracted too much attention. And he didn't want to be singled out for anything. If you were noticed, you were in trouble. It had always been like that. When he was a little kid, he used to hide in the house, close enough to hear what was happening but not be seen. Later, in the juvenile hall, there was no place to hide. Eye contact was a gamble. He turned his face from the officer, Skitter, the other men, and tried to go far away. The pain in his gut wouldn't let him.

He heard a GI crying. Then another. Soft boys, kids who never knew a beating or a day without three square meals. They had it the worst. Back home, they'd look down at Shard, pity him maybe, for all he had lost, all he would never have. But here, the tables were turned. They'd fallen so much farther, and it had to hurt deep down in their souls.

"Stop moving around, goddammit," Tiny growled from a few yards away. He was using another GI as a pillow, resting his head on his belly. The GI whimpered, his arms pinned behind his back, Tiny's weight on his gut.

"Hey, pal," a nearby GI said to Shard. "Did you know that guy they killed back there?"

"No. He wasn't with your unit?"

"No. Me and my buddy are from the 64th Field Artillery. We got overrun two days ago. They came outta nowhere. Name's Johnnie Collier. This here's Joe Martinez."

"I'm Shard, this is Skitter. We came up with a provisional company, got caught when they flanked us this morning."

"Most of these guys are with the 27th Regiment," Collier said. "I'll ask around."

"Why do you want to know?" Skitter asked, crawling forward to get closer.

"His folks will want to know. Somebody will want to know what happened out here. The Reds aren't exactly keeping records, in case you haven't noticed."

"Don Fuller," a voice spoke from one of the nearby prone forms. Collier repeated the name softly, and the date. Shard laid awake, listening to the groans rising up from the ground, hearing only Fuller's name, repeated again and again, until he wasn't sure if it was a bad dream or the corn churning in his stomach.

In the morning, their boots were gone. The officer was gone, along with the truck. Shouts roused the POWs, bayonets prodded their bodies, hurrying them to rise. The buckets were back, this time filled with water. A guard stood at each bucket with a wooden bowl, pouring water into each man's mouth as he filed by. One guard was careful, allowing each prisoner to tilt his head back and open wide before pouring the water. The other frowned and shouted, spilling half the water as he tossed it at the waiting, gaping mouths.

"No boots, no food, hands tied," Skitter said. "How far do they expect us to go like this?"

"I don't think they care," Martinez said. He and Collier fell in with Shard and Skitter. Most of the other men were from the same unit, so the four outsiders formed a natural bond.

"They have to care," Skitter said. "Otherwise, they'd have shot us all." He winced as he caught the sharp edge of a stone, nearly falling over as he fought to regain his balance. He'd been in handcuffs once, but they were in front. That had been nothing compared to hands tied in back.

"No," Shard said. "The problem with killing prisoners is that once word gets out, it makes your enemy fight harder. There's no alternative."

"So?" Skitter said, keeping his eyes on the roadway.

"So they don't care if they lose a few bodies on the way to the POW camp," Collier said. "It's not like anyone is going to find fifty corpses all laid out together. That's why I'm going to remember the name of every guy who doesn't make it. I have a pencil stub they didn't take. If I find any paper, I'll write them down."

"I got an empty cigarette pack they left in my pocket," Skitter said. "I'll give it to you. Later." They almost laughed, then realized that they were assuming the deaths of the men around them, which quickly led to the conclusion it could happen to them. They walked, heads bowed, in the most efficient posture they could muster, balancing the weight of their hands while keeping their eyes on the ground for anything that might injure their feet.

In a couple of hours, no one had much left of their socks. Their mouths were dry, eyes gritty from the dust kicked up by the shuffling march. Lungs ached from the altitude, each suffering step taking them higher into the mountains, where they had no strength to be.

The guards drank from canteens but seemed to have eaten no more food than the POWs. The main difference was they were alive, triumphant and armed. Not thirsty, perhaps, but they were not beaten and demoralized like the American POWs. All the water in Korea couldn't wash that stain away.

The sun was high in the clear sky when it happened. One of the GIs collapsed. Other POWs tried to get him up, cajoling him, trying awkwardly to pick him up with their bound hands, but the guards charged in, beating them away.

"Smitty!" One of the GIs yelled. "Get up!" He ran forward, a desperate look on his face, and jostled a guard who was kicking the nearly unconscious Smitty. The guard spun around and fired, hitting the GI square in the chest. He dropped to his knees and keeled over, a gaping hole over his sternum.

Everyone froze, the guard worked the bolt on his rifle, ready to fire again. Smitty moaned. Skitter moved back, away from the confrontation, but Shard pushed with his shoulder to keep him in place. "Don't move," he said. Another GI bent to examine the dead man, but the guard screamed at him, aiming his rifle.

Another North Korean, maybe a noncom, ran over and began berating the guard who'd fired the shot, pushing his rifle down to the ground. POWs began to edge backwards, away from the dead and dying.

"See," Skitter said, looking to Martinez. "He's getting holy hell for shooting that guy. You were wrong about them." The senior guard pointed at Smitty. The other man nodded and bayoneted him in the chest. Twice, the second time working the blade free by bracing his foot on Smitty's neck.

"Yeah," Martinez said. "Holy hell for wasting a bullet."

They marched, the sun burning their necks, the heat roasting their throats. Each man lost in his own thoughts, trying to make sense of the terror, to work out where it was taking them, what price it might exact. Names were passed up to Collier, and he began his chant.

Don Miller, George Ray Smith, Elgin Randall.

Sometime that afternoon, another prisoner fell. This time, no one moved to help. His pals called to him to get up, to hang in there, but he said he didn't care. Shard saw him squeeze his eyes shut as the guards rushed him. The bayonets did their work, and the column marched on.

Don Miller, George Ray Smith, Elgin Randall, Archie Closson.

The dead kept pace with them throughout the afternoon. As the sun dipped behind a high peak, and the column traversed a winding mountain road, the ghosts became lonely. Two men collapsed, one dead when he hit the ground. Guards rolled his body down a steep rocky ravine, then did the same with a second prisoner, who was gasping out his last request. *Water.*

Don Miller, George Ray Smith, Elgin Randall, Archie Closson, Joseph Morales, Fletcher Perry.

They stopped at twilight. The truck was waiting for them, parked beneath a tree in a small grove. The NK officer was there, grinning as he stood in his sturdy American combat boots.

"Hands," he said to the POWs. "Drink, eat, sleep here. I am Major Bak. You must obey my orders, or you die." With that declaration, he dropped the grin and got into the truck.

"Hands?" Skitter whispered to Shard. "What's he mean?" Shard shrugged, too exhausted to think. He watched eight new guards jump down from the truck and sling their rifles across their shoulders. They shouted orders, twirling their hands in the air, telling the prisoners to turn around. The men obeyed, meekly. Shard felt the wire untied from one hand, a length left dangling from his other wrist. He couldn't move his arms; his shoulders rebelled after being pulled back for so long. He grimaced, and Skitter helped him, moving one elbow forward, then the other.

"Thanks," Shard said, his voice a rasp. "You okay?"

"Soon as we get water," Skitter said. He rested his hand on Shard's arm, not trusting himself to stay upright, afraid of what a fall would mean.

"Say the names," Shard whispered to Collier. He did, all six names, twice. It was all they had to draw strength from, and Shard knew they needed to play every angle. Tonight might be time for a prayer, he thought.

Skitter whispered the names to himself. As long as he spoke the names, he wasn't one of them.

There were four buckets this time. Two filled with water, two with food. The guards put out the water first and left the POWs to work it out. "Two lines," Shard whispered, motioning the men forward. The water drew him in. He wanted to dunk his head and then drink his fill. It shimmered in the waning light, magical, beckoning him. "Two lines," he repeated. "Cup your hands, drink over the bucket, go to the end of the line." He'd thought it through, the best way not to waste a single drop. He'd always had that knack. To see exactly what had to be done. But sometimes, knowing what had to be done was a curse.

The line went around three times on each bucket. Even Tiny was compliant. No one had the strength to fight or complain. When it was Shard's last turn, he pressed his palms and fingers together as hard as he could, making a firm bowl of his hands. He sucked the water in, letting it sit in his mouth for a second, then swallowing the coolness. He licked his palms, taking in every bead of moisture.

Shard inspected the buckets. There was an inch or two of water left in each. He poured one into the other, telling the men they'd let the dirt from their hands settle. Skitter approached the guards, lowering his gaze. They motioned for him to take the food buckets, and he carried them to the waiting POWs.

"What the hell is that?" Martinez said. The buckets were filled with something yellowish and puffy.

"At least it ain't raw corn," Skitter said.

"That there's millet seed," one tall GI with sandy hair said. "We grew it on the farm for feed when we had a bad year. Stuff grows on damn little rain."

"What's it taste like?"

"Dunno," the farmer said. "The pigs never complained, that's all I can say."

"Millet seed?" Collier said. "I had a parakeet when I was a kid. That's what I fed it."

"I wish your parakeet was here right now," Shard said. "I'd eat it. But you guys know the drill."

"At least our hands are clean," Skitter said as they waited for the line to move along.

"Hell, things are looking up," Shard said as he took his scoop of the food. They found a rock and sat, letting their legs slide out in front of them. The millet was hard, maybe not cooked all the way, they had no way of knowing. It tasted nutty, at best, but that could have been from the dead insects. It sat hard in their stomachs.

Another truck came for the original guards and took them back toward the front.

"I hope they croak, long and slow," Collier said. "Maybe an artillery barrage."

"Or a P-51 strafing run," Martinez chimed in.

"Too quick," Skitter said, launching into a defense of shrapnel. There wasn't much else to do but talk and settle in on the hard earth under the leafy branches. Two guards patrolled the area, but they might as well have put their feet up. The POWs were as good as chained. Weak, dehydrated, their legs sore, and the soles of their feet torn and bleeding, they were no threat to go cross-country.

It rained during the night. Drops splattered on the leaves, dripping onto the POWs, waking those who managed to sleep, and soaking them all. The guards retreated to the cover of the truck, leaving the POWs alone in the baleful Korean weather.

That morning the truck returned. As they struggled to their feet, Shard saw that one man was still on the ground. Dead.

"Should we take his dog tag?" Skitter asked.

"No," Shard said. "I don't think the Reds would like that idea." Tiny knelt by the body and went through the man's pockets. He found a wallet and stuffed it in his jacket. He removed the man's belt, shirt and field jacket, tying it all into a bundle which he fixed to his own belt.

"Hey, he's not going to need this stuff. Any objections?" Some of the men looked to Shard, but this was not a battle he wanted to fight. He turned away from the big man and waited by the truck.

A grayish milky white liquid, bean milk, was doled out from the bucket in a wooden bowl, one man at time. Shard guessed it was about four or five ounces. The guards took what was left, then bound their hands again.

Don Miller, George Ray Smith, Elgin Randall, Archie Closson, Joseph Morales, Fletcher Perry, Charles Andrews. Collier chanted the names, softly, as they moved out, the corpse left where he died, half naked, arms spread wide upon the barren earth.

Chapter 4

April 18, 1953
Camp Eleven, North Korea

Shard stacked the wood outside their hut. The ancient iron firebox in the cramped kitchen space inside leaked smoke and looked like it had been used for generations. Shard tried to imagine a family living here, the sounds of gurgling babies, laughter and cooking filling the air. But it was impossible. Too much suffering and death had filled that small, pitiful space.

It had taken a while to get used to the Korean heating method. Gudeul, they called it. The firebox was in the kitchen and used for cooking. Vents took the heated smoke under masonry floors to a chimney on the other side of the hut. Theirs was in disrepair, the top stones broken and fallen in a heap on the ground. Backdrafts were common, sending the men outside, choking in the frigid air. But it managed to warm the hut enough to keep them alive, despite the Korean winter. This year, anyway.

"Remember that first winter, Skitter?" Shard asked as Skitter snapped a branch over his thigh.

"I'd rather forget it," Skitter said, tossing the wood onto the pile. "When the war's over, I'm going down south, someplace where it's always warm."

"South China?" Shard asked, smiling to let Skitter know he was joking. He sat down on a log, too big to cut, but a good place to rest.

"You know I'm not one of those," Skitter said.

"You're a progressive," Shard said.

"Plenty of guys are. Things would go easier for everyone if more were. Or at least if there were no reactionaries. They're the ones making it hard on us all."

"Like Shirt?"

"Yeah, like Shirt. And I got my reasons. I can think things out as well as the next guy. Truman rammed this war through the United Nations when the Soviet Union wasn't seated in the Security Council, so it's illegal, or immoral at least."

"That first winter, was that immoral or illegal?"

"That first winter was hell," Skitter said, sitting next to Shard. "No argument there. You know that better than anyone." He shivered at the memory of winter and trembled at the memory of the days after their capture.

"Yeah, I do. I wouldn't be here now if it weren't for you."

"It was no big deal," Skitter said.

"It was to me," Shard said. "Life is a big deal. Waking up in the morning, even in this pit, it's a real big deal." He thought about the guys who hadn't made it. The names. So many names, no one could remember them all. Somewhere around the fifty mark, they hadn't been able to recite them, not even Collier. But they were all on the list. "So I owe you."

"Forget it," Skitter said. "You stuck by me. You've been a real friend, Shard. The debt is paid."

"There are a lot of debts in this camp," Shard said. He stared off into the distance, where the Chinese were gathering around the recreation hall. It was the only building they'd constructed for the enlisted POWs. Not a lot of recreation went on there, unless you counted Russian propaganda films and diatribes against Wall Street imperialists and United Nations germ warfare. It was big enough for a couple hundred guys to sit and watch the latest newsreels of the victorious People's Army defeating the agents of imperialism. Red banners hung from the wood beams and trusses, reminding Shard of a festive bloodletting.

"You can't settle scores with them," Skitter said. "We'll be home and they'll be back in Red China. The North Koreans are to hell and gone. No way to take revenge on those bastards."

"There has to be an accounting," Shard said. "It's a matter of balance. Too many wrongs, not enough made right."

"It's hard to know, some days. What's right and what's wrong," Skitter said. He felt uneasy with this conversation, worn out by wariness. Was Shard talking about him? Or was this another in the long line of bull sessions he'd sat through? It was a way to pass the time, but Skitter preferred to talk about broads or booze.

"The Chinese are good at confusing you. I hear they're looking for POWs to refuse repatriation," Shard said.

"Yeah, I heard that too." Skitter didn't say it had come from Comrade Yuan yesterday. He'd made a pitch for the progressives to think about refusing repatriation to the United States when the war ended, and prisoners were exchanged. Chinese and North Korean POWs were likely to choose non-repatriation by the boatload, so the Reds were trying to drum up volunteers for a life in the people's paradise.

"Think anybody will take them up on the offer?"

"Couple of guys in class were talking about it," Skitter said. "Not serious, you know, just talk. What would it be like, that sort of thing."

"What would it be like?" Shard asked, keeping his eyes on the Chinese. Comrade Yuan had noticed them and was walking their way.

"I dunno. I'm pretty good with languages, so I think I could pick up enough Chinese to get by. I did okay in Japan, remember?"

"Yeah," Shard said. "I was impressed. You knew when to bow and all that."

"I've always been able to read the signs, figure out how to act and understand what people want. It's a good way to steer clear of trouble, right?"

"As long as you don't get into trouble giving them what they want," Shard said. "Speaking of trouble, here comes your pal." At the sight of Yuan, Skitter stood up.

"Shard, will you join our class today?" Yuan said by way of greeting. He wore a blue quilted jacket similar to theirs, but his was clean and the fabric soft. He wore black boots, and his hair was long, parted severely and brushed back. Long hair, as opposed to the shaved heads of most guards, was a trademark of the political officer. Not that the Chinese Army had officers or enlisted men; they were all comrades.

"What's the topic?" Shard asked, standing slowly enough to show his distain, but standing, nonetheless.

"Racial Discrimination in America," Yuan said with a smile. "Skinner is leading the critique. He is your friend, why do you not come and listen?" The Chinese only ever used last names. No ranks, no nicknames. POWs weren't soldiers or individuals. They were prisoners, reactionaries, middle-of-the-roaders, war criminals, or peace-fighters, depending on how compliant they happened to be.

"You mean about how bad we are to the Negros? How we make them live in separate neighborhoods, that sort of thing?"

"Exactly, Shard. The American capitalist system divides the people by class and race, isn't it so?"

"Hard to argue with that," Shard said. "Especially about dividing the people by race. Like you do, Comrade Yuan. Aren't all the Negro POWs put into their own separate camp? The Ku Klux Klan would applaud you for keeping the races separate in Korea. Hell, the US Army doesn't even do that anymore."

Yuan slapped Shard on the cheek. He had to reach to do it, but he had a lot of anger behind that open palm. "Why do you insist on this attitude? Have you not benefited from our lenient policies here? We let you gather wood. We provide you with decent food. We clothe you. Yet you mock the efforts of your comrades to educate themselves. What are you afraid of, Shard?"

"I like to look at all sides of an issue, Comrade Yuan."

"There is only one side to the question. We are a peace-loving people, but we do not like to be mocked. You must accept that. Skinner and the others are open to learning new truths, to seeing the true side of the question. You, Shard, are on the wrong side of history. You see only the old truths, the old lies you have been told." Shard could tell he wasn't expected to answer. But he did have something else to say.

"It may surprise you, Comrade Yuan, but Skitter—I mean Skinner—and I were just talking about non-repatriation. What it would be like to live in Communist China. He's good with languages, but I'm a slow learner. Probably be harder on me."

"But not hard for Skinner?" Yuan asked, surprised.

"He should think about it," Shard said. "Might be the best thing for him." Skitter stared, eyes blinking in disbelief. Shard smiled, watching Skitter and Yuan walk away, Skitter glancing back at him, worry splashed across his face. Yuan took him by the arm, leaning in to speak to him, perhaps sharing a secret about the delights of Mao Tse-tung's China.

Shard sat, loosening the top button on his jacket. It was almost warm in the midday sun. In half an hour, their noon meal would be delivered. Rice balls with millet for the reactionaries and middle-of-the-roaders, while the progressives ate rice with vegetables off real plates. It was tempting, so a lot of guys went for extra food. Many got kicked out. You had to show interest, be willing to criticize yourself, your buddies, your country, over and over again until Yuan was satisfied. But he was never satisfied. He always wanted more. That was the problem with giving in; the demands never ended. There was always another hurdle, another bit of your soul to surrender.

It almost made Shard nostalgic for the pure cruelty of the North Korean camp regime. Almost, but the warmth of the sun brought him back to the heat of the march when the hot summer sun scorched their skin and the only thing that held them together were the names of the dead.

July 1950
Crossing into North Korea

It was the third day of the march. The North Koreans halted them in a clearing not far from a mountain stream, the trickle of water lazily splashing over stones before vanishing into a culvert. The guards took turns drinking and filling their canteens, menacing the POWs with bayonets whenever they nodded toward the stream, their mouths open. With their hands tied behind them, it was the best they could do. Some guy said the Korean word for water was *mool,* but even saying that got no response beyond a threatening snarl.

They gave up asking for water and sat in the sparse shade, gazing at the brown and unforgiving landscape. Shard saw them first, coming in from an intersecting road. Another column of prisoners. Hundreds of them, GIs with a cluster of civilians in the center of the group. He rose, too weak to speak, then doubled over in pain, the morning's ration of corn and water churning his guts.

"Shard, what's wrong?" Skitter said, resting against Shard's shoulder as he kept his eyes on the prisoners coming their way.

"Same thing as Hardy," Shard said, unwilling to say it out loud. Dysentery.

"Hell, you haven't puked, have you?" Skitter said, his false smile the best he had to offer. "Hardy puked a bucket of blood before, well, before it happened." Hardy had refused to get up that morning, rolling on the ground and clutching his belly. Then he vomited red with flecks of yellow. The little food he'd digested passed through him at the same time. His pals lifted him up, but the guards forced them away. Hardy stood on his own, blood and feces staining his uniform, swaying slightly, one hand covering his eyes, the best blindfold he could manage. Two guards charged him, then stepped back laughing as Hardy flinched, expecting bayonets to end his misery. Then they poked him in the legs, jabs no more than an inch deep. He fell, clutching his wounds, begging his tormentors to finish him.

The POWs were too weak to protest, knowing that there was nothing to be gained. It would only anger the guards, waste their energy, and prolong Hardy's misery. The stood still, watching, praying for it to be over. More jabs to the ribs, and red bubbles burst from Hardy's lips. Growing tired of the game, one guard thrust his bayonet under the ribcage, up into Hardy's heart. He held his nose, laughing at the stench that flowed from the dead man.

No one went near Hardy. No one wanted to watch the end that might come for them in an hour or a day from now. Degradation, sickness, filth, and painful death were best viewed from a distance. Hardy was no longer a man or a fellow prisoner, he was a truth too horrible to witness. The guards tied the men's hands and angrily ordered the march to resume.

On the road, Shard began to feel the pain in his gut. Sweat broke out on his forehead, nearly blinding him as the droplets cascaded from his eyebrows. The last two meals, if they could be called that, were corn soaked in water. He'd been feeling sick since that first morning, the day after he'd gotten the dregs of the corn and dirty water. He had to force himself to move each leg, to take each step, to keep balanced with his hands tied tight. There was no stopping. It was painful movement, step by slow step, or death by bayonet.

The spasms came unbidden, sending streams of foul-smelling liquid and undigested corn down his legs, staining his already filthy uniform. He saw it happen to other men, but still he felt ashamed. It was like being a child in a terrible nightmare. Nowhere to go, no help to be found, no comfort, no solace. Not so far off from his childhood in Ohio, he thought. He might have laughed if he hadn't been in agony.

He'd been fighting the urge to collapse and be done with it when they stopped. He fell on the ground, the barest tuft of grass under his head. Major Bak stood away from his soldiers, eyeing the POWs. He studied Shard, who turned away from him, dizziness overcoming him when he closed his eyes. He forced them open but continued to look away from Bak. He didn't want the attention; he had trained himself to be invisible. That's when he spotted the approaching column.

"Maybe there's a medic or a doctor," Skitter said, hunching his body forward. Getting up was the hardest thing about being bound. "I'll see if I can find anything out."

"Be careful," Shard said, gritting his teeth against the pain. "Watch out for Bak." He felt foolish saying it. What could Skitter be careful of? He used to tell his kid brother to be careful every day. Be careful crossing the road, be careful when Dad's drinking, be careful not to wake him on Saturday morning. There were steps to be taken, things that could be done to stay safe. Speaking the things out loud had always made him feel secure, as if knowing the dangers, saying their names neutralized them. But not here. It was a crapshoot, living or dying, and at that moment, Shard didn't care much which way it went. Except for Skitter. He felt a responsibility for him. He didn't want to leave him behind. He couldn't leave him behind. No one got left behind, that was the rule.

Shard fell inside himself, his mind working its magic to disappear the heat, the thirst, the pain in his gut, the shame that coated him. He heard Bobbie's voice, calling to him, his thin, reedy country child yell drifting in from a distant field. He ached to hear that voice, missing it and hating it. That voice held everything: sweetness and joy, terror, and fear.

Someone was nudging his arm. Was it Skitter? Skitter had been a mistake. He should have let him take his lumps that day on the Ginza. He never should have taken on a friend. Now he had to watch out for him, and he knew Skitter would, in his own way, watch out for him. They would build a bond of dependence until one day, something would break. That day on the sidewalk in front of the PX, he'd been wonderfully alone. In a strange country, on the other side of the world from his home, money in his wallet, and a pack of Luckies in his pocket. It had suited him.

"Shard! Wake up!" Skitter pushed at him with his knees, kneeling at his side.

"No," was all Shard could manage. But he kept his eyes open. He didn't want to come back, but the new column held a small promise, maybe a false hope, but a hope, nevertheless. Something might be different; something might be better, fairer, kinder. He knew that was not possible, but still, he held his eyes open, watching, until the heat fluttered them shut.

It was night when they opened again. Pinpoints of light rose into the darkness as flames popped and snapped. Shard wondered if he had died and descended into hell. But if so, this was a kindly hell; a cup of warm broth was pressed to his lips as arms helped him to sit up. He drank, greedy for more.

"No, my son, that is enough for now," a voice said.

"You'll be okay, Shard," Skitter said from behind. He was holding him, Shard's head resting against his thin chest. As his eyes became accustomed to the darkness, he could see that the lights were sparks from the guards' campfire. "Father Cadars is going to take care of you. He's kind of a medic, right, Padre?"

"I have some medical training, yes," Father Cadars said. He had a French accent, but his English was clear and precise. Shard tried to focus on the haggard priest and what he was saying, but the taste of real food had disoriented him. "All I can do is pray for you. Major Bak has given you soup, which should help if you take it slowly. You need rest, as do we all, which I am afraid will not be allowed." He lifted the cup to Shard's lips and tipped it forward. It was warm and tasted of vegetables and rice. Shard felt the nourishment, his body soaking it in on the way down. Kindness. Had it really happened?

"Take some, Father," Shard said, pressing his hand against the priest's, noticing he was untied.

"It is forbidden," Father Cadars said, rubbing his hand over gray stubble. "I am being punished. I must look after my companions. Your friend can care for you. God help us all." He rose stiffly, almost falling over as he straightened his thin frame.

"Why are you being punished?" Shard asked.

"I gave last rites to Sister Mary Clare. She was dying. No surprise when you make a sixty-six-year-old nun march under these conditions. It was starvation; she'd given all her food to the weakest and kept none for herself. Major Bak said it was imperialistic superstition and ordered me to stop. I could not."

"What happened?" Skitter asked. Another priest approached Father Cadars to help him.

"Bak shot Sister Mary and asked if God would raise her from the dead. He beat me when I prayed for his soul," he said, allowing the other priest to support him as he hobbled away.

"He ain't had any food in two days," Skitter said. "Bak said if anyone gives him food, he'll execute ten prisoners."

"How long is he supposed to go without eating?" Shard asked, letting Skitter feed him, feeling the childhood helplessness all over again.

"Until he dies," Skitter said. They were both quiet for a while as Skitter gave him another small sip.

"Did you get soup?" Shard asked. "We can share this."

"No, I got some. You go ahead and finish this." Skitter's voice was almost a whisper.

"The other guys?"

"Millet again."

"What? Why did we get soup? What's going on, Skitter?" Shard struggled to rise, nearly knocking the cup out of Skitter's hand. He wanted to understand, but he wanted the soup too. Wanted it like an animal wants its kill. Logic and reason fought with desire as he took the cup in both hands and finished the broth, bits of vegetables tumbling into his mouth as he tapped the bottom of the cup. He ran his finger along the inside, capturing the last dregs. Only then did he turn to face Skitter, refusing the child's role a moment longer. "Tell me."

"I talked to Major Bak," Skitter said, leaning forward and whispering. "I suggested that it would be better if you were feeling well. I've seen him watching you organize things, and I figured he'd want a POW who knew what he was doing."

"Want him for what?" Shard asked, wondering what Skitter had gotten him into.

"Nothing bad, don't worry," Skitter said. "I said the men looked to you for guidance, and that you kept things steady. It'd be a shame to lose you, that sort of thing."

"What did he say?"

"Nothing. He spoke to the guards, and one of them got Father Cadars to look at you. Another gave me a cup of soup, and one for you. I was worried we were too late."

Shard had been worried too. But now there was a different worry. He looked at the men collapsed on the ground, hunched together in small groups, some moaning, some weeping, most silent. What did they think? Skitter read his mind.

"I told the guys the priest set it up," Skitter said. "Martinez and Collier anyway."

"And what did you say about your soup?"

"That Bak ordered me to take care of you, so you could be our section leader. I had no choice."

"Section leader?"

"Yeah. Just like you've been doing, really. But now you can keep your strength up."

"Courtesy of Major Bak, the psychotic nun killer? Are you crazy, Skitter? The best way to survive this is to keep your head down and your mouth shut. Now Bak will be on us like a fly on shit if something goes wrong. And the other

POWs will hate us for getting better rations and working for the Reds."

"You may be right about that," Skitter said. "But you forgot one thing."

"What?" Shard said, the bitterness sharp in his throat.

"You'll be alive in the morning."

Skitter was right. They were both alive the next morning. The new prisoners were spread out on the roadside in three separate groups. The handful of priests and nuns were nearest to Shard's dwindling group. Further down the road, he could see another line of guards and a smaller contingent of POWs.

"Who are they?" Shard said as Skitter came to his side.

"Officers and sergeants," Skitter said. "They're keeping them separate."

"Yeah, who needs sergeants when the Reds have their own section leader?" Shard stared at Skitter, still angry at him for the deal he'd made, even though he might be dead otherwise. He could see Collier, Martinez, and the others glancing at them, then looking away. Only Tiny met his gaze and held it. Whether it was from admiration or hatred Shard could only guess. "There's no way these guys are going to listen to me now."

"Maybe, maybe not," Skitter said. "I did point that out to him."

"What the hell? Did you two go out for dinner and drinks? When did this all happen?"

"You were unconscious, Shard. I was worried about you, so I decided to give it a shot. Without you, Tiny would probably take over, and I'd never get enough to eat." That was true enough, Shard knew. Tiny was big enough to take on all comers and leave them broken. Not dead, but beaten. Dead, there would be no rations to steal.

"Okay," Shard said. "At least that makes sense."

"How are you feeling?"

"Woozy. But as you pointed out last night, alive." Shard looked at the half-dead prisoners scattered across the dusty, barren landscape. How many would make it? Half or more had stained pants like his. Dysentery was a killer, and it would only get worse.

A truck rumbled down the road, bouncing over the ruts and washed-out holes. Major Bak waved it down, and North Korean soldiers dismounted, off-loading large pots. Breakfast, Shard hoped. Guards distributed the pots to the different groups, the smallest to the priests and nuns, then the officers and sergeants. The remainder went to the larger group on the roadside.

Major Bak approached Shard, two guards trailing him with a basket. "You are Section Leader," he said. "No trouble, you eat. Trouble, no eat." He spoke quickly to the guards, who set down the basket. It was filled with bread. Round yellowish rolls. "One," Bak said. "One man, one bread."

"Form a line," Shard said, trying for as much authority as he could pack into his quivering throat. Bread. He'd never seen anything look so good. "One per man." He stood aside as the POWs rushed to the line, watching and calming the men, telling them everyone would get a piece.

Six men were too weak to stand. Shard asked if their bread could be brought to them. No. No stand, no bread, according to Bak. Shard asked for volunteers to carry the men, but no one wanted to leave the line. He pulled Skitter along with him and lifted one of the sick prisoners, dragging him into line between them. The man could almost stand on his own once he was up. Other men left the line and helped the sick, until only one was left.

"He's dead," Collier said. "Anyone know his name?"

"That's Cleon," a voice called out. "Cleon Raborn."

"Cleon Raborn," Collier repeated, memorizing the name. He had all the other names written on the paper from a pack of cigarettes Skitter had given him. He'd add Cleon's later.

Collier was last in line, Martinez ahead of him. There were plenty of rolls left. Made with yams, someone said. Martinez took his, but before Collier could do the same, Major Bak shouted orders to the guards, grinning as he did, his eyes narrowing in on Shard. They knocked Collier to the ground and tore off his jacket, searching his pockets, ripping his shirt, all the while punching and kicking him. Finally, a guard held up what they'd found. One pencil stub and a carefully folded piece of paper. It was from a pack of Lucky Strikes.

"What is this?" Bak demanded. He unfolded the paper, holding it so the red target with the black lettering faced the prisoners. "What do you write here?"

"Names," Collier said. "Only names." He grimaced and held his ribs as he struggled to stand.

"We feed you, and you hide names?" Bak asked, incredulous. "You are all war criminals! But we do not shoot you, we give you food, the people's food. And this is what you do? You make propaganda?"

"No propaganda, only names," Collier said, finally on his feet.

"You are war criminal," Bak said. "You insult the People's Democratic Republic with your secrets. Are you a spy?"

"They are only names," Collier said, his voice a blend of repressed anger and pleading.

"Major Bak," Shard said, raising his hand in what he hoped was a calming gesture. "It was only so the families of the men would know when they died." Bak didn't have to order the guard to slam his rifle butt into Shard's stomach. He fell back, gasping for air, feeling like he'd never breathe again.

"You do not speak unless I say to," Bak said. "Now this spy must die." He drew his revolver from his holster and aimed it at Collier's heart. Collier's eyes widened as the men gathered around him went silent, bread stuffed in their mouths, and clenched in their fists. Bak squeezed the trigger.

Click.

The chamber was empty. Bak laughed and the guards joined in. He holstered the revolver and spoke, raising his voice so all could hear. "The Korean People's Army is lenient and peace-loving. This spy may live. For now." He laughed as he translated for the benefit of the guards.

"Bastard," Skitter whispered as he helped Shard stand up. Shard hobbled over to Collier.

"You okay?"

"I didn't get any bread," Collier said, his voice trembling. He held his ribs, wincing with every breath. His face was swollen, and a cut on his forehead dripped blood, a steady patter like rainwater overflowing a gutter. "Bread."

Shard tore off a piece of his and gave it to Collier. Skitter edged away, but Shard grabbed him by the arm and pulled him toward Collier. Skitter gave a small piece up. Shard looked at the others. Martinez did the same, and so did a couple of other guys. A few said theirs were all gone, but Shard knew they'd hidden bread away in their pockets.

"Go to hell," Tiny said, stuffing the last of his in his mouth.

"Form a line at the stream," Shard said. "Get a drink. Make it fast."

"You gotta ask the guards," Skitter said, his eyes darting between the guards and Major Bak.

"No. They've had their fun. We have a few minutes. Now!" Shard said, with authority.

The men obeyed. Even Tiny. It was so orderly the guards didn't take notice. Their energy had been spent, the great charade the high point of the morning. They were stowing bedrolls and getting ready to move out. Major Bak watched the prisoners for a moment, then lit a cigarette. Even at that distance, Shard could make out the pack. Lucky Strikes. Bak smiled, happy with his handiwork, happy with his man in charge of the section.

The priests and nuns joined the POWs at the stream, but one. Father Cadars lay on the ground, unmoving, his hands folded on his chest, his rosary wound through his fingers.

The men's hands were tied again, the communications wire pulled tight around their wrists. The guards enjoyed it, laughing as the men winced in pain. When they finally marched off, names were whispered, a reconstruction of the list that had been confiscated.

Shard told Collier the name of the nun who had been killed earlier. He nodded; the names repeated through his swollen lips like praying the rosary.

Don Miller, George Ray Smith, Elgin Randall, Archie Closson, Joseph Morales, Fletcher Perry, Charles Andrews, Edgar Hardy, Thomas Jones, Joseph Lebiedz, Lloyd Bolles,

Willie Kingsley, Cleon Raborn, Sister Mary Clare, Father Joseph Cadars.

Shard's section was at the end of the column. Dust choked parched throats. Collier kept up the drumbeat of names until each one was burned into his brain, until nothing was left but names and stumbling steps toward the unknown.

Chapter 5

April 18, 1953
Camp Eleven, North Korea

Shard waited for Skitter near the recreation hall, the Chinese flag fluttering above him, blood red silk and golden stars. He sauntered past the kitchen, waving to Horseface, who pointedly ignored him. It must mean someone important was close by. Shard glanced in the windows and saw Commander Peng with his staff in tow. Comrade Peng, he corrected himself. Peng was small, with a wispy mustache, thick lips, and round cheeks. He'd been wounded in battle and walked with a limp, courtesy of a P-51 Mustang, or so the story went. Peng was a hard man, and Shard thought the pain brought out the worst in him. Or maybe it was the job. This command was his reward, or his curse. Was he glad to sit out the grinding combat in the mountains? Did he pine for home, far across the Yalu River? Or did he dream of killing American imperialists?

Shard moved on, approaching the administrative offices, hospital, and supply rooms housed in a concrete building, low, squat, and ugly, much like Peng himself. As always, a guard was posted at the door. Shard asked for permission to visit the hospital, where at least two POWs were laid up with complications from beriberi. Not that the hospital provided much in the way of treatment, but rations were slightly better, and they slept in a real bed.

The guard waved Shard through. Shard was of no concern to him, especially since Peng and his pals were on an inspection tour of the kitchen building and weren't around to reprimand him. Which is what Shard had planned on. He walked to the hospital wing through a narrow hallway that led to a large room that held ten beds, four of which were empty. Chinese orderlies crowded around one bed where a POW was vomiting loudly. A desk stood by the door, its chair empty, the orderly on duty holding a bucket and looking away from the contents.

An apple sat on the desk. No one noticed Shard, their attention focused on the patient and avoiding the puke that spewed out of him. Shard swept up the apple, dropped it in his pocket, and turned smoothly, leaving the room. No sudden sharp moves, nothing to draw the eye. He strolled down the hallway to the storeroom, where another guard sat in a chair, smoking a cigarette. Sitting and smoking were both against the rules, so Shard nodded and smiled, not worried about this kid, who looked maybe eighteen or nineteen.

"Can I have a cigarette?" he asked, not expecting the kid to understand. He put two fingers to his mouth, the international sign of smokers. The kid waved him off, muttering something in Chinese. Shard smiled and left, happy to be told to leave rather than be asked why he was there. He continued through the outer offices where clerks were busy with paperwork, like in any army. Not too many people, and the atmosphere was relaxed with the bigwigs gone. Shard waved across an empty desk to one stocky woman, her quilted jacket buttoned up tight. She frowned and looked away, and as she did Shard's hand fell from the proffered greeting, scooping up a pack of cigarettes from the desk. He shoved both hands in his pockets, a practiced dejected POW look on his face.

Not a bad haul, he thought, as he returned to the recreation hall. About a dozen smokes left in the pack by the feel of it. He watched Skitter come down the steps, Comrade Yuan at his side. Yuan patted him on the back and smiled as he walked back to his office.

"You must have raked the Wall Street racists over the coals," Shard said. "Yuan looked happy."

"What gives with the non-repatriation talk?" Skitter demanded. "Now he's all over me about what great opportunities there are in the People's Republic for a guy like me. Jesus, Shard."

"Just having some fun with you, Skitter, don't get all nervous. Come on, let's see if Shirt is up and about." They walked through the crowd of progressives who had attended the session. Most turned away from Shard; all had a fullness to their faces from the extra midday rations. Shard got whatever fullness he had from thievery, while other POWs suffered with gaunt, sunken cheeks, night blindness, and swollen gums.

Skitter followed, hands stuffed in his pockets. His shoes scuffed the dry ground, the same demeanor as when he was a sullen kid from the Michigan woods, resentful, ready for trouble, afraid to be alone. He didn't like Shirt, but he didn't like being away from Shard either. Except in the recreation hall. There, he was somebody. The Chinese respected him or played at respecting him. He knew it was a game, but he enjoyed the attention. With Yuan as his mentor, he got enough to eat. With Shard as his protector, he would live. It was a delicate balance, but Skitter knew how to walk that tightrope.

"Maybe I can get a few favors from Yuan if he thinks I might go to China," Skitter said as they covered the ground between the enlisted men's camp and the sergeants' compound. "They can't make me go, can they?"

"Yuan doesn't like to be disappointed," Shard said. "Makes him look bad."

"Yeah. Good point. I won't take it too far, maybe tell him I'm thinking about it. Can't hurt, right?" Shard didn't answer.

Shard and Skitter kept walking, picking up twigs and dead branches to look like they were still on a firewood expedition. "How'd we ever make it that first winter?" Shard said, once they'd turned around. It had been bad. With the wind, the temperature was below zero most nights. They were allowed to go out once a week to forage for firewood. There was never enough. "No boots, rags for shoes, never enough to eat. I can't believe we lived through that."

"You taking a trip down memory lane today, Shard?" Skitter hefted his twigs, a good supply of kindling to get the fire going tonight.

"Bad memories never go away," Shard said. "We had some good times in Tokyo, lots of fun. But it all blends together, doesn't it? I can't recall half of what we did: the girls, booze, gambling. That wasn't important enough to really remember, the way I remember everything that's happened since we were captured. The bad things are burned in, like a brand."

"I try not to think about it," Skitter said.

"Does that work?"

"No. Not really."

"You got boots that winter, didn't you?" Shard said.

"Yeah. Traded a pocketknife to a guard."

"I pegged you as a born businessman the first time I met you, Skitter. And a survivor."

"I hope you're right on both counts," Skitter said.

"Time will tell. You were lucky that guard didn't turn you in."

"That was Cho, remember him? Crookedest Commie you'd ever want to meet."

"Yeah, Cho. He'd trade anything, not that we had much," Shard said, scanning the sergeants' compound for Shirt. POWs walked listlessly within the enclosure, looking alarmingly alike. Blue quilted jackets, blue caps, sunken cheeks. "How'd you get that jackknife anyway?"

"Traded up for it, I think. Started out with hard candies from that one Red Cross parcel we got. Christmas, remember? Then got some cigarettes, and the guy who'd smuggled the pocketknife in was dying for a smoke, so he traded. I showed it to Cho, and he wanted it right away. I knew he wouldn't snitch, since that way he'd get a pat on the head but no jackknife. He came through with the boots and a couple pair of socks, remember? I gave you a pair."

"Best Christmas present of my life," Shard said. All POWs had been stripped of their combat boots, many of them marching in snow and ice barefoot to get to this camp. Upon arrival, Shard had been given a pair of worn-out North Korean sneakers, the kind their soldiers wore in the summer. With the wool socks, he had an edge, enough to avoid frostbite. Skitter had played the angles and won.

"Hey, Shirt!" Shard yelled, keeping his eyes fixed straight ahead. "Incoming." The guards patrolling ahead of them, their rifles held lazily across their shoulders, weren't paying attention. Shard took the apple from his pocket and threw it over the fence, in a high arcing curve, right into the waiting hands of First Sergeant Hector Kelso.

"He's got beriberi," Shard said by way of explanation.

"Shirt? I thought he was invulnerable," Skitter said, looking back to see Kelso staring at him, the apple already hidden. "Where'd you get the apple?"

"Somebody left it sitting on their desk in the admin building."

"Are you nuts? Stealing in there?"

"Scored some smokes too. But Shirt needed the apple. It's supposed to help with the beriberi. Vitamins or something."

"Jesus, you take some risks, Shard."

"Sometimes you have to," Shard said, holding his bundle of twigs under one arm as they walked. "Like you took a chance to get those boots. Cho could have turned you in; you didn't know he'd be willing to trade when you approached him, right?"

"Yeah, sure. But stealing from the head office, that's nuts."

"What do you think the North Koreans would have done to a prisoner with a weapon?"

"Aw hell, it was only a little pocketknife," Skitter said, whining like a teenager making excuses.

"We've seen them beat and bayonet men for less," Shard said. "That was brave of you. You took a risk. That's all I did."

"I thought I might get frostbite and lose my feet," Skitter said, his head hung low. "It wasn't brave."

"I know what you mean," Shard said. "Who did you trade with? For the knife."

"Schuman. John Schuman," Skitter said, after a moment's thought. "I think he was a corporal. He didn't make it through the winter."

"He should have traded for boots," Shard said. They walked in silence back to their hut, memories of that terrible winter swirling in their minds like remnants of a nightmare, a vision that remains even as you tell yourself you are fully awake.

"Yeah," Skitter said, glancing at Shard. But Shard's eyes were elsewhere, gazing into the past. Back before that first winter when they'd had their baptism in the Brick Camp. Their communion with confession.

August 1950
Brick Camp, North Korea

Shard's section arrived at the temporary camp after a week on the road. More names were chanted that first night, the roll call sounding like attendance in elementary school, except no one answered. Collier shuffled along, nudged forward now and then by Martinez, the pain from his broken ribs sharpened by the pull of his bound hands.

The camp was an old brick factory, half in ruins, whether from decades of neglect or thirty seconds of a bomb run, no one could tell. No one cared. The wooden roof was rotten but kept most of the rain out. Kilns were smashed, anything useful carried away long ago. The prisoners were told to clear the rubble away in a series of rooms and make them habitable. Habitable was a relative term. Here it meant a space cleared of broken bricks and splintered timbers.

Shard's section—now down to thirty-five after Nick Garza fell dead at the side of the road not one hundred yards from the Brick Camp, as the POWs dubbed it—was assigned to a gloomy chamber with a hole in the roof, an empty wooden workbench, and bird shit on the floor. They were told to clean it for inspection in one hour. No tools, no gloves, no food, no shoes.

"Christ," Skitter muttered. "What are they going to inspect? There ain't nothing here."

"Let's not give them any excuse to punish the section," Shard said, loud enough for all to hear. "Form a line and let's move through the room. Use those pieces of wood and bricks lying around to pick up what you can."

"I ain't cleaning nothing, and you can't make me," Tiny said. He folded his arms across his chest and leaned against the wall.

"Any man too weak to work, stand with Tiny," Shard said. No one did. Shoulder to shoulder, they moved through the room, picking up debris, scraping bird droppings loose, and tossing handfuls of refuse out the single window, incredibly still intact. Tiny brought up the rear, making a big show of picking up nothing in particular.

"Good," Major Bak said from the doorway. Good enough for POWs, but not so good that he wanted to walk through the remaining filth in his newly acquired American combat boots. He snapped his fingers, and guards moved into the room, depositing straw mats for each man to sleep on. "Food and water come soon," he continued. "This is rest camp. We stay here two, three days. Then trucks take us to POW camp. Good food, doctors, clothes for you."

Bak left, and Shard could hear echoes of the same cheery report down the hallway, his voice bouncing off the concrete walls. A guard remained at their door, another outside the window. Boiled millet and water were brought in, a bucket of each. By now everyone's hands were encased in dirt and waste, but there was barely enough water to drink, and none to be wasted on washing. No utensils either, so it was the hand scoop again, road dust and bird shit for seasoning.

The food tore through half a dozen men immediately. They made for the door, asking where the latrines were. The guard had no English, but he didn't need it. He held up one finger, meaning one man at a time. The latrine was a room that hadn't been cleaned. No holes in the floor, nothing but cracked concrete and cries of agony as abscesses caused by dysentery wreaked havoc in their intestinal tracks.

"Stay by the door!" Tiny shouted, the waiting men doubled over in pain, the smell overwhelming as bodies involuntarily voided bowels which had refused to digest the seedy mixture. He backed away from them, seeking the outside air by the window, propped open by a miraculously intact brick. The outside guard hit the brick with his rifle butt, and the window slammed shut.

Shard shook, the tremors in his gut threatening to rip him apart. He broke out into a sweat, and huddled against the cool wall, unable to help the others, barely able to look at them. The stench intensified from the cascade of putrid bodily fluids, as if the men were rotting from the inside out.

Skitter ate, doing his best to remind the others to take one handful only and pass it on. But he wasn't Shard. He was Shard's sidekick, and that's as much attention as he got. Tiny grabbed the bucket and held it up to his lips, the gruel dribbling down his cheeks. He set it down and chewed a giant mouthful, disdainful of stares and murmured protests. With Shard down for the count, he could do what he wanted.

"Shard," Skitter said, shaking him by the shoulder. "You gotta do something."

"Can't," Shard gasped. "Hide in the pine tree, Bobbie."

"Bobbie?" Skitter said, confused. Shard was sick, he knew that, but now he worried about him going off the deep end. He expected Shard to get better, he had to. When they got to the new camp there'd be doctors and decent food. Bak said so. What point would there be in lying? He got two straw mats and rolled one out for Shard, pushing his limp, reluctant form onto it. He laid next to Shard, listening to men bicker, moan, argue, and weep. Skitter felt the hunger pull at him, the desire for real food mingled with the pain from the millet coursing through him. He knew he was lucky. He probably had dysentery, but it was mild. Impossible in these conditions not to get it. The trick was to live through it. Shard could help him, watch over him; but not if he went crazy and died.

In his fevered dream, Shard watched Bobbie run out the back door, screen door slamming behind him. First mistake, he thought. But Bobbie was thin and swift; a seven-year-old flying like a bullet down country lanes. He'd be in the pines in a flash, scampering up their special tree, the tallest around. There'd be plenty of places to hide in the crook of a thick branch, shielded from the world as the wind whispered through the verdant green needles that hid him from the stumbling whiskey-fueled anger of the man they called Daddy.

Shard knew Bobbie was in for a beating. Daddy had come home drunk that Friday night and kept taking swigs from his whiskey bottle. The booze was fetid on his breath, stinking through his sweat and swears, words he'd tanned their hides for saying when he cared enough to take the switch to them.

Why couldn't he move? Where was he? Stuck in the hallway upstairs, outside their attic bedroom? He felt the boot into his ribs, and the pain felt familiar. It felt like home. He looked for Mom, but she was nowhere to be seen, not behind Daddy pulling on him, telling him to come into the kitchen, or the bedroom, anywhere the boys weren't. And it wasn't Daddy either, and this was no place like home.

"Get up!" Major Bak screamed as the guard kicked him again, followed by a bucket of water tossed on his head. His first thought was why were the North Koreans wasting water on him? It felt good, cold and clear on his face. Why didn't Bak just shoot him? "You are Section Leader! Get up!"

Skitter helped him up, draping one of Shard's arms around his shoulder so Shard could stand. "He's up, Major."

Bak slapped Skitter. "I ask, you answer. No more." Skitter bowed his head in submission. "Good. Section outside, now."

Guards herded the prisoners into the dirt courtyard formed by the L-shaped building. Dead trees lined the exterior perimeter, the inner marked by garbage piles beneath the windows. Two tables were set up on a loading dock that jutted out from the center of one wing.

"They gonna feed us?" Skitter asked as the guards hurried them along with bayonets and rifle butts.

"No," said Shard. "This is trouble." He didn't know what it meant, but it wasn't good. All the enlisted men, a couple hundred, were ordered to line up facing the loading dock, section by section. No sergeants, no officers. No witnesses other than the North Koreans. Not a good sign. The pain in his gut was like broken glass. He leaned on Skitter, who was practically hopping from foot to foot, eager to run with nowhere to go.

Shard's section lined up as best they could, five lines of men leaning on each other, miserable in their grimy, tattered clothes, barefoot, fear etched on their faces. Shard figured this might be a mass execution, machine guns opening fire on them from the windows of their prison. But the Reds had something else in mind.

"Before we go to your camp," Bak said from the loading dock, "before trucks and doctors, you must confess." Soldiers carried out two tape recorders, unspooling electrical cords behind them. Microphones were placed in front of each recorder, reels of tape set in place. "You are only enlisted men in the service of the capitalist aggressors. The peace-loving people of North Korea can forgive your warmongering for Wall Street. But only if you confess."

No one spoke. Each man knew enough by now not to speak unless it was an answer to a direct question, and it was the answer the Reds wanted to hear. Skitter had gotten off easy; Bak must have been in a hurry to get to the confessions.

"Each section must give two confessions," Bak continued. He unfolded a sheet of paper and read from it. "You must tell the world how you invaded North Korea in an attempt to overthrow the Democratic People's Republic and depose our Great Leader, Kim Il-sung. You must call upon American forces to quit Korea and apologize for this unwarranted aggression." He refolded the sheet and placed it in his pocket. "You have five minutes to select those who will speak. They will read confessions as they have been written."

"What the hell?" Skitter said, turning to Shard. "They invaded, didn't they?"

"Doesn't matter," Shard said. "They want this stuff for propaganda broadcasts."

"Who the hell would believe it?" Collier asked.

"Doesn't matter," Shard said again. "They want it."

"Who's going up there?" Tiny wanted to know. "Not me."

"We can't do it," Martinez said. "That's aid and comfort to the enemy. Hell, it's probably treason, ain't it?"

"The army will court-martial anybody who reads that crap," said Vernon Stallings, a buck private with a slow southern drawl.

"Maybe someone should read it," Skitter said. "The rest of us could back him up, say he was forced to." They talked, but Shard didn't listen. It was useless to talk. He was sure they'd be killed here, confessions or no.

"Time!" Major Bak shouted. He looked to Shard's section first. Shard shook his head, then stared down at the ground. No confessions. Bak shouted orders to his guards, who ran at the men, slamming them with rifle butts, grabbing the first POW they could by his legs and dragging him up the stairs onto the loading dock. It was Stallings. They threw him into the chair facing the microphone. "Speak!" Bak said, drawing his revolver. "First name, rank, and where you are born. Then read confession. When you are done, you must sign." He pointed the barrel of his pistol at a pencil next to the paper.

Stallings was confused. He looked Shard but there was no help from that direction. Shard didn't know what to do or say. If he encouraged Stallings, he'd be a traitor. If he told him not to speak, Bak might kill them both.

Bak pointed his revolver at Stallings's head. Shard prayed it was another trick like the one he pulled with Collier, but he doubted it. There were too many men watching, too much at stake for this to be simply a cruel joke. He watched Bak's finger tighten around the trigger, and his words burst out of his mouth before he could stop them.

"Read it," Shard said. "You have to do it."

"No," Stallings said, folding his arms across his chest. Bak swung his arm back and smashed the butt of the revolver against Stallings's face, his own face a snarl of anger. The impact sent Stallings flying, spitting blood and teeth, a large open gash on his cheekbone, the confession fluttering to the ground. Bak stood over him, the pistol again aimed at his head.

"Next man," Bak ordered.

"So we should do it?" Skitter said to Shard, pulling at his sleeve. Shard watched Stallings roll on his side, his hands holding his ruined jawbone in place, hacking up blood. He wanted to answer yes, we should, but he couldn't. He'd learned early in life that there was no end to the brutality after you gave in. It was only different. He shook his head.

They came for him, bayonets pushing the others back. But Skitter hadn't earned his nickname standing in one place. He sidestepped the guards and bounded up the stairs, his hands held high.

"I'll confess," Skitter said. "I'll read it, whatever you want."

"No!" Shard shouted, but the guards lifted their rifles, aiming at his chest. He backed off, words dying in his throat.

"Good, good," Bak said to the entire group. "This man knows the truth. Very good."

The charade played itself out along the courtyard. One section had two men ready to go. Another section refused, and three POWs were nearly beaten to death before one prisoner volunteered for the confession.

When it was his turn, Skitter read the text that had been prepared for him. About how the Americans had armed the South Koreans and helped them to invade the North. How sorry he was for his crimes against the North Korean people, who were treating him well in captivity. How the United States should leave Korea immediately and allow all the Korean people to live in peace. How the American enlisted man was glad to stand with the peace-loving peoples of the world and demand an end to this aggression.

Oddly, the words filled a place in Skitter's heart. They meant the salvation of Shard, who never would have given in. They meant trucks and food and medical care. They held the promise of better treatment now, even if there was some vague future threat of a court-martial. You have to be alive to worry about a court-martial, right? Peace-loving peoples. It had a nice ring to it. Skitter watched Bak smile as he read. Perhaps Bak was only doing what he was told to do. That slap had been a gift, not a punishment. Skitter read on, his voice soaring, willing himself to believe every word, every promise, listening as he finished for the sound of trucks coming to take them away. When he was done, he was eager to sign. The pencil had been lost in the tumult, but Bak found one for him, smiling like a schoolmaster as Skitter carefully signed his name.

There were no trucks. The sections were sent back to their rooms with promises of good food to celebrate the confessions. It was sorghum grain with a few kidney beans scattered about, thickened with a fine powder of rice husks. Insects crawled out of the gelatinous mix. The POWs called it bug dust and dug in.

Skitter took his handful to a corner of the room and leaned against the gritty concrete wall, his hands to his mouth, gazing at the other POWs. Shard was tending to Stallings, using a dirty handkerchief to staunch his bleeding wounds. Stallings was thrashing his legs, clawing at his face with his hands. Martinez tried to calm him, but Stallings was in agony, shrieking in a strange, choked voice, his broken jaw and teeth unable to give proper voice to his pain.

Shard got up and approached the guard at the door. "Do you have a doctor? Medic?" He pointed to Stallings and tried to get through to the stone-faced soldier. "Red Cross? Hospital?" Another guard looked into the room and walked away, shouting a stream of Korean at somebody.

"I think someone's going to get help," Shard said, kneeling at Stallings's side. He took his hand and squeezed it. "You told them, buddy. You did good." It was meaningless. Or maybe not. Whatever he said seemed to calm Stallings. His breathing slowed to jagged rasps and he squeezed Shard's hand in return. Shard and Martinez tried to give him water, one man lifting the wounded POW, and the other tipping his cupped hand into the good side of Stallings's face. He took a little and choked.

A commotion sounded in the hallway. "This might be help," Shard said, hoping that the example Bak had set in front of the men was enough for him. If Stallings could get patched up, he might make it. For now.

"You ask for doctor," Bak said from the doorway, his voice neutral.

"Yes, please," Shard answered, lowering his head in what he hoped was obedience. "This prisoner needs medical care."

"We take prisoner to doctor," Bak said, giving orders to his men. Two of them entered and dragged Stallings into the hall. Bak spat out another order, and Stallings was on the floor, screaming, as a guard lunged at him with his bayonet. Two thrusts to the chest and the screams ended.

"We have doctor ready for any prisoner who needs him," Bak said, looking back into the room. "Doctor Bayonet." Bak edged out of the room, his teeth bared in a snarling laugh.

"Bastard," Martinez said, his voice a narrow hiss. Tiny turned away. Collier lay flat on the floor, his arms wrapped around his broken ribs. The room went silent. No one looked as guards dragged Stallings off by his feet.

Skitter hugged his knees to his chest, his face buried. He was afraid he'd be blamed for Stallings's death, but it wasn't his fault. Shard should have insisted Stallings read the confession right away. His silence had given Stallings the idea he could resist. As if he had a choice. No one did. But Skitter was the one who had confessed, and guilt settled over him like a shroud. The words had come easily. But now that it was over and Stallings's blood was drying in the hallway, he didn't feel as certain. Of anything.

Shard sat next to him, his hand on Skitter's shoulder. They didn't speak for a long time.

"I should have done it," Shard said. Skitter was silent, his head still on his knees.

"No one blames you," Shard continued. "It had to be done."

"But you didn't do it," Skitter said. "None of the other guys did."

"Guys from the other sections did."

"Did you notice?" Skitter said, raising his head. "Did you notice Bak asked for two men per section, but he didn't always get them? And no punishment."

"You're right," Shard said. "He asked for more than he expected."

"Which means there's a way to deal with him. Give him something, but not everything," Skitter said, excited as if he'd discovered a great truth.

"It's dangerous," Shard said. "He's always going to want more. When the war's over, someone's going to have to pay."

"Pay? What do you mean pay? He's forcing us to do this. You've seen Bak kill. They gutted Stallings! Are we supposed to be tortured and killed rather than read a phony confession that no one is going to believe anyway?"

"I don't know," Shard said. "But I know the army. This makes the army look bad. The brass won't like it."

"The brass ain't here," Skitter said. "The brass wasn't on that hill when we took out that tank. The brass is having lunch at the officers' club while we're here eating out of a dirty bucket. The hell with the brass."

Shard had no response. It didn't feel right, but it made sense.

Collier groaned as he rose, taking small steps to a wooden workbench built into the wall by the door. It had been stripped clean, but Collier wasn't looking for tools. The interior wall was made of wood, papered over with faded wallpaper, peeling away in great chunks. Collier winced as he reached for a strip and tore it off, watching the door for a guard to make an appearance. He brushed the remnants of dried glue from the backside of the wallpaper and folded it into quarters. He sat against the wall, using the workbench to block the view of the guard in case he came into the room.

Shard watched as Martinez moved next to Collier and took an object out of his shirt. The pencil. The one that had gone flying when Bak knocked Stallings over. Collier opened the stiff paper and began to write, as Martinez chanted the names, beginning with Vernon Stallings and working backwards to Don Miller. There was plenty of room left when he was done.

Chapter 6

April 18, 1953
Camp Eleven, North Korea

It began to rain on their way back to the hut. Fat raindrops splat against their cotton jackets, and they made it behind the thin rice-paper door seconds before the gray skies opened and sheets of rain, freshly chilled in Siberia, let loose over the compound.

"Hey, O'Hara, how's things?" Shard asked. Seated next to Collier was Mike O'Hara, one of the prisoners from the original group.

"Hanging in there," O'Hara said. "Thought I'd drop by and see if you heard any scuttlebutt about the peace talks."

"Nothing new," Shard said. "They're still arguing about repatriation. Where've you been?"

"The Chinese took a truckload of us down to the Yalu River. Unloading barges at night," O'Hara said.

"Anything good to steal?" Shard asked.

"Would have been if we were brought back here at night. But they kept us in bunkers near the river, so there was no place to stash anything. It was mostly food, some medical supplies. We got some apples on the first day but had to eat 'em fast. They were watching us pretty close."

"Feed you okay?" Shard asked.

"Yeah, we ate pretty much what the soldiers ate. Rice with beans and some kinda greens thrown in. Wasn't bad," O'Hara shrugged. "Not as good as what the birdies eat, though. Skitter, you're looking well."

"Listen, O'Hara," Skitter said, hunching forward in the tight confines of the hut. "You were there at the Brick Camp. I didn't see you refusing, like Stallings did. So don't criticize. I probably saved your life."

"I didn't refuse, I didn't offer," O'Hara said. "But whatever you did that day—and I'll admit it had to be done—you kept on doing it. Why do you still go to those classes?"

"I'm open to new ideas," Skitter said, settling back down now that O'Hara had agreed with him about the confession. "And I don't mind eating their food. Small price to pay."

"You're putting yourself in a bad position, is all," O'Hara said. Skitter glanced at Shard, who'd said much the same thing earlier. He shrugged. "Unless you're going to refuse repatriation."

"Hell no," Skitter said. "I'm going home." Alive, he added to himself.

"Good to hear," O'Hara said. "I'll be glad to get home too. After I see my folks, I'm heading up to Vermont to see Schuman's family. We promised each other if one of us didn't make it, the other would visit his folks."

"Oh yeah," Shard said. "I'd forgotten. You and Schuman were buddies, right?"

"Yeah. We were together since basic."

"When did he die?" Shard asked.

"Winter of '52," Collier said. "January." Schuman was on the list, of course.

"Me and Skitter were talking about him this morning," Shard said. Skitter shuffled his feet in the enclosed space. The rain had lessened but was still drumming down on the rice straw roof. It smelled like rotting hay. "Skitter traded with him about then, didn't you?"

"Yeah," Skitter said.

"I told him a million times, he was taking a chance with that jackknife," O'Hara said.

"That's what he traded with me," Skitter said, looking to Shard.

"Couldn't be," O'Hara said. "His granddaddy gave him that knife. Schuman was proud he'd hidden it from the Reds all those months. He called it his good luck charm. He'd never have given that up. That's what the Chinese threw him in the turnip hole for. They searched him one day and found it. Threw him in the damn turnip hole for that little knife."

"No, really, I traded with him," Skitter said. "I gave him stuff from my Red Cross parcel. Food. Maybe he decided to trade the knife to survive. A pocketknife doesn't do you much good if you starve to death, does it?"

"Where's the knife now?" O'Hara asked.

"I traded it on to Cho. For boots."

"They shipped Cho out last spring," Collier said. "Too bad we can't get the knife back. He was always good for a trade."

"He really wanted that knife," Skitter said.

"Those boots?" O'Hara said, pointing at the worn combat boots Skitter wore.

"Yeah. I needed them. My feet were in bad shape," he said. Skitter sat motionless, afraid of saying the wrong thing. All he could think about were his feet and how much they'd hurt after the march from the Brick Camp. How he could have lost them. He'd watched men with black, frostbitten feet wrapped in rags dragging them through the snow as tears froze on their cheeks. Saw them fall and welcome Doctor Bayonet.

November 1950
Brick Camp, North Korea

Brick Camp was home for weeks, then months. Major Bak carried out daily interrogations, demanding more precise confessions: details about war crimes, killing civilians, invading peaceful North Korea, anything and everything. He cursed them for not admitting their crimes, forgave them for working as tools of the capitalist bosses, berated them for their stupidity, beat them for nothing, and occasionally gave the most cooperative among them cigarettes, extra food, and always, the promise of better treatment.

"They call you Skitter, because it means fast?" Bak asked one day. They were alone in the interrogation room. One table, two chairs, one door. No window, no witnesses.

"Yes," Skitter said, avoiding the comparison to a crab walking sideways. Bak's English was improving, but there was no percentage in confusing him.

"You are fast to learn, a good progressive prisoner," Bak said. "You wish to leave here?"

"For where?"

"Ah, Skitter must mean cautious also," Bak said with a sharp laugh. "The Democratic People's Republic will soon release some prisoners as a gesture of good will. We do not want any criminals who will spread lies about how our guests are treated. You must think about this. How can we trust you? How can we be sure you would be a good candidate?"

"I don't know."

"You must think of a way if you want to be considered. Now go."

"I need shoes," Skitter said, in a low voice. "Please."

"Go!"

As Skitter left, he saw North Korean soldiers huddled together, whispering. A truck was being loaded with boxes of files, supplies, and bedrolls. He slowed, kneeling to tighten the rags wound around his feet. The soldiers looked scared, their movements quick and jumpy, a change from the sudden rage or bored indifference that made up their two normal emotions. Change was never a good thing in a POW camp.

He approached Shard in their room. The concrete was cold, chilled by the autumn winds, still seeping water from the night's rain. "It looks like we're moving out," he said. "They're packing up trucks, and the guards seem nervous."

"We might know why," Shard said. "Coupla new prisoners were brought in. Tankers with those new Pershing heavies. MacArthur landed at Inchon, took back Seoul. The Marines hooked up with our guys in the Pusan Perimeter and are chasing the gooks north. These guys were in the spearhead when their tank broke down. They grabbed a jeep but took a wrong turn and got nabbed."

"What are they going to do with us?" Skitter asked, not caring about the tankers. Now he knew why Bak mentioned a goodwill gesture. North Korea wanted to show how nice they were to American POWs before MacArthur had the whole damn country in his hands.

"Take us farther north," Shard said. "They're not done yet. We may have become more important to them as bargaining chips."

"Or less important, if they don't want witnesses," Martinez said, as the small group sat in a corner of the room. "They still haven't put together a list of our names for the Red Cross. No one outside of this place even knows we're alive."

"So what are you going to do, Shard?" Tiny's voice boomed out from over their heads. "You're our damn section leader. Talk to these people."

"There's no talking to these people," Shard said. "We need to stand together, that's all we can do."

"Half of these guys can't even stand," Tiny said with a bitter laugh. "Stand together? Fall down together, more like."

"So what's your answer?" Collier asked.

"Give them what they want, and plenty of it," Tiny said. "The army can't court-martial a corpse."

"No," Shard said. "Once we give in, they'll be done with us for sure." Skitter stood and moved away from the group. He didn't want to go over the same issues again and again. Their opinions were all the prisoners had, the only thing of value. He didn't care. He cared about his feet, the cut on his ankle that wouldn't heal, the gnawing hunger in his gut, the lice that were hatching in the rotting seams of his uniform, the same uniform he'd donned on board ship before they landed at Pusan. He cared about the cold, about the approaching winter.

The new prisoners were obvious. Not so much by their distinctive tanker's overalls, but by their short hair and cleanliness. None of the other POWs had shaved or had a haircut since their capture. Their clothes were ragged, stained, and torn, their feet caked in dirt, covered in scars and scabs.

"Miller," said one of them when Skitter sat and introduced himself. "This is Lefkowicz."

"You've been interrogated?" Lefkowicz asked. He was almost clean-shaven, hardly a stubble growing on his young cheeks.

"Yeah, about a hundred times," Skitter said. "You get used to it." He eyed their socks. Thick wool socks. They wouldn't last long on the road, but in this damp, cold chamber they looked like bedroom slippers. "You guys take out any T-34s? Me and Shard did, with a bazooka."

"No, we never had the chance. Shot up a few trucks the day before we were captured, though," Miller said. "We were way the hell up front when our transmission went. Me and Lefty took a jeep and tried to get back to base and bring up an armored recovery vehicle, but we got lost. Next thing we know, we're on the ground, beat senseless. They only thing that stopped 'em from killing us was them fighting over who got our boots."

"Yeah, they love Uncle Sam's boots," Skitter said.

"Think they'll give us any shoes?" Lefty asked.

"Dunno," Skitter said. "They promise, but you know what that's worth. I hear those new heavy Pershing tanks are really something, big enough to take on the T-34."

"Yep," Lefty said, still capable of excitement. "The T-34 can't penetrate our armor, and our 90mm gun with the high-velocity round can go right through those Russian tanks."

"Okay, simmer down," Miller said. "Let's not mention the Pershing, okay?"

"Why not?" Skitter asked.

"We told the Reds we had Shermans, medium tanks. They'd probably like to hear about the new heavies, and I don't want to be the one to tell them. They believed us, had no reason not to. We complained about having old equipment from the last war. They ate it up."

"Smart," Skitter said. "Real smart." He appreciated a guy who knew how to play the angles.

Over the next few days, Major Bak became increasingly agitated. He'd bring a prisoner in for questioning and slap his face for an hour, pausing only for an occasional cigarette. He had a POW beaten unconscious when he asked how the war was going. Even the guards steered clear of Bak whenever they could. More equipment was moved out, new guards brought in, some still bandaged from recent wounds. Rumors flew thick, but the North Koreans refused any information except for the silent fear their faces betrayed.

Bak had the section leaders brought to his office early one morning. Shard could smell the coffee Bak had left in his cup, a delicate piece of china, so out of place. Bak sat back and lit a cigarette. As required, the ten section leaders stood at attention.

"The North Korean People's Army, in keeping with our lenient policy, will share our supplies with you for the upcoming journey. We will be going north, closer to the Yalu River. I have ordered shoes to be distributed, but unfortunately, due to the indiscriminate bombing of our civilian centers, we do not have enough for all. Therefore, you will distribute what I give you as you see fit. But first, all prisoners must sign a peace petition. There will be no exceptions. There will be a special midday meal in the courtyard to celebrate the signing. Assemble your sections at noon. I will read the petition, and section leaders will sign first. Then your sections. Then food. Then shoes."

Bak turned his attention to the last of his cigarette. His men pushed the POWs out of his office, out of his sight.

"We're leaving," Shard said to the men in his section. The weakest lay on the floor, their eyes studying the cracked ceiling, their minds far away from whatever Shard had to say. "Bak said he had shoes, not enough for everyone. Each section will get some to hand out."

"How are you gonna decide?" Tiny demanded.

"We'll see how many there are," Shard said. "But first, he wants everyone to sign a peace petition. Then we get some special food, or so he says."

"What's the petition say?" Miller asked.

"I don't know," Shard said. "He's going to read it out. Whatever it says, the other section leaders and I decided we all have to sign."

"What the hell, Shard?" Collier said. "Have you gone over to them?"

"If we all sign our names, it will be the first time the outside world hears we're alive. And if we all sign, no one person gets the blame." Shard looked around the room. "Every man signs, no matter what it says."

The next morning, after their breakfast of millet and sorghum, guards ordered the prisoners to fall out with all their belongings. Two of Shard's men curled up, faces to the wall, and refused to move. They were sick, they said. Shard knew they wanted to die, that they'd welcome a quick bayonet. If they died on the march, so be it. But he wouldn't walk out of the Brick Camp knowing they were cowering in a corner. He talked four men into dragging them to the formation, ignoring their pleading and groans.

"You'll stand up, goddammit," Shard said. "Stand up and sign the petition. Then there'll be extra food and maybe shoes." He hated himself for parroting what Bak had promised, but he needed everyone to be in on this. If the men died by afternoon, at least their families would know something about their deaths.

POWs lined up in the courtyard by sections. A few stood erect. Most leaned on each other. All had their feet wrapped in whatever rags or strips of clothing they'd been able to salvage from their own uniforms or those of the dead. Beards and hair hung ragged, framing vacant eyes and thin, grimy faces. One man collapsed, but his pals lifted him up, pressing close to keep him upright. Foul smells rose from the ranks, dysentery wracking bodies already weak from near starvation. Screams echoed from inside the building as Doctor Bayonet made his rounds.

"Today we leave for a new camp," Bak announced from his perch on the loading dock. "To show our solidarity with you as members of the working class, the Korean People's Army will give you extra rations. And shoes for the journey." Bak halted, looking out over the lines of prisoners as if he expected applause. But he had lied so many times that even if Shard hadn't spread the word to go along with the signings, he would have been ignored. "But first, you must all sign a peace petition. Every man must sign. No exception."

Bak read the statement. It called for peace between the Democratic People's Republic of Korea and the United States. In return for peace, the United States must withdraw from the Korean peninsula and apologize for the aggression against the North Korean people and the massacre of thousands of innocent civilians. The declaration went on like that for a while, stating the same thing in as many different ways as possible. It closed by describing the undersigned as freedom-loving former soldiers.

When Bak finished reading, he glared at the assembly, daring any man to resist. The prisoners were silent. Bak seemed at a loss, surprised at the lack of response. He snapped orders for the guards to bring men to the tables arranged in the courtyard where stacks of peace petitions were waiting.

"Write your name clearly and sign!" Bak yelled. "Hurry."

The lines moved as fast as the men could hobble and carry the sick. Three trucks spewing exhaust fumes drove into the courtyard and came to a halt at the loading dock.

"Food and shoes, you think?" Skitter asked as they moved closer to the petitions.

"I haven't seen three trucks' worth of food since Japan," Shard said. He glanced back at Miller and Lefkowicz, who were helping one of the sick men. Lefkowicz shook his head as he held the lifeless man upright. Miller lifted the man's head, felt for his pulse.

"Dead," Miller said.

"At least he didn't get the bayonet," Lefkowicz said. "That's something."

"Hurry!" Bak yelled as the small group huddled around the body. "You two men, here!" He pointed at Miller and Lefkowicz, barked orders to his men who grabbed the two tankers and forced them to one of the waiting trucks.

"They haven't signed," Shard said, stopping himself from going after them. A guard advanced, bayonet leveled, and Shard stepped back, hands held high.

"You sign," Bak said to Shard. "Now." Miller and Lefkowicz stood at the truck, the smallest one of the three. Worry and confusion played across their faces. Shard took the pencil and wrote out his name as the others had, in block letters so they'd be easy to read. Then he signed with a flourish.

Lines of prisoners moved to the tables, signed, and returned to the formation. Another man died. Prisoners descended on both bodies, shredding rotten and lice-infested uniforms and wrapping the rags around their feet. The dead were laid to the rear of the formation, pale skeletons in the dust.

Everyone waited for the last man to sign, eyeing the trucks, wondering if Bak would keep his word. The petitions were collected, guards counting the names on each piece of paper. It took some time, a good deal of screaming on Bak's part, and a head count of the prisoners until he was satisfied. All the time, Miller and Lefkowicz stood against the tailgate of the truck, two guards facing them.

"Good," Bak finally said. "You have taken the path of truth and peace. All have signed."

Shard struggled to speak, but he couldn't bring himself to say a word. Only the dead hadn't signed. And the two tankers. Protest was useless, even deadly. Miller and Lefkowicz stared at Bak, not yet comprehending.

"Your first reward is shoes," Bak said. "Each section will receive six pairs of shoes from the People's Army. In addition, those prisoners who signed the previous confessions voluntarily will receive new shoes. Consider this a gift from your comrades-in-arms." Bak smiled broadly. This time he really did expect applause.

Guards unloaded wooden crates from the trucks and carried one to every section, dumping the contents on the ground. Six pairs of worn-out North Korean Army sneakers. Heels flapped loose, laces gone, holes worn at the edges. Their gift from Bak. He grinned as he lit a cigarette, enjoying the looks on the prisoner's faces.

"Now you will see the reward for real cooperation," Bak said. "The ten men who voluntarily signed confessions previously will receive brand new shoes." He snapped his fingers, and guards raced through the formation, grabbing Skitter and the nine other men who'd signed the confessions at the last assembly. They were allowed to go through a box of sneakers on one of the truck beds until they found their size. They smiled and congratulated each other, until they turned and faced their fellow POWs, who'd just sold their souls for a few pairs of rotting sneakers.

"Hey, it ain't our fault," one of the men hollered. "Any of you coulda volunteered to sign, but you were too chicken." There was enough truth in what he said that they were allowed back into their sections without a fight. It was true that a few of them had been eager to sign. But most had done so to take the heat off their buddies. They'd all seen what had happened to Stallings.

Everyone had thought the confessions were forgotten, but now Bak used them to break whatever bond the prisoners had formed. For a few brief minutes, it had been us against them, Shard thought. Now the POWs were once again divided, even if most grudgingly accepted that the ten men who'd signed the first confession weren't to blame. Blame didn't matter. They had good shoes. Good enough to get to the new camp.

Shard looked at the pitiful pile of six pair for his section, while everyone else eyed Skitter as he put on his new shoes.

"I ain't giving them up," he said to no one in particular. "I practically stopped a riot by signing that thing. Nothing wrong with having these."

"If you say so," Tiny said. "None of them Chink shoes gonna fit me anyway."

Shard gave a pair to Collier. He didn't say why, but everyone knew Collier kept the list in his head. No one knew the names like he did. He gave the other five to men whose feet were still cut up, or who needed help walking.

"You are going to a new camp," Bak said, once the commotion over the shoes had settled down. "Obey your guards, or you will die. Do not stop, or you will die. I will greet you there in several days. As you march out of camp, each man will be given one apple. As I promised."

Bak turned on his heel, marching to the truck where the tankers stood. Guards pushed them into the vehicle and climbed in behind them. Bak got in the passenger's seat, and the little truck took off, leaving a gray haze of exhaust behind. Guards pulled bushels of apples out of the lead truck and hastily collected the petitions. They went in the truck with the guards' gear and supplies. That done, there was nothing left in the Brick Camp but death.

"Wonder what they wanted with those guys?" Martinez said.

"Interrogate them about the new Pershing heavy tanks, probably," Shard said, as they began to file out of the courtyard, heading north.

"But they told them they had Shermans," Skitter said, falling in next to Shard.

"Someone talked," Shard said. "Or maybe the North Koreans knew they were up against Pershings and figured it out. Who knows?"

"I got their names," Collier said. "Taken away from the Brick Camp, October 3rd, 1950."

Guards handed out apples as they stuffed their own pockets full. They were gnarled and spotted, but fresh. Each POW got one and ate it on the march. The apple tasted cool and refreshing in Shard's mouth, the momentary feel of crisp autumn air on his lips. It was fleeting. Shard crushed the seeds between his teeth and ate them along with the core.

Bak's truck was nowhere to be seen, probably speeding to their camp or an interrogation center. Bringing in two Pershing tankers would make Bak look good, Shard thought, wondering if the North Korean army was different than any other when it came to politics and getting ahead.

Guards took turns riding in the two trucks, munching on apples and tossing out the cores, enjoying the anguished looks on the prisoners' faces as they had to pass by the remnants. No one was allowed out of the line. The North Koreans hadn't bound their hands this time; the POWs were too weak to think of escape. The farther north they went, the more certain they were never to make it back to their own lines.

Shard felt his stomach begin to contract. The acidic apple had not set well. It was the first fruit he'd eaten since when? Japan? He couldn't even remember when that had been. He saw other men clutching their bellies as he felt his own bowels loosen. Had this been a trick of Bak's, or was it coincidence? There was no stopping allowed; Shard and the others stumbled forward, streams of foul-smelling brown liquid trailing them.

The road was a rutted gravel bed at best. The trucks lurched ahead, kicking up dust for the POWs to swallow. The march went into the mountains, along a barren valley road marked by rockfalls and dying vegetation. They had made ten miles when a halt was called near a stream for the midday meal and a rest. Rice balls were handed out, the gummy rice filled with kidney beans. The guards, perhaps because Bak was away, were lenient and let the POWs drink from the stream, but only after they'd drunk themselves.

A snarling drone rose from the south. Men looked around, unsure of the sound. A guard yelled, incomprehensible, but everyone understood the tone and the arm pointed skyward. Aircraft.

Guards ran away from the trucks, which stood out on the rocky terrain. POWs ran or cowered where they were, too weak or afraid to move. Skitter dashed past Shard, then turned back to help, taking him by the elbow, propelling him forward, up the slope to a rock outcropping.

As the roar of the planes grew, Shard couldn't help raising his head above the rock. Two P-51 Mustangs, bright silver in the sunlight, lined up for a strafing run on what they thought was a column of retreating Reds. Flashes sparked from their wings, the sound of machine guns echoed along the valley as rounds hit the ground, sending up plumes of dirt, stitching a line through the POWs and right to the trucks. One exploded, a hit on the fuel tank sending up a ball of fire. The other shuddered as the .50 bullets shredded it, leaving a smoking riddled heap behind.

The Mustangs peeled off, heading north, in search of more impressive prey.

Shard watched the POWs as they stood, all but the dead and the writhing wounded.

"Help me up," he said. Skitter pulled him upright, and Shard hobbled to the stream. He took off his trousers and washed himself, soaking his pants in the flowing mountain stream. He figured he had five minutes before the guards rounded everyone up. Five minutes while they assessed the damage, dealt with the wounded, and cursed the American air force. He squatted in the cold water, not caring about the death and agony yards away, thankful only to be able to wash away his own filth.

"You gonna make it?" Skitter asked as Shard wrung out his trousers.

"Yeah. I think the worst is over. Pain's not so bad now. How about you?" Shard asked as he pulled the wet pants on.

"The apple set okay, I guess. No problems," Skitter said. They walked to the road as the guards shouted at them, gesturing with their rifles to hurry up. Other guards walked among the dead and wounded, bayoneting them all, to be sure no one was left alive.

Three men were dead from Shard's section. The machine gun rounds had shattered their bodies, leaving legs and organs dangling, one head severed. Tiny was busy going through their pockets where he could, taking the small treasures hidden there. A wallet with a sawbuck and a picture of a pretty, young girl. Wooden matches. Tiny pulled the wrappings off the feet of the largest corpse and added them to his own. Then he stood and stared down the other men, silently daring them to say a word. As he walked away, they fell on the dead, ripping off clothing left unstained by blood, leaving behind naked bodies on the glistening, red rocks.

As the column passed the burning truck, guards prodded them along, fearful that the fighter planes might return. Ash settled from the fire. Bits and pieces of burning debris, borne skyward by the heat from the fire, fell on the prisoners like a gentle snow. Shard caught a smoking fragment, swirling and dancing in the air. It was paper, and he could make out enough of the words to know the outside world would not yet know their names. They were marching through the ash of the peace petitions.

Chapter 7

"Let's go see Smitty and Hughes," Shard said. "They'll want to trade for these cigarettes."

"You could trade with half the guys in here," Skitter said. "Why them?"

"Because they're new," Shard said. "They haven't had time to shake the nicotine habit, so I'll get the most from them."

"Yeah, they came in a coupla months ago, right? Makes sense. And the sooner you ditch those Chinese cigarettes the better." Skitter shoved his hands in his pockets and hunched his shoulders against the wind. "Why are we making the grand tour today, anyway? We've been from one end of camp to the other."

"To stay on top of things," Shard said. "You never know when someone's going to have the real lowdown." Camp Eleven was a sprawling encampment, made up of dozens of huts for the enlisted men, the sergeants' enclosure, the officers' section, administrative offices, barracks, storehouses, and kitchens. The newest prisoners were housed in sheds thrown together with scrap lumber and topped with rice straw roofs.

The lacked the gudeul heating system that the older huts used, but each had an ancient firebox and stovepipe chimney which managed to generate some warmth.

"Nobody knows anything," Skitter said. "And a trip down memory lane is the last thing I need."

"Hell, Skitter, we don't have much to show for the last few years except memories. Besides, I like seeing Shirt. Never thought I'd see him again after what happened in that pesthole of a camp. Besides Callahan, he's the only one of our original company left."

"Nothing but bad memories," Skitter said, glancing away as they walked.

"Happy New Year," Shard said, waving to a knot of prisoners gathered outside their hut, roasting two rats on a spit over an open fire. Catching, gutting, and cooking a rat without the benefit of a knife was a valued skill in Camp Eleven. Country guys were the best at it, and this hut was lucky enough to have three farm boys from Georgia and a short order cook from Savannah on the roster. Negro GIs who'd been captured a few months ago, they seemed to know how to survive. Shard thought that might have something to do with making it out of the Deep South in one piece.

Singed rat hair smelled awful, which was one good reason to cook it outdoors. Protein was protein. Someone said that roast rat was a tradition on Chinese New Year, so anytime rat was served, New Year's greetings were in order.

They found Smitty and Hughes sitting outside, backs against their shed, faces lifted to the meager sunlight.

"Hey, guys," Smitty said, raising a hand in greeting. "Have a seat, take a load off." Shard and Skitter sat on a log that had been left after the land was cleared for additional prisoners. Smitty grinned as if they were guests at a picnic. He was thickset, with dark wiry hair, and grease still in the creases of the skin on his hands. Hughes was younger, thin, and more wary. He nodded a greeting and went back to staring off in the distance.

"Thought you boys might want to trade for some smokes," Shard said, after they'd all settled into the silence for a while. "Chinese cigarettes, a dozen."

"Wouldn't mind," Smitty said. Hughes nodded his assent. "What you want?"

They settled on a package of crackers and a cube of cheese from a recent Red Cross packet. Shard passed them the cigarettes, the pack decorated with a picture of a pagoda and Chinese letters.

"Don't hang onto that pack," Shard said.

"Don't worry, we'll put the butts in our packs and burn this later," Smitty said. He gave one cigarette to Hughes, took one himself, and struck a match to light both. He put the pack away inside his tanker's overalls as he drew on the cigarette with a denied smoker's delight. Hughes took a drag and blew smoke rings. He was good at it.

Shard stashed the food away in his jacket. Skitter eyed him, hoping he'd break open the crackers and share, but the food vanished inside the folds of the quilted coat.

"Not a lot of tankers in here," Shard said. "You ever notice that, Skitter?"

"Yeah," Skitter said. "There's one guy I know of, but you're right."

"Occupational hazard," Smitty said. "If a tank is hit, the whole crew might go up with it. If they bail out, there's usually a whole lot of small arms fire going on. Tanks draw fire like bees to honey. Doesn't make sense, but infantry tends to shoot at armored vehicles. No big deal if you're inside, but hell to pay if you gotta get out."

Hughes nodded.

"How'd you get captured?" Shard said. "I don't recall."

"We were on point and hit a mine. Blew a tread clean off. Me and Hughes got out to check things out, and artillery starts dropping all around us. The column backed up and got off the road, since they were all bunched up. We dove into a ditch, and the next thing we know a round hits our Pershing dead center, and it starts to burn. No one got out. The Chinese swarmed all over us. We didn't have a chance."

"You were lucky," Skitter said. "Sort of." Hughes nodded. Luck was a relative thing. Here he was, smoking and getting a tan. His pals were decaying somewhere in the Korean hills. Lucky indeed.

"We knew a couple of guys back when we were first captured," Shard said. "They were a Pershing crew too. Remember them, Skitter?"

"Yeah, I think so. What were their names?"

"Miller," Shard said, "and Lefkowicz. You guys know them?"

"When was this?" Smitty asked.

"Back in '50, late September," Shard said.

"Never heard of 'em," Smitty said, blowing smoke. "Hell, Hughes was still in high school back then." Hughes nodded.

"First time the North Koreans took them away for interrogation, they said they were from a disabled Sherman tank, and the Reds believed them. But one day, the commander of the camp left with them. I guess they figured out they'd been in a Pershing."

"Pershings were new to Korea back then," Smitty said. "The Reds, Russians included, would want everything they could get on the latest version of the Pershing. That 90mm gun really chewed them up."

"You get any tanks?" Shard asked.

"Yep. Two T-34s. Lit 'em up like roman candles." Hughes nodded, taking a careful last drag off the remnants of his cigarette.

"Miller and Lefkowicz," Smitty repeated. "They on that list of yours?"

"Yeah."

"How many names you got?"

"Four hundred plus," Shard said.

"That's a dangerous list," Smitty said. "Lot more dangerous than carrying Chinese smokes."

"That's how the list started," Shard said. "The first few names were written on the back of a cigarette pack."

"Helluva tombstone," Smitty said. Hughes nodded.

December 1950
Mining Camp, North Korea

The list increased on the late November march north. The guards grew mean and surly, angry at the loss of their gear in the trucks. Some food had been salvaged, and the North Koreans kept most of it for themselves. Ten men were killed before the column stopped for the night. Remnants of rice balls were doled out to each section, barely a handful for each man.

Collier still had the pencil. He wrote in tiny letters on scraps of paper salvaged at the Brick Camp. Name, rank, date. He'd chanted the names of the day's dead until he could write, avoiding the nervous glances of the guards.

Shard stumbled on, weak with hunger, the days blurring into one long stretch of pain, misery, hunger, thirst, and shame. He wondered if he was dying, and if that would be such a bad thing. Food came intermittently, raw corn one day, millet the next. Rice balls became a long-ago luxury. He felt Skitter at his side guiding him, his arm draped over Skitter's bony shoulders. The road beneath his feet became a slog of dust and worn bloody wrappings which had fallen away like a snake sheds its skin. He couldn't see anything except ghosts, couldn't hear anyone except Bobbie, calling to him from a distant field, always out of reach. He walked on, beyond pain, beyond understanding.

"Here, eat." He heard the words and felt food on his lips. Awareness came slowly. He was inside. He felt hard dirt beneath him. An enclosed space. Cold. It felt like a grave.

"You have to eat," the voice said, insistent. A hand lifted his head, and he felt metal touch his mouth. A spoon. He hadn't felt a utensil against his lips since he was captured. How long ago? He had no idea. He opened his mouth and let the food in. Like a baby. It was soft, not millet or sorghum or raw corn. It was good, and he did think he might have died. Heaven could be a real spoon and soft food.

"Shard," the voice said. He expected to hear Bobbie, but he knew it was Skitter. Skitter was a lot like a little brother. Always around, a lot of trouble, but there when he needed him.

"Yeah," Shard said, trying to open his eyes. They fluttered and he caught a glimpse of Skitter. Tiny loomed over him.

Then it was night, and then day again. He was still on the ground, but he felt a straw mat under his body.

"Shard," Skitter said. "Have a drink. Here." He felt his head lifted as water filled his mouth, the liquid seeping into his body, filling it as if it were a dried-out husk. "Where are we?"

"Who knows?" Skitter said. "It's an old barracks, for mine workers, someone said."

Shard tried to rise but got as far as one elbow before falling back on the mat. He looked around, willing his eyes to stay open. Wood plank walls. One window. One door. The room was maybe eight by eight feet. Tiny took up a lot of it. Collier and Martinez, Skitter, and one guy lying down with his face to the wall. "Who's that?" Shard asked.

"Kiser," Collier said. "Henry Kiser. He's dead."

"Why is he still here?" Shard croaked out.

"He stays until he smells bad," Tiny said. "They count how many in a room before each meal. We get his food."

"Welcome back," Skitter said. "It's been ten days. You almost died."

"My tough luck," Shard said, and closed his eyes.

He awoke alone, except for Kiser. He ran his hands over his face, pinching his skin, feeling for signs of life, not knowing if he should be glad or disappointed. Either emotion seemed to demand more energy than he had to give. He rolled over and pushed himself up, his legs weak and wobbly, his body stiff from the cold ground. Straw mats lined the dirt floor. Except for Kiser's body, there was nothing else in the room. Shard moved to the grimy window and through the gloom saw blurry figures trudging by a long building. Kiser was beginning to smell, so he tried to open the window. Either he was too weak, or it was nailed shut. He left the room, entering a long, narrow hallway. Identical rooms continued off the corridor, some with prisoners lying on mats, moaning. The smell here was as bad, either from other corpses still drawing rations or the filth of the living.

Outside, gray clouds hung low over buildings, rows and rows of identical barracks of weathered wood and tar paper roofs. As he walked between the buildings, Shard could make out slag heaps at the bases of hills rising up from the camp. Mining. He shivered as winds blew along the walkway between the buildings. POWs in small groups passed him, heads bowed, apathetic. He didn't recognize any of them. He came to a large clearing and a roadway splitting the camp. The Chinese flag flew from a pole attached to one of the barracks. Not the North Korean flag, but the blood red banner of the Chinese Communists. No more Major Bak.

A long line of men waited at a hand pump by the road. They drank, washed themselves, and moved on through the mud around the ancient, rusty pump. He wanted water, but he couldn't wait. He had to find a familiar face, he had to know he hadn't been left behind, alone with a dead man.

Further on, POWs squatted over a trench latrine overflowing with shit. Others defecated on the bare ground, unable to make it to an open spot. Dysentery didn't wait. The stench was awful; the misery on the men's faces worse. He came upon a dead man, his trousers down, only yards from the latrine. Flies buzzed around his open eyes, and Shard stepped around him, wondering if perhaps he really were dead. If this wasn't Hell, he hoped he'd never see it.

Dozens of POWs stood in rows, listening to a prisoner standing on a chair and reading from a newspaper. There were five groups, spread apart, sections maybe. Guards walked behind them, watching the readers. Chinese guards, Shard reminded himself, their green woolen uniforms markedly different than the North Korean's pale brown. What had happened? Was this China?

He approached the sections, finally recognizing familiar faces. Then he heard a voice. Skitter was one of the readers, perched on a chair, holding a newspaper. Another Chinese soldier, his neat uniform with red piping on the collar marking him as an officer, stood behind him. The guard nodded along as Skitter's halting narrative described how the Tibetan people had welcomed the assistance of the People's Liberation Army in driving warlords and bandits from their land. Shard squinted to read the masthead as Skitter turned a page to start an article about a new hydroelectric dam. The *Shanghai Times*. Why was Skitter reading this crap?

A guard roughly pushed Shard in line, smacking him in the back with the butt of his rifle and pointing to the other POWs standing at attention. Skitter looked at the commotion and saw Shard. He stumbled over the words, but the soldier behind him rapped the chair and pointed to the paper. Skitter read on. The POWs—Shard's section—didn't turn, didn't acknowledge him. He stood at attention, his knees slightly bent so they wouldn't lock up, arms straight down at his side. The words buzzed in his ears, dull recitations of tons of wheat harvested, steel mills meeting quotas, and the wisdom of Chairman Mao in guiding the Chinese people to prosperity. He closed his eyes, but within a minute the rifle butt was back, the guard shaking his finger. No sleeping on your feet.

Shard struggled to keep standing, wishing he were lying on the dirt floor next to a corpse. His legs shook, sweat broke out on his forehead, and the ground came up to meet him as Skitter read the headline, People's Volunteer Army Aids in Heroic Defense of Korea.

Water splashed on his face. He felt it run down his chest as he licked his lips for the moisture.

"He's sick, Comrade," he heard Skitter say.

"If he was out of his room, then he is not sick," the Chinese voice said in precise English.

"Where am I?" Shard said, shaking his head like a wet dog. He was seated in a chair in a small room, like the other rooms, except that this one had a wood plank floor and a wood stove in the corner. Skitter stood with his hand on his shoulder. An empty glass sat on the desk in front of Shard, and he wanted to reach out and drink the drops at the bottom. Behind the desk, the Chinese officer sat smoking a cigarette, watching him.

"You are in the care of the Chinese People's Volunteer Army. I am Comrade Wong. You are Shard, section leader, correct?"

"I am Ethan Shard, Private First Class, serial number—"

"No, no, no," Wong interrupted, wagging his finger. "You are no longer a soldier. There are no ranks among prisoners. You are all war criminals until you prove otherwise. No officers, no sergeants, no privates. You must not speak of rank."

"Are we at war with China?" Shard asked, confused by Wong's accusation.

"Do you wish to invade China as you invaded the Democratic People's Republic?"

"Please, Comrade," Skitter pleaded. "Shard is not well."

"It does not matter," Wong said, crushing his cigarette. "Well or unwell, he is either a war criminal or not."

"I can't argue with that," Shard said, trying to find a common ground. "I don't want to invade anyone. I only want to know what's happened. Are we in China? Where are the North Korean guards?"

"Skinner tells me you are a good section leader, that you controlled your men and oversaw the distribution of food well. These are excellent attributes. We need section leaders who can guide men to the course of right thinking."

"Thank you," was all Shard could think to say.

"So I will brief you," Wong continued. "Since you arrived here and fell ill, much has happened. Chairman Mao has allowed our volunteer soldiers to come to the aid of our Korean comrades. This was necessary as the imperialist lackey MacArthur was about to invade the People's Republic of China. Chairman Mao showed great forbearance and kept the struggle contained here in Korea. So no, you are not in China. Another world war has been averted due to the Chairman's peaceful approach to this crisis. Do you favor peace or war, Shard?"

"I already signed a peace petition," Shard said.

"Yes, unfortunately the petitions were destroyed. For now, be assured your treatment will be most lenient. The Koreans are more primitive than we Chinese, and I regret your suffering. If you cooperate, your situation will improve. Now leave and resume your duties as section leader." Wong ground out his cigarette and opened a file on his desk, done with the Americans.

"What the hell is going on?" Shard asked Skitter as soon as they were clear of the headquarters building.

"The Chinese are running the show," Skitter said. "You weren't making a lot of sense when we got here, so you probably didn't notice. The NKs handed us over to the Chinese and took off. Scuttlebutt is they're pretty much out of the fight, but the Chinese have picked up the slack."

"What do you mean, not making sense?"

"You were talking to someone named Bobbie, but there wasn't anyone there. Who's Bobbie?"

"I must have been delirious. What is this place?" Shard asked, leaning on Skitter as they crossed the main road. Military trucks drove slowly past, Chinese soldiers gazing at them with contempt.

"Wong said it's a temporary holding camp. Gotta be a coupla thousand guys from smaller camps. You won't believe who's here."

"Who?"

"Kelso."

"Take me to him," Shard said.

"Okay, but don't call him sergeant," Skitter said, his voice low as he leaned close to Shard. "This is an enlisted man's camp. He's trying to organize things, but it's not working. Anyway, his guys call him Shirt. Something about an old army name for a top sergeant."

"Yeah, I heard that one. Since the only guy on a work detail with a clean shirt would be the top kick. Get it?" He leaned on Skitter as they walked past their barracks, his breath coming in ragged gasps.

"You should have stayed inside," Skitter said. "We were getting sick rations for you."

"I remember eating something. It was warm."

"Boiled turnips and grains. You get it if you're sick. That's about the extent of the medical care here."

"Look," Shard said as they turned a corner. "There's a red cross on that building. Is it a hospital?"

"Stay clear of that place. Scuttlebutt is they experiment on patients. Most POWs who go in never come out. No one's sure if those Chinese are real doctors or not."

"I think I'm beginning to miss the North Koreans," Shard said as Skitter opened a barracks door. He knocked as they entered a room as small and dismal as theirs. Five men sat on mats, their backs to the wall. Shard hardly recognized the prisoner who rose and extended his hand.

"It's good to see you alive, Shard," First Sergeant Hector Kelso said. "A little worse for wear, I'd say."

"Same here, Shirt. We tried to get to you on that ridge, you know."

"I know. Skitter told us, and Callahan here saw you get that tank." Kelso gestured to another prisoner that Shard recognized through the beard and grime covering his face.

"Vic Callahan, right? How's Hanson? Did he make it?"

"Nope. Our rounds bounced right off those damn tanks. We took off when you did, but we got caught by the Reds coming up that road. They shot Hanson and took me prisoner. I still don't know why it wasn't the other way around."

"Have a seat, boys," Kelso said. Shard and Skitter squeezed in next to Callahan. "Far as I know, I'm the only noncom in this camp. The Reds are keeping ranks separated and telling our boys they don't have to follow orders. They're trying to break us. What we need to do is keep military discipline if we're going to survive."

"How?" Skitter asked. "We can't salute or anything."

"It's not about saluting," Kelso said. "It's about not becoming a mob. We need to police ourselves, quietly. Our guys need to know that they're still in the army, otherwise the Chinese will have us eating out of their hands in no time."

"We can't go up against them," Skitter said. "They're crazy about this indoctrination stuff. The North Koreans were unpredictable, but the Chinese are serious trouble."

"We don't go up against them," Kelso said. "But we need to deal with the mob mentality. One place to start is with one of your men, Shard."

"Who?"

"Tiny," Callahan said. "That big bastard is intimidating everyone. He's made a business out of delivering sick rations."

"If you're officially sick, you have to have someone go get your rations," Skitter explained. "Like I got yours."

"Tiny beats up anyone who doesn't stop carrying rations for the sick. He cornered the market and keeps a quarter of each ration for himself," Kelso said. "That has to stop. We can't let the strong bully the weak."

"Okay, but how?" Shard said. "I'm not in shape to do anything about it."

"Deliver the message," Kelso said. "Let him know he's being watched. Tell him the bigger they are, the harder they fall."

"Does he know about you being here?" Shard asked.

"No," Kelso said. "Only the men in this room. Skitter here recognized me, and Callahan has been with me since the beginning. Keep it a secret, okay?"

"Okay, Shirt." Rain began to splatter against the roof. Big fat drops that quickly turned into a downpour.

"Outside," Kelso said, and they scrambled out of the room. Shard followed the group as they stripped off their clothing and stood naked in the rain, holding their mouths open and scrubbing their stained trousers.

"Why are we doing this?" Shard said, raising his voice to be heard over the rain.

"Every sick dogface in this god-forsaken camp is washing by that one pump, every hour of the day," Kelso said. "Where do you think all of the germs and filth end up?"

"In the ground," Shard said. "Then in the water."

"Right. That's the next thing we need to do. Find buckets and organize a location for washing away from the pump before everyone dies of disease. Get the section leaders to talk to Wong. He might listen."

"What about you," Shard said, rubbing his body in a useless pantomime of lathering soap. "Aren't you a section leader?"

"Nope. I'm just plain Kelso, war criminal." He grinned, and Shard smiled, too, cheered at the semblance of a plan, a sense of order amid the chaos. The rain was cold, but it felt good. He felt alive. It was an odd sensation, he decided.

"What are you going to do?" Skitter asked as they made their way back to their barracks, the rain having turned to a light mist.

"Try to get rid of these lice," Shard said, squeezing one between his fingernails.

"You know what I mean."

"I'll talk to Tiny," Shard said. "He's got to know there will be consequences when we get out of here."

"Tiny doesn't think about consequences," Skitter said. "He thinks about today." They walked on, wringing their threadbare clothes, working lice eggs out of the seams as best they could.

"Why did you call Wong *Comrade*?" Shard said. It had been bothering him ever since he heard Skitter speak the word. It came out of his mouth much too easily.

"It's what they like. I figured it might help you if I showed a sign of respect. It's just an angle, Shard. We have to think about today too."

When they got back to the room, Kiser's body was gone. The odor of death lingered, a familiar fragrance by now. Collier, Martinez, and Tiny sat listlessly, knees drawn up to their chins against the damp chill rising from the dirt floor.

"Didn't know if you'd ever get up again," Martinez said. "You okay?"

"Good enough," Shard said, hoping it was true. He sat down on his mat, his clothes in front of him. "We need to get rid of the lice. If we don't, they'll breed in here and suck us dry."

"I don't got to listen to you," Tiny said. It was his first reaction to any idea, no matter how sensible.

"Yes, you do. I'm section leader here, and I just met with Comrade Wong. Disobey me, and I'll have him deal with you." He stared at Tiny, willing his nerves to hold.

"Don't get all hot and bothered," Tiny finally said, taking off his shirt.

Skitter managed to pry a rusty nail from the wall and dig a small trench in the floor. They worked for hours, going through their clothes and bodies, snatching the little bastards as they crept out looking for blood to feed on. Quick pressure between fingernails, and they went into the trench. The nail was passed around to work the tiny white eggs out from the rotting seams of their garments, sweeping them into the pint-sized mass grave.

It needed to be done, but Shard also wanted Tiny to agree with him about something, anything, before he delivered his real message. It might help, it might not. He warned them about the water and hinted that he and Wong were about to do something about it.

"Glad to have you back, Shard," Collier said. He inspected his trousers, gave them a shake, and put them on. When everyone was done, they covered the lice casualties with dirt, and Tiny made a little joke how much fun it was to kill North Koreans, even if they were lice. It wasn't that funny, but the others appreciated his effort and laughed.

"When's chow?" Shard asked.

"About an hour before sunset," Skitter said. "Not much longer. You got sick rations this morning, but that's probably over now. And Kiser's too."

"We'll make do," Shard said. Tiny rose and left the room. Shard got up slowly, wincing at the pain in his gut, and followed. "Tiny, hold up."

"What? I'm busy," Tiny said, not breaking his stride.

"That's what I want to talk to you about," Shard said. A shiver ran through him, the still wet uniform cold and clammy against his body. Scattered raindrops fell on his face as he hugged his body, hoping to keep some warmth in and rain out.

"Talk then."

"You've got to stop taking rations from the sick. I heard about your scam. It has to stop."

"No, it don't. I got a responsibility," Tiny said, his lips curled in a sneer as he turned to look down at Shard.

"I know you're a big guy, and you need more food. But you can't take it from the sick."

"I got news for you, Shard. The sick are going to die anyway. I got a chance, and I'm taking it. And you're not going to stop me." Tiny pushed his finger against Shard's chest. It wasn't much, but it almost knocked him over.

"I can get Wong to stop you," Shard said in a low voice, glancing around to be sure no one heard. "Or I could get him to help you. Extra rations, maybe."

"I'll cut my own deals, Shard. You mind your own damn business. Otherwise, you might get sick and die, real sudden like." Tiny turned and stalked away, his fists clenched at his side. Shard hadn't expected obedience, but he wasn't ready for the threat. What deal? Information was the only currency a POW had. What did Tiny know?

"Collier," Shard said from the doorway when he returned to the barracks. He nodded his head toward the hallway.

"Yeah?" Collier said when they were alone.

"I think you should hide your list. Make a copy if you can."

"I already wrote all the names out on that wallpaper I found at the Brick Camp. I still have the scraps of paper I started with. I could add the rest of the names to those."

"Good. Let's find a hiding place once you're done. But don't let anyone know, okay?"

"No one?" Collier asked.

"Just to be safe," Shard said. "Not a soul. Not Martinez or Skitter, for their own good. Where do you hide the stuff now?"

"I got the pencil stub in my shoe. The original list, far as it goes, is on a bunch of cigarette packages. I keep them folded up in my pocket like they're junk I haven't thrown away. Hidden in plain sight, you know?"

"Smart. What about the full list?"

"Right here," Collier said, tapping the large side pocket on his fatigues. "Wrapped up in a handkerchief I traded for."

"What'd you have to trade?"

"That apple they gave us. It had a worm."

"Hell, I would've eaten the worm," Shard said.

"That's what the guy wanted the apple for," Collier said.

Back in the room, they waited for the evening meal, not that it deserved the name. And for Tiny's return. The food came first, delivered by guards who counted out balls of grain from a bucket, leaving them on a chipped bowl.

"What are these?" Shard said. "No rice?"

"Soybeans, mixed with our old pal millet, plus corn and sorghum," Skitter said. "Wong said they grow a lot of soybeans around here."

"When'd you get so chatty with Comrade Wong?" Shard asked.

"Getting you on the sick list," Skitter said. Then they were silent, each man focused on the soy ball held in the palm of his hand, licking up each fallen morsel as they eyed Tiny's portion sitting alone in the bowl.

"Where do they store the food?" Shard asked, after everyone was done licking scraps from their hands.

"The building Wong took you to," Skitter said. "It's the same as all the others, except they had wood floors put in and a stove for heating and cooking. They use one room to prepare the sick rations. That's where they boil up the grains and turnips. Then a couple of other rooms are used to make this soy crap."

"Who does the cooking?"

"Locals, I guess," Skitter said. "They look Korean. It's forbidden to talk with them. They look as afraid of the Chinese as they are of us. I doubt we'd have a chance with them."

"A chance at what?" Collier asked.

"A chance to steal food," Shard said. "Skitter and me were pretty good at it in Tokyo. Helped to have a truck and ready cash, though."

"Well, well, a couple of wheeler-dealers," Martinez said. "Is that why you were so chummy with Wong and his pals, Skitter?"

"Just trying to work the angles," Skitter said. "And I had to be sure Shard was listed as sick. He needed the food. Still does."

"We all do," Shard said. He lay down on the mat and tried not to think of the gnawing pain in his gut. Hunger, diarrhea, dysentery, he couldn't tell them apart anymore.

"I'm going to stretch my legs," Skitter said. "One hour after dinner we have to be inside."

"Okay," Shard said, feeling the sweat break out all over his body. Collier and Martinez left, too, and he shivered alone on the floor, thinking things through, wondering if there were any angles left to play.

Dreams flitted across his eyelids, so real that he thought he was awake, or at least the visions would still be there if he opened his eyes. He could feel the damp earth beneath him, but then it became a soft meadow on the sloping banks of the river by the farm. Bobbie was fishing. He could only see the back of his head and wished he'd turn around. He rose and walked closer. Bobbie's hair was filled with lice, crawling down his shirt, coming out his pant legs. He ran, and suddenly he was in the rain, washing mud from his arms.

"Shard, Shard," Skitter called, shaking him by the arm. "Are you all right?"

"What?" He was in the barracks, surprised to find himself back here.

"You were having another nightmare. Who the hell is Bobbie, anyway?"

"Just a bad dream, I'm okay." He turned away from Skitter, pretending to sleep. His heart pounded so loudly he was certain everyone in the room could hear it. Everything hurt from his guts to his heart to his searing memories. He didn't know if he could do it. Hold it together. Help Skitter along, control Tiny, support Shirt in what he was trying to do. All he could think about was pain. Pain now and forever.

In the morning he decided. If he was going to die, it might as well be for something. Death had become so commonplace that it wasn't such a farfetched thing to think about. Not like bullshitting in a bar back home, talking about dying for country or kinfolk. This was real. He was probably going to die here, or in another camp like it. So why not stand up? Saint Peter might take note and weigh it against his other sins.

Shard stood, his knees a sharp ache as he rose from the ground. His ribs hurt, his side hurt, and he realized there was less and less flesh every day between his bones and the cold, damp ground. So why not? What did he have to lose?

"Skitter," he said as he braced himself against the door. "Go out and spread the word. Tiny's not carrying sick rations anymore. For anyone."

"But Shard—" Skitter said, looking at Tiny who was on his feet, his mouth twisted in anger.

"Now!" Shard said, hoping his voice carried authority rather than the quavering desperation he felt. With a nervous glance at Tiny, Skitter darted out of the room, squeezing past Shard.

"Get out of my way," Tiny said, advancing on Shard.

"No. I told you yesterday. It's over."

"Who says?" Tiny snarled into his face. He loomed over Shard, his grimy hair matted above his thick brow.

"What is this, a schoolyard?" Shard said. "Is that all you got?"

"No," Tiny roared, and picked Shard up in a bear hug that burst the air out of Shard's lungs. Tiny carried him down the corridor, kicking the door to the outside open. Shard's arms and legs flailed, but Tiny laughed and squeezed harder. Shard began to see stars as he gasped for air.

"Let him go!" Collier cried, while Martinez tried to pull Shard free. But Tiny was too strong, and they were far weaker. Shard heard more voices, excited Chinese jabbering, and then heard a loud *thump* before he hit the ground, half a second before Tiny's body fell on top of him, his bear hug finally broken.

For the second time in as many days, Shard found himself slumped in a chair in Wong's office, consciousness slowly returning. A Chinese medic was winding a tight bandage around his ribs, tying off the ends. He looked at the medic and thought it might be a woman under the quilted wool. It was hard to say, but soft, small hands gave her away. A woman is touching me and Tiny didn't kill me, Shard thought. My lucky day.

"It is a grave offense for a prisoner to attack a section leader," Wong said, without preamble.

"I thought it was pretty grave myself," Shard said, smiling at the medic. She took no notice but pulled the bandage tight. Shard winced, wondering if his ribs were bruised or broken.

"Ah, a joke," Wong said. "Not a good one, but it shows you are resilient. Now, what provoked this attack?"

"We don't like each other," Shard said.

"No, that is not the correct answer." Wong walked around the desk, spoke to the medic, and she quickly gathered her things and left. "The correct answer is the truth. There must be nothing between a section leader and the camp commander. Otherwise, I will get a new section leader. And please note, it is not an offense for one common prisoner to attack another. Do you understand?"

"I do. But you must understand, a section leader who informs on one of his own men will no longer have their respect. So you'd have to get a new section leader anyway."

Wong lit a cigarette and studied Shard. He exhaled and looked at the ceiling, as if Chairman Mao were there, ready to dispense some of that famous wisdom. "You are correct. And I am satisfied since you spoke the truth. You would be useless to me if you told me more. So the prisoner—you call him Tiny, another joke, yes—will be punished simply for assault. He will be in special solitary confinement. Whatever other infractions he committed can be set aside. For the moment."

"Thank you," Shard said. He didn't like saying it. He didn't want to be beholden to this man, but he had no choice. "May I ask a question?"

"Yes, quickly."

"The water. Men are washing next to the pump. Everything goes into the ground, lice eggs, and maggots. Then it's pumped back up, they drink the water and become sick. If we had some buckets, the men could take water and wash elsewhere, and it would reduce illness. It would be good for everyone."

"It is up to you to reduce illness!" Wong lunged around his desk and slapped Shard twice, back and forth with the palm and back of his hand. "That is what section leaders are for. Do not come to me with your petty troubles. Do you think the Chinese people can spare hundreds of buckets? That we should ship them from China, instead of supplies for our own soldiers? Do you wish to undermine our struggle against imperialism?"

"No. I am only addressing a health issue," Shard said quickly, stunned by the sudden outburst. "Perhaps if there were another water source, one could be for drinking and the other washing."

"There is another pump, in this building. It is for the People's Volunteer Army. Go. I am tired of your complaints. You Americans are too soft. We will make you harder." Shard rose, surprised at how swiftly he moved. He was getting used to obedience. Wong was right, they were too soft. It took a hard man to survive Korea.

Shard walked down the main road looking for Skitter. There were no newspaper readings today, nothing but a knot of guards standing off to the side of the road. He walked closer and saw Tiny. He was digging a hole. The guards looked at Shard, menacing snarls forming on their faces. He turned away, eyes to the ground, his back tensing for the blows that did not come, as he wondered if the hole was Tiny's solitary confinement.

Shard approached Kelso's barracks. As he was about to enter, the door burst open from the inside and two guards dragged Kelso out. His hands were tied, and he was bleeding from a cut above his eye, his head hanging low. A third guard followed, holding a submachine gun, screaming at the prisoners. Everyone dove for cover, expecting him to open fire.

Shard crouched down but kept his eyes on Kelso, who was blinking away the blood seeping into his eye. He mouthed *someone talked,* and then the third guard kicked Shard in the ribs. That was when he knew they were broken.

He staggered back to his barracks, where Skitter was waiting along with Collier and Martinez.

"Who called the guards?" he asked as he slid down against the wall, wincing in pain.

"Dunno," Skitter said. "I was on the other side of the compound, putting the word out like you said."

"They're around all the time," Collier said. "They could have seen it on their own. What did they do with Tiny?"

"He's digging a hole. I think it's going to be his solitary confinement."

"For how long?" Martinez said.

"Don't know," Shard said. "But I think the real question is, how deep?"

"Christ," said Skitter. "Are they going to bury him alive?"

"I don't think so," Shard said. "Wong wanted to know what we were fighting about, but I told him I couldn't be a good section leader if I squealed, so he let it drop. For now."

"Here, eat," Skitter said. "We saved your breakfast. For you and Tiny." Skitter handed the bowl to Shard. "Maybe we could split his."

"No," Shard said. "Why don't you and Martinez see if you can find out what's happening. Maybe they'll let you give it to him."

"Okay," Skitter said, cupping the soy ball in his hands. "Tiny hurt you much?"

"Only when he fell on me. And a guard kicked me a few minutes ago as they were taking Kelso away. A guy Skitter and I knew in Japan," Shard explained to the others. He wasn't entirely certain the Reds knew Kelso was as sergeant, and there was no reason to spread it around. "Remember him, Skitter?" Shard said, his eyes telling Skitter to stay mum about Kelso's rank.

"Yeah," Skitter said. "Shit. What he'd do?"

"No idea. Go on, see what you can find out about Tiny."

As soon as they were gone, Shard pulled Collier in close. "Hide the damn list. Now." His hand shook as he grasped Collier's shirt. He let go and fell back, the room swirling around him, centered on the spasms in his gut. He heard a shriek, his own, as if from some distant place. The pain nailed him down, the ground cold as a grave.

Chapter 8

April 18, 1953
Camp Eleven, North Korea

"You sure the list is safe?" Skitter asked as they stopped to watch the feast in progress. Men were peeling off tiny shreds of meat and licking rat fat off their fingers.

"We're okay, don't worry," Shard said. "Why would the Chinks even know about it?"

"Can't help but worry," Skitter said. "Now that the peace talks are moving along. If they find that list now, there'll be hell to pay."

"You scared they'll kill us after all this time?" Shard said. "We made it this far, a few more months should be easy."

"Not with a bullet in your head," Skitter said. "I know it's important to get that list back home, but it's important for *us* to get there too. I'd like to be sure they can't find it."

"Don't worry. If they do, I'll take the blame," Shard said.

"You and Collier," Skitter said.

"Yeah, if it comes to that. Bak knew about the list, but who knows what happened to him, or if he thought we'd go on with it? They didn't keep any records, that's the whole point of having the list."

"Yeah, okay," Skitter said, his voice dropping to a whisper. "Yuan gave us some news this morning."

"What?" Shard said, gripping Skitter by the arm. "Is something happening?" He moved him away from the knot of men around the fire. The greasy smoke sought them out, filling the empty space where they had stood.

"There's going to be an exchange. It sounds like they've made some sort of agreement about repatriation. They call it Operation Little Switch. It's for the sick and wounded. If that goes well, it's on to Operation Big Switch for the rest of us."

"Why didn't you tell me before?" Shard said, his voice shrill with disbelief. "This is big news."

"We weren't supposed to say anything," Skitter whispered. "He hinted that some progressives might be released with the sick cases. He wants guys who won't bad-mouth the Chinese before the main release."

"Worried it'll hurt your chances if they find the list?" Shard asked.

"That doesn't matter now that you put that bug in his ear about me going to China, for Christ's sake," Skitter said. "He'd never select me and give up on that. I don't want anything to mess things up. We're close, Shard, real close."

"I'm not going to destroy the list, Skitter, if that's where you're going."

"No. The only place I'm going is home. Just don't let them find it. Not now."

"I'm careful," Shard said. "Very careful." He moved closer to the fire, watching one guy toss rat bones into the flames. The fire danced higher, charring the carcass until there was nothing left but blackened ash.

December 1950
Mining Camp, North Korea

After Kelso was taken away from the Brick Camp, Shard worsened. Collier found Shard delirious, telling someone named Bobbie to watch out, to run for it, don't get caught. "Shard, talk to me," he said, dragging him to his straw mat in the corner, leaving a trail of brown liquid. Shard's guts were giving way. "Shard, I hid the list. You have to wake up so I can tell you where. Shard!"

"What happened?" Skitter said, Martinez at his heels.

"I dunno," Collier said. "I found him on the floor like this. He's got the dysentery real bad."

"Maybe we can get him back on sick rations," Martinez said. "He needs decent food and clean water."

"I'll try," Skitter said. "I'll tell Wong it's an emergency. He might go for it."

"Don't get yourself killed trying," Collier said. "These bastards don't give a crap about any of us. Remember Doctor Bayonet."

"I think the Chinese are different," Skitter said. "They have to be." It was wishful thinking. But wishes were all they had.

Skitter was gone an hour. He came back with a black eye and a chipped enamel pot. POWs followed him into the room, trailing the scent of hot food. Martinez pushed the other prisoners out into the hallway and blocked the door.

"What happened?" Collier asked.

"I got soup," Skitter said. "For all of us." He opened the lid, and hot steam wafted out. Green vegetables floated in a broth that might have once had chicken somewhere close to it.

"Jesus," Collier gasped. "Is that real?"

"Yeah," Skitter said. "It cost me, though." He pointed to his black eye.

"Damn, I'd trade a shiner every day for a pot of soup," Collier said. He raised Shard as upright as he could while Skitter held the soup for him to smell. Shard opened his eyes.

"Drink, Shard," Skitter said. "It's still warm." He held the rim to Shard's lips and tipped the pot, letting a little of the broth into his mouth. With no cups or utensils, they passed the pot around, taking small sips.

"How'd you do it?" Collier asked after half the soup was gone.

"I asked Wong for sick rations for us, so we could take care of Shard. I said we were all in bad shape. He had a guard whack me one and toss me out of his office. I thought it was over, but then they took me to the kitchen and gave me the soup. They had to escort me back here, otherwise I never would have made it alive."

"They want him as section leader that bad?" Martinez said.

"Who the hell knows what they want?" Skitter said.

"Good work," Collier said. "We need to get the vegetables out. Who has the cleanest hands?"

"Me," Skitter said. "They let me wash up in the kitchen. Figured we wouldn't get anything to eat the soup with, so I asked the guard, and he said okay—far as I could tell." Skitter reached in and took out a leafy green that reminded him of celery. He fed it to Shard, telling him to chew and swallow. He gave him another swig of broth and handed out a round of vegetables. He felt proud. He was pulling his weight, doing what needed to be done. Who else was eating this good tonight?

Shard felt the warm broth in his belly, heard the voices in the room, and rolled the unfamiliar taste of greens around in his mouth. He didn't understand, but took the food in eagerly, desperately, feeling his ruined innards soak up the soothing warmth. The image of a wilted plant in a glass jar flitted through his mind, long buried amidst childhood memories best forgotten. He'd found it when he was a little kid, some early spring day by the recollection of sunlight on his face and muddy dampness on bare knees. It was on a shelf in the barn, an old jam jar filled with powdery dry dirt. The few leaves were yellowed and wilting, the root tendrils curled thick at the bottom of the jar. He'd filled it with water from the pump and watched as the soil drank it up, the roots seeming to thicken and come alive as the nourishment reached them. That was how he felt. Every small sip went where it was needed. If someone could sit him outside in the sun, like he'd done with the little plant, he'd be fine.

Except if his Pa came along. Two days after he'd discovered the plant, when it was already greening as the sunlight fed it and little Shard watered it, Pa came along and threw the jar into the woods. Shard could still hear the shattering of glass on rock and Pa's whiskey voice telling him to get to work and not be foolish, some things weren't meant to be saved, and he might be one of them.

He was right about not being saved, Shard thought. He didn't know how right he was.

"Who's right?" Skitter asked. "You awake?" Shard tried to answer, but he couldn't. It made no sense. When he didn't mean to, he spoke. When he wanted to, he couldn't. He raised his hand and felt someone take it. Too far gone? Not meant to be saved? We'll see.

They fed him broth every day. It came in place of their evening ration. Soy balls in the morning, vegetable soup at night. Shard grew stronger and the dysentery lessened, his system tolerating the warm and nutritious soup. He dreamed of the plant. He wondered if it might have taken root in those woods, freed of the confining jar. Maybe it was a small tree now, growing next to that rock, the broken glass covered by years of fallen leaves. It was the only reason he could think of ever going back there. He imagined the tree, fifteen or sixteen years old, cracking the rock with its strong roots, the bark smooth even as leaves fluttered to the ground, covering the evidence of a violent beginning.

Shard slept, dreamed, ate, and drank. The sleep was fitful, the dreams nightmares. He heard Collier reciting names, a whispered prayer in the dark.

Robert Nichols, Basil Varney, John Baron. One night he heard Collier speaking names of guys he didn't know. Time must have passed. One morning he sensed his tattered uniform being removed. He was cold, his pale, dank skin stretched thin over bone, his whole body shivering on the straw mat. Someone covered him with another straw mat, speaking soothing words. As he slept, dreams of winter snows and frigid winds haunted the night. He sensed light and was fed, pieces of soy ball stuffed in his mouth. Warm water followed and it felt clean, free of grit, odorless.

Hands pulled at him, and he felt his clothes being put back on. The seams were damp. Someone had washed his clothes, or what was left of them. He managed to force his eyes open, but it was already dark. Skitter was lifting a tin cup to his lips. Soup. How long had he slept?

"Eight days," Martinez said. Shard didn't understand him, but then realized he must have spoken out loud. His throat constricted as he tried again, letting little more than a croak escape. Skitter tipped more soup into his mouth. He swallowed the liquid, the warmth soothing and pleasant, strange sensations after all these days and weeks. He looked at Skitter and tried to smile his thanks, but it faded into a grimace. He raised his hand to Skitter's arm and patted it, the most he could do. His hand fell to the ground, and as he fell into a strange slumber, he felt Skitter place the bowl to his lips again. He took it in, gulping with his last waking breath.

"What happened?" Shard asked, his eyelids fluttering open. The light was different in the room. He'd slept, but he had no idea how long. His back ached and his muscles rebelled at any movement.

"You almost died," Skitter said.

"Somebody said eight days, I remember," Shard said as Skitter helped him sit against the wall. Other figures moved in the dark, hazy background, but he couldn't focus on them.

"That was three days ago," Skitter said. "You've been out for eleven days. Welcome back."

"You cleaned my clothes," Shard said, feeling the worn, thin fabric against his thighs.

"Purely in our own self-interest," Collier said. "I wouldn't call them clean, but we boiled out the lice."

"Did you get buckets?" Shard asked.

"Yeah, big iron pots," Martinez said, kneeling next to him. "Wong gave one to each barrack. Told us not to wash near the pumps. He said it was time we learned how to stay clean. They let us build fires outside so we could kill the lice. Even the guards were itching."

"He slapped me silly for suggesting it, right before I passed out," Shard said. "I guess he's the kind of guy who likes an idea to be his own. What else happened while I was out?"

"Guys are still dying every day. Dysentery, starvation, the occasional bayonet," Collier said. He didn't mention the list, and Shard didn't ask.

"Better food ought to help that," Shard said. "Any news of Kelso, Skitter?"

"Haven't heard a thing about him," Skitter said. "Must be in another camp."

"They found a sergeant," Collier said. "Guy named Cooper. Skitter said you and he knew him too."

"He was in with us?" Shard asked.

"Yeah. He bunked with Kelso. The guards came the day after they grabbed Kelso," Martinez said.

"And?"

"They shot him. Right in front of his barracks. Wong announced that all officers and noncommissioned officers were war criminals and got what they deserved," Collier said.

"Wonder if Kelso knew and talked?" Martinez said.

"No," Shard said. "Not him."

"You can't tell," Skitter said. "You don't know how people will react, especially when they're tortured." A look passed between him and Shard.

"No, you can never tell," Shard agreed. "Hey, what happened to Tiny?"

"I'm here," a voice said from the shadows of the far corner of the room. It wasn't the booming bully voice Shard was used to. It was meek, as if Tiny was about to weep.

"What did they do?" Shard asked.

"He just got out of the hole yesterday," Skitter said.

"The turnip hole," Collier said, as if that explained things.

"They made him dig a hole twenty feet deep," Martinez explained. "Barely wide enough to swing a shovel. They rigged a bucket on a pulley for him to get the dirt out. When he got to twenty feet, they pulled up the shovel, threw a turnip at him, and left him there for ten days. Rainwater to drink and sit in and one raw turnip to eat."

"Christ," Shard said.

"He ain't here," Tiny mumbled, then groaned as he tried to stretch his cramped limbs. No one liked Tiny and many were afraid of him. Tiny might have been a bully and a thief, but he'd been strong. The Chinese made him weak. It was an omen of what they could do.

In the morning, Shard got up for the first time in twelve days. He waited until everyone but Skitter was gone, then rolled over, pressed his palms against the floor, and pushed his body up. His arms quivered under the weight. Skitter took him by the arm, but Shard shook him off.

"Leave me alone," he said, the words nearly exhausting what little energy he felt. "I have to do this myself." He rocked back on his legs, halfway up. He took a deep breath and rose from the floor, steadying himself like a tightrope walker. He made it to the wall, one arm pressed against the rough wood. Sweat broke out at his temples, and his heart slammed against his chest with each ragged beat.

Skitter gave him a pair of Chinese sneakers. They were ragged and dirty, but better than nothing. Socks as well, and a field jacket. "The Chinese gave out sneakers last week," Skitter said. "The guards got winter boots, so we got the hand-me-downs. The new POWs are coming in with their boots on."

"That's good news," Shard said, balancing as he put on the socks and shoes. "Where'd you get the other stuff?"

"The dead," Skitter said. "You're lucky to get a jacket."

"You're taking clothes from the dead?" Shard said, hesitating as he took the jacket.

"Stripping them bare. If we don't the Chinese will. We started bringing bodies to a hill at the south side of the camp. They wouldn't let us bury them, so we left them in rows. The next morning every stitch of clothing was gone, and the bodies were scattered everywhere. They got no respect."

"Why am I lucky to get a jacket?"

"Because most of the dead are guys who were captured in the summer. Hardly a stitch of warm clothing on 'em. Newer POWs with jackets and boots are doing better. But this poor bastard hung himself. Couldn't take it."

"How'd he manage that?" Shard put on the jacket. He was cold, and maybe the guy wasn't wearing the jacket when he died. There was enough bad luck around without taking on any a dead man might have left in his pockets.

"Got up on one of those beams in the hallway," Skitter said. "Tied his pants around the beam, stuck his head in the noose and dropped."

"Lucky me," Shard said, still leaning against the wall. He waited a minute, then stood on his own, his hands at his side. "Not so bad," he said, walking out with the deliberate gait of a drunk who knows he might collapse at any moment.

First, he headed to the latrine. It was nothing but a narrow, long ditch on a downward slope. He squatted over it and held his breath against the stench. To his surprise he produced something close to a normal crap, a shock after the tortures of dysentery. He nearly passed out when he finally had to gasp for air, the putrid odors of decay and waste assaulting his senses. All around him men were groaning as they voided, diarrhea and dysentery churning through their intestines and sending out gushes of brown liquid, flecked with blood in the worst cases. Some couldn't make it to the ditch and lay on the ground, gripping their bellies as their diseased bodies turned on them. Shard stood and walked away, the foulness lingering after him, almost embarrassed at his moment of normality. One POW had gotten his trousers down ten yards short of the latrine and squatted, his eyes clenched shut in misery. His diarrhea was copious, decorated with yellow kernels of raw, undigested corn. Two other prisoners knelt behind him, jostling each other as they picked through the mess and filled their palms, their fingers daintily plucking each kernel, little fingers extended as if they were at a tea party hosted by Satan himself.

Shard looked at Skitter, his brows furrowed. He didn't understand. He'd seen Skitter and the others eating the same soup they fed him. Why were these guys so sick?

A rock sailed through the air and clipped Skitter in the neck. He stumbled, his hand held against the bruised skin. Shard looked around, but the POWs near the latrine were either engrossed in their own business or studiously looking away. Skitter hunched his shoulders and picked up the pace.

"What's going on?" Shard asked. "Who's got it in for you? Why are all these guys sick? Isn't everyone getting the same rations?"

"You were out a long time," Skitter said. "It hasn't been easy."

"What hasn't?" They came out between two buildings, near the main roadway that split the camp.

"Holding it together, Shard. The Chinese keep pressuring us, for confessions, all sorts of stuff. Everyone's taken a beating or two."

"But the food's better, isn't it?"

"No," Skitter said, coming to a halt. He gazed at a group of vacant-eyed POWs gathered around a prisoner standing on a chair, reading a newspaper. From the looks on their faces, it was an English-language Chinese or Russian paper. Guards patrolled the perimeter of the group, prodding men with their bayonets to keep their attention focused. "I talked Wong into it. I said we needed it to nurse you back to health. And to be strong enough to protect you."

"From who?"

"From anyone jealous of you being a section leader."

"You mean from anyone who thinks a section leader is a traitor?"

"I guess. Lots of guys are upset that we got the extra rations. The guards had to escort me back to the room every day," Skitter said. His eyes flitted about, turning to check the POWs who walked behind them, watching for any threat.

"Hey, punk," shouted a POW. "You singing for your supper tonight?"

"Yeah, birdie," his pal said. "Who you gonna rat out now?"

"Shut up," Skitter said, leaning in closer to Shard. "You're just sore you ain't smart enough to get decent chow." The two POWs cursed Skitter but kept moving.

"Who are they talking about?" Shard said. "Who was ratted out?"

"Maybe Cooper, I don't know," Skitter said. "The Chinese take POWs away every day. Like you said, I doubt it was Kelso who gave him up, but you never know, especially if he was tortured. Coulda been anyone, but I make an easy target carting in those extra rations."

"Sure," Shard said, pulling his jacket tight to his neck. A cold wind was blowing down the road, scattering dust and dirt, sending it pelting against their faces. "Where's the rest of our guys?"

"Thought struggle class," Skitter said. "That's what the Chinese call it. We need to go. There'll be trouble if they find you up and not in class."

"What does thought struggle mean?"

"It means they keep at you until you understand that America started the war, that we foolishly fight and die for Wall Street imperialists, and that Communism is the way of the future and the only path to peace," Skitter said, with a grand flourish of his hands at the end.

He led the way to one of the administration buildings. A classroom of sorts had been set up, about thirty guys seated on chairs, a Chinese instructor at a podium. Comrade Wong stood in the back and looked pleased when he spotted Shard taking his seat along with Skitter. No one else acknowledged them. Everyone kept their eyes on the lecturer.

He was Chinese American, or so he claimed. He had returned to the People's Republic out of patriotic fervor and wanted to share the message of Communism and Chairman Mao's wisdom with his fellow Americans. He was smooth, talking about how his village now had enough food, how Mao had fought the Japanese in the last war, just like America. They'd been allies then, so why were they enemies now? On and on about peace and how that could only come about with an understanding of how the war began when Truman tricked the UN and sent forces storming across the border into the North. Peace and freedom. The words were used a lot, and they sounded good in this heated room. Some of the guys nodded. Maybe they were putting on a show, maybe they liked hearing a pleasant Chinese man saying nice words instead of beating or bayoneting them. Or maybe they agreed.

The class ended. The POWs left slowly, reluctant to leave the warmth of the room. A group spoke to the instructor, calling him Comrade Lee. Their interest may have been canted toward the small coal stove he stood by, but they smiled and nodded enthusiastically, their hands held low against the rising heat.

"Shard, I am glad to see you are better," Wong said, heading them off as Shard and Skitter made for the door. He lit a cigarette with his American Zippo lighter. "You will now attend class every day and be certain the prisoners in your barracks do so as well. They must pay attention."

"These boys were pretty attentive," Shard said, looking back at the dozen or so men clustered around their instructor.

"Perhaps that is because one of them had to be disciplined," Wong said. "He was disrespectful and uttered counterrevolutionary sentiment. The rest of the class went well after that."

"What happened to him?" Shard asked, opening the door and looking for a body or a beaten prisoner.

"You call it the turnip hole," Wong said with a smile. "I call it a place to cultivate right thinking. If prisoners showed respect and worked for peace, there would be no need for it." He drew on his cigarette and blew out the smoke with a laugh.

"Goddammit," Shard muttered as he followed Skitter to the turnip hole. "They can do anything they want and there's not a thing we can do."

"How about not mouthing off? If it did any good, I'd be all for it," Skitter said. "But it's useless."

POWs were gathered around the turnip hole. A circle of packed dirt enclosed it, not more than three feet across. Shard pushed his way forward and peered into the darkness. A form looking like so many filthy rags lay curled up twenty feet down, moaning softly.

"Hang on, Rivera," one of the prisoners shouted. Shard remembered him from the march. Fernando Rivera. He'd turned twenty-one the day he was captured.

"I think my leg's broke," Rivera answered, weakly.

"What'd he say to get thrown in here?" Shard asked one of the prisoners who had been in the class. Mulligan, he thought his name was. A guard pushed him back roughly as Shard strained for a closer look.

"He asked if they believe in peace so much, why did they kill his buddy when he asked for water? That was on the march here," Mulligan explained.

"Stupid," Skitter said, shaking his head. No one disagreed, but no one acknowledged him either. The guards began to laugh as one of their number pushed his way through the gathered POWs and lifted a turnip high above his head, throwing it into the hole as hard as he could. Rivera howled as it hit home, which the Chinese thought hilarious. The guards grinned, pointing to the hole as if the gathered POWs simply didn't get the joke.

"He's from our barrack, right?" Shard asked.

"Yeah," Skitter answered. "What are you going to do?"

"I'm going to suggest to my friend Comrade Wong that mercy will make more of an impression than punishment," Shard said, turning to go. "What good is it to be a section leader if you don't try to help your men?"

"What a laugh," Mulligan said. "You get the best chow, you and your buddies. You kiss Chinese ass, that's what's good about being a section leader."

"Why don't you show us how it's done?" Shard said, turning back and going chest to chest with Mulligan. "I kept you alive, didn't I?"

"Okay, okay, no need to get hot under the collar," Mulligan said, backing away. "I don't want to give your Red pals a chance to beat my head in."

"Come on," Skitter said, taking Shard by the arm. "Let's give it a shot. You never know."

"Fine," Shard said as they crossed the main road. "I wish Wong would get another section leader. It's a thankless task."

"Well, he did have one while you were sick," Skitter said, staring at the ground. "You're wearing his jacket."

"What?" Shard stopped and grabbed Skitter by the arm. "I thought you said it was a new guy."

"He was. Name was Blanchard. He'd been in charge of his group on the way in. Wong put him in with us and said he was temporary section leader. Blanchard said he didn't want to do it, and Wong had him beat, then showed him the turnip hole. He had no choice."

"Why did he hang himself?"

"He couldn't take it. They'd killed a lot of his men on the march, no matter what he did. He kept saying he wanted to be left alone, but Wong was always after him about the classes and right thinking. That last night he was happy. I thought he'd calmed down, but I guess he'd made his decision."

"Why didn't he pick you?"

"Aw hell, Shard, you know no one listens to me."

"Wong listened," Shard said, his hand resting on Skitter's shoulder as they walked. "Okay, let's see how valuable I am to them." Shard knocked on the door of the administration building. Skitter backed off, shaking his head, before darting away.

"Shard," Wong greeted him after keeping him waiting for an hour. "What do you want now?"

"It's about Fernando Rivera, the man you put in the turnip hole," Shard said, standing in front of Wong's desk.

"What about him?" Wong said, lighting a cigarette. He played with the American lighter, twirling it between his fingers. "Other than he is very foolish."

"He's what you might call a proletariat. He's Mexican American. His people are oppressed."

"He did look dark-skinned," Wong said, squinting one eye against the cigarette smoke. "But it is the duty of all oppressed peoples to struggle together against the oppressor. Rivera is a lackey, as are you."

"When he gets home, wouldn't it be better if he told his people about the kind treatment he received?" Shard said, desperate for some advantage, some rationale that Wong would buy. "I'm sure he'd see the error of his ways if he was taken out of the hole."

"No," Wong said, flicking his hand in dismissal. He drew long and hard on his cigarette. The embers glowed.

"He's not used to being in the classroom," Shard said, trying one last argument. "He worked on a farm all his life, like many Chinese young men. He had no chance to learn and understand how to respect his instructor. Please give him a chance to learn about Communism properly." Wong probably didn't know Rivera's leg was broken and wouldn't care. Shard's best bet was to appeal to his beliefs.

"You want him taken out of the hole?" Wong said.

"Yes, please." The words spilled out. Shard had begged so many times as a child that the pleading tone and downcast eyes came naturally.

"Very well. Rivera will be removed immediately," Wong said, crushing out his cigarette in an ashtray overflowing with ash and butts. He yelled orders in Chinese and guards rushed to the door to do his bidding.

"Thank you," Shard said, bowing his head with practiced humility.

"But there is something you must do," Wong said. "As section leader."

"What?"

"Rivera's punishment must be carried out, if not by him then by another. Choose a man from your barracks. Not yourself, Shard. Do you understand?"

"No," Shard stammered. He thought he'd pulled it off, but this was worse than Rivera in the turnip hole. At least it had been Wong who put him there. "I mean yes, I understand. But who? I can't pick a man to take that punishment."

"That is not my concern. It is yours. Select a replacement now for the ten-day sentence. If you do not, Rivera will be shot. You are dismissed."

"I don't want to be section leader," Shard said, his voice trembling with fear. He thought he'd fooled Wong, but all he did was make things worse. If Rivera's leg was broken, he probably wouldn't make it anyway. Now another man was going into the hole, and what happened to him would be Shard's responsibility. Why were decisions forced upon him? He never asked for it, never wanted to be responsible for anyone else. He'd learned that lesson long ago. Still, the burden stayed with him, even here.

"You will be a good section leader," Wong said, rising from his chair. "Or I will execute Rivera and your comrades myself. Now go!" He drew his pistol from his holster and aimed at Shard's chest. "Go!"

Shard went, wishing Wong had pulled the trigger.

"What's wrong?" Skitter asked, appearing from nowhere. He'd kept himself far away from the administrative building but sidled up to Shard as soon as he was ten yards from the place. Shard walked on, unable to speak. Skitter cocked his head to look at Shard, studying the expression on his face as he hurried to keep pace with him. It was grim. "What happened?"

"You happened, Skitter!" Shard turned on his heel and stopped in front of Skitter, jabbing him with his finger. "I knew you were trouble when I first laid eyes on you in Tokyo. You should have left me alone to die in peace. It'd be better than this."

"Jesus, Shard, what's got into you?" Skitter said, backing away. "I kept you alive. What did I do wrong?" His voice was shrill and plaintive as he stared into Shard's looming face.

"That's it. You kept me alive, and right now I'd rather be dead. But I don't even have that choice unless you want to die too." He turned away, heading for the turnip hole, trying to figure out what to do. His mind raced, sorting the options, failing to find one less desirable than the others. He was vaguely aware of POWs and guards running in all directions, shouting incomprehensively, but he couldn't break out of his churning thoughts. Noise buzzed above him as he stalked on, determined to get this over with.

"Wait!" Skitter yelled. Shard ignored him. "Shard, wait."

Shard felt Skitter pulling at him, screaming in his ear, not understanding why he couldn't hear what he was saying. Skitter forced him to the ground as the noise grew into something recognizable, a roar of snarling engines. Shard looked up and saw a line of fighters swooping low, their wings evening as they started in on a line of attack. Shard could make out bombs slung under their fuselages. Three, four, five of them, P-51 Mustangs, headed straight for them.

The fighters dropped their bombs, increasing altitude as the planes were freed of the heavy loads. Explosions shook the ground, sending dirt, smoke, and debris skyward. The P-51s sped over Shard and Skitter, breaking into two groups and circling around for another run. Machine guns opened fire, each plane's six fifty-caliber guns spewing hundreds of rounds into the camp, chewing up men and spindly wooden buildings as if they were matchboxes.

Then they were gone. Off over the horizon, back to their base for hot chow and coffee.

The suddenness and ferocity of the attack was followed by a dead calm as men tried to grasp what had happened. Guards stood, stunned, open-mouthed, and gripping their rifles with white-knuckled hands. POWs tried to gather their wits and look for some advantage in the chaos. Among the dead, shattered bodies, grotesquely inert among welling pools of blood, it was nearly impossible to tell American from Chinese, fifty-caliber slugs being the final equalizer.

The quiet was shattered by cries from the wounded. Whether they had just started, or had been screaming the whole time, Shard didn't know. The sounds were everywhere. Bodies thrashed in the road, some with legs or arms shot off, others grasping gaping wounds in a vain attempt to staunch the flow of blood. From within a burning barracks, terrible sounds arose, shrieks amidst the crackling of burning timbers. Men, bloodied and scorched, stumbled about, black smoke drifting off them, their eyes wide with shock.

"My God," Skitter said, helping Shard to stand. A Chinese guard walked between them, holding his severed forearm tucked under the remaining stump, his left hand clasped over his wound, blood spurting between his fingers, an eerie look of utter calmness on his face.

"Let's get to the barracks," Shard said. Skitter didn't know what to say or do. He still wanted to apologize to Shard, but he didn't know what for. Instead, he draped the jacket over Shard's shoulders and followed.

It was still standing, no sign of damage. Everyone was accounted for. Except Rivera, still in his hole.

Collier and Skitter followed Shard as he made his way to check on Rivera. The Chinese were taking their wounded away and ignoring POWs as they pleaded for help. Shard saw Collier taking in the scene, memorizing names, murmuring them to himself as they moved along. There'd be more names by morning as the wounded bled to death.

POWs crowded around the turnip hole. The barracks next to it had been hit by a bomb, one wall falling onto the hole.

The prisoners were at work clearing away the smoldering timbers, but it was no use. The explosion had collapsed the hole, covering it with burning debris.

"Fernando Rivera," Collier whispered. "Fernando Rivera."

Chapter 9

"Where are we going now?" Skitter asked. "I'm tired of walking around this damn place."

"There's a new guy I want to see. Transferred in from another camp. He knew Cooper."

"Coop?" Skitter said. "Jeez, I haven't thought about him for a long time. Poor guy."

"Yeah, he deserved better," Shard said.

"Don't we all," Skitter said, his shoulders hunched against the wind blowing in from the north. He followed Shard. He always followed Shard. It was automatic, like taking a piss in the morning. Get up, see what Shard is doing. Stick close to him. Stay in his shadow. Watch his back, but always have a clear getaway plan. It had worked so far.

Back in Japan, Skitter had wanted to be the boss, the brains of the operation. But here, in the depths of North Korea, being the boss meant you had an even bigger and meaner boss to watch out for. Brains meant nothing if you weren't as tough as rawhide. Skitter had always known his chances would be better with Shard. There was not a chance in hell without him. But that street went both ways. He was

Shard's guardian angel, holding the key to survival. Stay in the boss's shadow and help him, any way you can.

"How'd this pal of Coop's find you?" Skitter asked.

"He asked around when he was brought in," Shard said, picking up the pace. He buttoned his jacket at the neck and turned the collar against the chill as the sun worked its way toward dusk behind the mountain peaks. "He'd heard Coop was missing in action and hoped he was here."

"That's a long shot," Skitter said. "Hey, what's the hurry?"

"We got a job to do," Shard said. "We're late."

"What kinda job?"

"Hauling supplies into the officers' camp. We'll meet this guy on the job."

"You lined this up so we do some trading, right?"

"No," Shard said. "Hurry, the trucks are here." He pointed to a line of trucks in front of the camp gate. The officers' compound was surrounded by barbed wire six feet high, same as the sergeants' area. To protect the common soldiers of the working class from the corrupt ruling class officers, according to their lectures. A lot of guys liked that. If you had to be a POW, they reasoned, at least you only had to worry about the Commies bossing you around, not your own brass as well.

"You gonna lift something?" Skitter said as they broke into a trot. Shard wasn't big on stealing from other prisoners, but maybe he made an exception when it came to officers.

"You never know," Shard said, giving a nod to Horseface as he slipped him four cigarettes, the going rate for a spot on the supply gang. No mercy if you were caught talking with an officer, or pocketing supplies, but the understanding was that Horseface wouldn't act unless he had to. A dance of deceit for everyone involved.

"So we see Coop's buddy after this?" Skitter said as he shouldered a sack of soybeans.

"No," Shard said. "He's here. A lieutenant with the 5th Marines."

"Jesus Christ," Skitter said, walking through the gate under the scrutiny of guards, their bayonets fixed, and their eyes tracking his every step.

Officers were housed in a series of dilapidated farmhouses and outbuildings, not much more than mud huts with straw roofs. But they were allowed to cook their own food in order to save the Chinese from delivering cooked food from the kitchen at the other end of the camp. One structure that might have been a halfway decent barn at one time was the storeroom. Skitter and Shard carried in supplies: burlap bags of soybeans, kidney beans, turnips, sorghum, and one case of canned meat.

POWs checked off the items on a list and showed the enlisted men where they should be stacked. The guards watched for any communication other than a finger pointing to a shelf. Horseface strolled around the room, checking supplies, and watching the prisoners. When the last of the supplies had been brought in, he ordered the other guards out. Shard and Skitter were left in the room with one officer holding a clipboard. Horseface took one of the tins of meat and put it in his pocket, gave a nod to the officer, and left.

"We have three minutes," the officer said. "I'm Lieutenant John Cooper. You're the guys who knew Freddie?"

"Yeah," Shard said, giving his name. "Me and Skitter were in his company."

"You mean Coop?" Skitter said. "Never got his first name. You related?"

"Yes," he said. "He was my cousin. I heard he was taken prisoner, but he's listed as missing in action. You guys were in the Mining Camp with him?"

"I was half-dead with dysentery," Shard said. "I never even saw him. Skitter did."

"How was he?" Lieutenant Cooper asked Skitter.

"Not too bad, considering," Skitter said. "He and Kelso had gotten in among the enlisted prisoners and were trying to organize things. Someone must have spilled the beans. First, they came for Kelso and took him away. Then they shot Coop."

"Do you think Kelso talked?" he asked.

"No," Shard said. Skitter shook his head in agreement. "Not Kelso."

"Any idea who did?"

"Coulda been anyone," Skitter said. "The guys in his barracks all knew. Hard to say." He looked around nervously, waiting for Horseface to come in and beat them for talking.

"Well, there's no way I can talk to Kelso," Cooper said. "It was hard enough to arrange this. Anything else you can tell me?"

"He was a good sergeant," Shard said.

"Yeah, everyone liked him," Skitter said, his eyes darting to the door. Voices sounded outside.

"What would it take to sell someone out like that?" Cooper asked, not expecting an answer.

"Food. Warmth. Clothing. The promise of life. It can bring out the worst in men," Shard said. "Sorry we can't tell you more."

"You're certain he's dead?" Cooper asked, a hint of desperation and hope flashing across his face.

"Saw the body myself," Skitter said, walking to the half-open door and peeking outside. "We should go."

Shard nodded to Cooper, who returned the gesture. The lieutenant ignored Skitter and went back to his clipboard, tapping the pencil stub against it.

"What was that all about?" Skitter whispered to Shard as Horseface hurried them out of the enclosure with a few obligatory blows from his rifle butt.

"He wants to know what happened to his cousin," Shard said. "Can't blame the guy." Guards hustled the POWs into the empty trucks. Horseface announced they had another job for them and got in up front. It was turning colder, and Skitter pulled his cap down tight.

"There's been so many dead," Skitter said. "It's hard to get upset about someone who's been gone almost three years. Coop missed a lot of suffering."

"True," Shard said. "But he also missed everything good that could happen after the war. Home, family, freedom."

Skitter didn't answer. Those things were so distant they seemed unattainable, unworthy of comment. If things couldn't keep him alive today, they had no value. He knew what happened to guys who forgot that. They drifted into apathy. *Give-up-itis* the POWs called it. He'd never give up. He'd never take his eyes off the grand prize of life.

January 1951
Mining Camp, North Korea

Guards were vicious and the weather worse after the P-51 attack on the Mining Camp. Ten POWs had been killed by bombs and strafing, and another sixteen died of their wounds within days. Medical treatment was nonexistent. Some of the wounded died in agony, moaning, shrieking, begging for morphine and their mothers. Others, through some unknown mercy, slipped quietly away from blood loss and shock. POWs from the bomb-damaged barracks crammed into other buildings already jammed with prisoners. The only good thing was the added body heat in the cold quarters.

Tiny, never one for sharing much of anything, got in a fight with one of the new men. Hawkins had stepped on Tiny's foot when he got up to go to the latrine in the night. Tiny was recovering from his time in the turnip hole, but he was still big and mean enough to do real damage. He threw a few punches before Martinez and Collier stopped him and let Hawkins out of the room.

"It's not worth it," said Diekman, one of the men who'd come in with Hawkins, as Martinez held Tiny down. "He's a progressive. Tiny, the Reds will beat the crap out of you if you hurt him."

"A what?" Shard asked.

"What the Reds call guys who go for their Commie line. Hawkins's the teacher's pet in our indoctrination class, one of the star pupils," Diekman said. "They'll come down hard if you hurt him."

"Shit," Tiny said, pushing Martinez away and retreating to his corner of the room. A sliver of light from a full moon in the clear, dark sky illuminated his scowl.

"Doesn't mean you have to talk to him," Diekman said. "We all give him the cold shoulder."

"Wong told me fights between prisoners weren't a punishable offense," Shard said.

"Yeah, but progressives are a special case," Diekman said. "It's a crime to touch anyone who's seen the light and knows China is a worker's paradise. So watch what you say around Hawkins. From his lips straight to Wong's ass."

Hawkins came back from the latrine while they were still laughing and asked what was so funny, his voice betraying a tremor of fear. No one replied. He hunched in a corner, the whites of his wary eyes visible in the moonlight as they moved from one man to the other.

Shard watched as Diekman sneered at Hawkins, his lips turned down in a venomous yet silent threat.

Skitter's head rested on his arms, his knees drawn up, conserving what little body heat he had. Shivers ran through his torso, shaking him uncontrollably. He caught Shard's eye and smiled. That made him feel better, and he tried to laugh, but it came out as a ragged cough. When he looked again, Shard was asleep, and Skitter felt the cold flood through his bones.

Shard wasn't sleeping. His hooded eyes watched Hawkins, trying to find evidence of what made a man turn on his own people, the mark of Cain or a scar of childhood pain. He saw a roundness in his face and a slight plumpness in the cheeks. That gave him his answer. Food. Survival. A little twist on the law of the jungle; here it was inform or die, much more subtle than kill or be killed. Cooperate or risk death. Who wanted to die? Shard didn't. But he knew he couldn't betray his men either. If a guy was tortured, maybe then the rules changed. But Hawkins didn't have the haunted look of a physically broken man. All he looked was well-fed.

The moonlight faded, and the room became dark, nothing but plumes of frosted breath visible as they drifted past the window. Shard thought of Skitter's face. It wasn't plump at all, but that wasn't how Skitter was built. In the best of times, he burned energy standing there, tapping his toes, nodding his head, rolling back on the balls of his feet, ready to skedaddle. Skitter scatter. Shard fell asleep on the cold floor, dreaming of what they used to steal in Tokyo. Warehouses of canned food, cured hams, cases of whiskey, the delights of the Orient, and the plenty of America. His dream moved to steaks on the grill at a party, all shouts and wood smoke.

He awoke to a gnawing hunger in his gut and sniffed the air, wondering if he were still dreaming. Smoke. He smelled smoke. The air was hazy, and a faint glow crept under the hallway door.

Fire.

Shard couldn't move, couldn't speak.

Fire.

Someone coughed and cursed. Shouts and pounding feet echoed in the hall.

"Get up," Martinez shouted. He was closest to the door. "Fire!"

The small space became a blur of men and choking smoke as soon as Martinez opened their door. Prisoners spilled out of their rooms, packing the narrow hallway, shouts and cries nearly drowning out the growing roar of flames. The opening of doors acted like a blast furnace, feeding the flames, and fanning them into ferocity.

Tiny rushed out, elbows flying, pushing his way through the crowd, forcing his body toward the outside door, not caring about the men he cast aside or stepped over. Shard was last out, his jacket over his nose, gasping as smoke wreathed his body.

"What happened?" Collier said from ahead of him.

"Some assholes lit a fire," a voice said. "They brought in wood and thought the window would vent the smoke out. Christ!"

Shard could see the flames working their way overhead, the bare wood splintered and dry, perfect conditions for a fast-moving fire. There'd been plenty of broken pieces of wood from the barracks that had been hit in the raid. He might have been tempted himself to dig a fire pit in the bare earth floor and start a fire if he'd had matches and no previous experience with a burning house.

But he had. He knew what could happen and yelled for the crowd to move, but it was like pressing against a stone wall. The guards. What were the guards doing? Did they think it was a riot? Or were they going to let everyone burn? He thought he could make out the room where the fire had started. Behind him, in the center of the barracks. The doorway was a mass of flames, and the fire licked upwards, into the rafters, then moved in both directions, overtaking the men below as they streamed to the exits. Flames burst from cracks in the brittle wood and engulfed whole sections of the ceiling, almost alive in its desire to rush ahead and consume everything in its path.

"Shard!" It was Skitter's voice, from up ahead, panic catching in his throat. It was bad news if a guy like Skitter couldn't work his way out.

"Follow me!" Shard shouted, grabbing Martinez by the collar and hoping Skitter and Collier were close enough to hear and see him. He pushed his way back into the least crowded section of the barracks, near the origin of the fire. He kicked at the wall, once, then again, with what strength he had. Planks of wood engorged with flames fell inward, revealing the room where the fire had begun. The heat was searing, and the others backed off, uncertain of what Shard was doing.

"It's the only way," he shouted, unable to see who was still with him. "Come on, follow me!"

Shard ran at the outside wall opposite him, targeting the spot where the window had been. It was all flame, a sheet of yellow, red, and orange, vivid and clear like a sunset on a clear summer day. Shoulder down, he barreled ahead, thrusting himself forward at the last second, eyes squeezed shut, chin tucked low, all his energy directed at the area where the fire had been consuming the wooden frame.

He was suspended in the flames and then rolling, the ground hard and cold, his clothing trailing embers and smoke. Behind him, other figures burst through the side of the building as it collapsed, the last of the weight-bearing wall gone from flame and force. Sparks arced skyward, followed by a flume of fire sucking in oxygen, following the path of least resistance.

"Skitter?" Shard asked. "Skitter, you here?" He blinked his eyes against the sudden brightness, saw guards surrounding them, bayonets menacing them as if they'd broken some rule by surviving.

"No," Collier said, grasping Shard and pulling him close. "Me, Martinez, and Hawkins. That's all who came through."

Collier opened the palm of his hand, then slid it quickly into his jacket pocket. He'd gotten the list.

"We gotta find Skitter," Shard said, getting uneasily to his feet. One guard stepped forward, bayonet leveled at Shard's belly. Shard brushed it aside. He knew that this was a moment he could get away with it. The guards only knew how to guard. They weren't prepared for the unusual. For the most part they were illiterate country kids, not good enough for combat. Surprise and determination worked in his favor. The ring of guards parted, their faces lit by the fire, mouths half-open in awe at the spectacle.

"Skitter!" Shard hollered, searching through the group of POWs at either end of the building. He found Tiny, standing with his arms crossed, watching the building burn. Shard asked if he'd seen anyone from their room. Tiny shook his head as if the question bored him.

The guards were now working to keep other POWs in their barracks, leaving the survivors of the fire alone for the moment. The two exit doors were spewing smoke, and men were dragging bodies out of the cramped hallway. Shard walked through them. Some were dead, others burned, a few breathing raggedly. Skitter was nowhere to be seen.

He looked at the building, afire along its entire length. It would collapse soon. Anyone left alive would be burned to death.

Fire. The thing he feared most, more than the North Koreans and Chinese combined. The fire of guilt and loss that burned in his heart, a low smolder that never went away. But he couldn't leave Skitter behind. You don't leave anyone behind.

He heard himself telling Bobbie that as he held his jacket over his mouth and nose and walked into the smoke. Or maybe it was the guys yelling at him to come back, it was useless, no one could be alive in there. Maybe. But he had to know.

He got down on all fours in the doorway and was soon on his belly, crawling over tangled bodies. He could see the smoke rising, venting through the openings that the flames made. There was a foot of visibility at the ground, the fire casting an orange light. Sparks and embers fell on his back as he slithered forward, calling for Skitter.

"Here." He heard a faint voice call out.

"Louder, dammit!"

"Here! Over here." Skitter's voice came from the left. Shard crawled to the next room and found Skitter. He was flat on the floor, against the outer wall that wasn't yet burning.

"Let's go," Shard said, grabbing Skitter by the arms.

"No," Skitter said. "We'll never make it." His eyes were wide with fear. "It's okay, this room is safe."

"Look," Shard said, pointing up, one hand still gripping Skitter's arm. Skitter rolled over and glanced at the ceiling. Fire was eating through it, dropping red-hot coals around them. There was no time to argue, no time to convince Skitter he was right. Shard wasn't going to be trapped in a burning room for the fire to consume him, roast his body to a crisp.

Flames snapped and popped the dry wood, sending explosions of sparks showering down over the two men. Shard dragged Skitter behind him, moving as fast as he could out of the room, through the smoke-choked hallway as timbers fell and walls collapsed behind him. Eyes shut tight against the fierce heat and the black, thick smoke, he trod on bodies as he vaulted out of the inferno, onto the cold ground. He felt blows raining down on his head and back and realized the men were extinguishing flames. Someone worked his fingers loose from Skitter's arm, and he let go as he pressed his face into the dirt, sobbing with memories.

Fire. Bobbie.

Shard lay there for a long time. He heard voices, American and Chinese. Soothing and harsh. He closed his eyes and fell into himself, far down, tumbling into the depths of his soul. It was like rolling down a grassy hill on a summer day with Bobbie laughing and shrieking behind him. Dizzying and farther than you thought it would be.

He felt a jolt and remembered Bobbie colliding with him at the bottom of a hill in the woods behind their farm. Bobbie had hit his head against his older brother's and cried, but not for long. He was eight, almost nine, far too old for a country boy to be bawling over a little bump.

Shard heard tears, cries of pain, and knew it wasn't Bobbie. But he couldn't swim up from where he was, couldn't break the surface of his eyelids. He didn't want to.

Minutes, hours, days, he had no idea. Once he felt water put to his lips and the involuntary swallow as it filled his mouth. Was someone holding his head? Why couldn't they leave him alone? He squeezed his eyes shut as he descended inward, far away from the distant voices, rough hands, and an insistent pain that broke through every barrier he erected. Farther into the depths of memory than he'd ever gone before.

Shard fell and fell until his feet landed on the bare wood floor of the kitchen. He was barefoot and the window over the sink was open, curtains fluttering in the warm breeze. Ma was bringing a bottle on a tray to Pa in the living room. Her faded cotton dress brushed Shard on her way by. Once red flowers, now the faintest hue of pink, like leaves fading in late fall. She smelled of soap and fresh earth, like she always did coming in from the garden. A bowl of freshly picked pea pods sat on the worn table waiting for her to hull them.

But that would come later. Pa had his demands, like drinks while he listened to the radio. The wireless, as he insisted on calling it. Nothing newfangled passed muster with Pa. Ma held the tray gracefully, balancing the bottle and glass like a waitress in a fancy restaurant, fancier than anything within an hour's drive of Blue Rock, Ohio. Pa liked her that way, a servant delivering his cheap booze and fancy glass. Shard remembered that glass. It was crystal; a tumbler, Ma had called it. She'd picked it up at a yard sale, and Pa had snatched it out of her hand when she'd come home. Since then, it never knew anything but rotgut whiskey. It was the same with his bottle of Chivas Regal. Pa liked the look of the bottle, but Scotch whiskey hadn't graced it since Pa drained the dregs after he'd come home with the bottle years ago. A guy driving drunk had crashed his Pontiac into a tree near the farm gate, and Pa had dragged him out, gave him a dirty handkerchief for the cut on his forehead, and flagged down a driver to fetch the sheriff. Pa claimed the man had given him the bottle in thanks. But doing that much of a good deed was so out of character for his Pa, that Shard knew he'd taken it while the man was passed out. Maybe along with the cash from his wallet while he was at it.

For the last few days, the Chivas Regal bottle was filled with white lightning, moonshine from a pig farmer over in Coshocton County. Pa was particular about his moonshine and didn't buy it from anyone who used a car radiator as a condenser for their hooch. Lead in the pipes could kill a man, he'd say, as he burned off moonshine in a bowl. Lead burns red and leaves you dead, Pa recited each time. It was about the only thing he taught his boys. He never failed to test the booze, even the jars from his trusted pig farmer.

Sobs came from the far corner of the kitchen, near the screen door. It sounded familiar, but Ethan couldn't see who it was. The room was hazy, like a dream or a memory you can't quite summon up. He knelt in the shadows and put his arm out. It was Bobbie, his face turned to the wall, knees to his chest. Like Skitter. When was that?

Ethan was confused. Where was he? He felt a hand on his shoulder, shaking him, but when he turned the kitchen was empty. Then Bobbie had his arms around his waist, his head buried in Ethan's belly. Shouts and curses came from the den, sounds that Ethan heard every night. He looked at Bobbie's face and saw the swollen eye, the bruised cheek.

He'd been here before, saw this before, and remembered it in every dark nightmare. He didn't know if he was crazy or dreaming, but he knew it wasn't right either way. He spoke to Bobbie, but the words floated away in the summer air, and all he had was Bobbie's touch and sad eyes. Ethan took him by the hand, and as they'd done so many nights, went outside, careful to not let the screen door slam. Ethan led the way to the big rock by the pond, along a curving path that followed the gurgling stream. Originally it fed into the Muskingum River, not a mile away, but Pa had dammed it so the livestock could have fresh water. The boys fished and swam in it all summer, diving to the deepest part at the center where they'd touch the rocks and then push off, racing to the surface, lungs bursting, and laughter dripping from their lips.

The sun began to set, reds and burnished oranges against the bluing sky. It was beautiful, but Ethan was uneasy. Bobbie tossed pebbles into the pond, as if black eyes were nothing to worry about. What happened next? Ethan thought he might know, that it might come to him if he tried hard enough to remember. But he didn't want to know. He wanted the dream to stay right here, to enjoy the sunset, watch the ripples as stones settled into the cold depths.

Their mother called them. Ethan didn't want to go, but Bobbie ran off, quick like a rabbit. Like Skitter. That confused him more, and he shook off the name like a bad dream within a better one as he followed Bobbie into the kitchen. Clothes. Ma would tell them to change their clothes. How did he know that?

Ma had her own bruise now. Her cheek was discolored, the way it was after a hard backhanded slap. Ethan knew enough about Pa to tell what kind of hurt he'd inflicted by the marks he left. The worse ones were when Ma showed no marks but walked with her hand clutching her side.

Ma told them to get dressed, to change from their play clothes into their visiting clothes. Not Sunday church clothes, but their newest shirts and pants. Socks, too, and shoes. Bobbie asked if they were visiting Aunt Mary. Ma didn't answer.

Ethan helped Bobbie change. Bobbie wanted to take his teddy bear, but Ethan told him no, he wouldn't need it. They weren't visiting Aunt Mary, not with Pa drunk and snoring in the den with the keys to the truck in his overalls. They left the teddy bear on Bobbie's bed, the button eyes intently watching Ethan who was now dressed in corduroy pants and a green shirt. Something wasn't right. Ethan felt as if he should understand something, but he was only twelve years old, and there was plenty he didn't know. Pa told him that nearly every day. As they left their bedroom, he saw himself walk down the hallway, shepherding Bobbie along, tiptoeing, even though Pa's snoring was loud enough to beat the band. But he wouldn't take a chance on waking Pa up drunk. Sober was bad enough.

The hallway was long, like a tunnel cut through a mountain. Was this his house? He touched the walls as he walked, paint chips flaking off at his fingertips. He'd seen a hallway like this one, but it wasn't back home. It was another place, another kind of terror. Terror for a full-grown man.

Ethan was afraid.

Bobbie pulled him to the stairs, and down they went, past the open front door, sneaking by the den and bursting into the kitchen, ready for a surprise. Ethan tried not to look at Ma's bruise as Bobbie pulled at her skirt and asked where they were going. She'd changed her clothes, too, Ethan noticed. She wore a bright blue gingham dress, and he wondered if they were going to a party after all. She told them to wait outside, down by the barn, and she'd be there in a minute. Stay together, she said. She had one more thing to do, and she'd be right out.

Fear grabbed hold of Ethan, a cold sweat breaking out in the small of his back, his stomach clenched. He took Bobbie by the hand, working at keeping his own from trembling. What was he so afraid of? Pa drunk and dead to the world, nothing new. Bobbie with a black eye was different, but Ethan was about the same age when he'd gotten his first shiner from Pa. His mother taking charge like this, sending them outside in their good clothes? That was new, and it scared him. What would Pa do when he woke up?

Standing in front of the barn, Ethan could see his mother moving about in the kitchen. Why didn't she come outside? He told Bobbie to stay put and ran up to the house, close enough to see through the kitchen window. Ma carried two open mason jars of Pa's moonshine out of the kitchen, toward the den, and out of Ethan's line of sight. He ducked when he saw her return, then edged close to the window to peek inside. Two more mason jars. She poured these out on the floor by the hallway. Ethan watched her walk to the stove where she opened a box of wooden matches.

He saw the moment in desperate clarity, his vision focused on the tiny sparks as she drew the tip of the match across the striker strip and the explosion of flame blossoming at the end of the arc. Ma held the match for a second, the flame biting into the wood, before she tossed it into the hallway, her eyes wide and her mouth open as if she were about to cheer.

A fireball went up, sending a sheet of fire into the kitchen, then retreating into the hall, licking the ceiling and walls before another explosion sounded, a *whump* sounding against the door and echoing through the open windows and doors. The mason jars in Pa's den. Every window and door was open, feeding the flames with a cross breeze of soft summer air. Ma stepped outside as smoke crept into the kitchen, billowing behind her, building into a wall of swirling gray cloud so at odds with her pretty blue dress.

The fire was full of roar and crackle, but another sound broke through, a heavy thrashing that reminded Ethan of an enraged bull in a narrow pen, kicking in every direction, seeking a way out. It ended quickly, and soon only flame and smoke poured out of the old house, the only sounds the crack and snap of burning wood.

Ma looked shocked and happy, both at the same time. She took the steps slowly and carefully, as if she were on a stage and an audience was waiting to applaud. She looked along the driveway toward the road at the end. She smiled, and the shock left her face, leaving only a dreamy gaze to take in the destruction of her home and the path that would take them away from it. She saw Ethan, finally, and her eyes softened for a second before hardening into a searching stare. Where's Bobbie, she wanted to know?

Where's Bobbie?

Not where Ethan left him out by the barn. Nowhere in sight. Ethan looked in every direction, until it hit him. Teddy. Bobbie went back for Teddy. He raced to the front door, his mother at his heels, shrieking from the depths of her soul, calling for her baby, her face a rictus of regret. Ethan halted at the door, heat and smoke enveloping him. His mother went straight inside, calling Bobbie's name. Ma had told him to stay with Bobbie. It was his responsibility. He grabbed her by the arm and pulled her out, pushing her back into the yard. He went in, feeling his way to the stairs, calling out Bobbie's name. Each time he took in smoke, choking and coughing until he could try again.

Ethan found him at the top of the stairs, Teddy firmly in his grasp. His face was tucked into the corner, like he always did after Pa got after him. Ethan shook his shoulder, but then decided all that mattered was getting out. He was sure he was alive, but they both needed to stay that way. His eyes stung from the smoke, and he heaved in a coughing fit as he carried Bobbie down the stairs, holding him tight against his chest, Teddy tucked between them. The wall was hot, smoke forcing its way out between cracks in the horsehair plaster. Ma was calling for them outside the front door. Ethan did his best to answer, but between his choking and the roar of the spreading fire in his ears he wasn't sure he'd made any sound at all.

He felt the bottom step and turned toward the front door and escape from the acrid smoke and intense heat. It was seconds away; a few steps and they'd be breathing clean air.

The wall collapsed in a shower of sparks, flames, and debris. It came from the direction of the den, where the fire was most furious. Ethan felt hot cinders on his neck and smelled his hair burning. Bobbie whimpered. He swatted at Bobbie's head, dusting off bits of smoldering plaster and wood, then fell across a burning timber, protecting his brother's head with both hands. Another section of wall disintegrated, sending out fingers of flame, licking at the two of them as Ethan crawled to the doorway, burning planks falling on his back. Bobbie's whimpers became screams, and the heat was searing and sharp like glass.

He fell onto the front stoop, rolled away from the fire, then felt his mother smothering flames as he wondered what was burning. Bobbie was screaming. Ma pulled at Ethan, trying to break his grip on Bobbie. He let go. Where Bobbie had laid against his chest, his shirt was charred, smoke drifting up from burned flesh and fabric. Ma brushed Bobbie's cheek, red and black with burns. A piece of splintered, smoking wood had been stuck between them. The closer Ethan held his brother to his heart during the last moments of their escape, the more he'd burned Bobbie's cheek and his own thin chest.

He didn't feel the pain, although he knew it would come. He followed his mother as she ran with Bobbie in her arms, taking him to the pond and the cooling water. Smoke trailed them from Bobbie's smoldering clothes, and Ethan brushed at his pants and shirt, putting out his own small fire. He saw men running across the fields from the neighboring farm, the smoke rising like a signal in the country sky. Cars raised dust on the county road, heading their way. A distant siren sounded, a sure sign someone with a telephone had seem the fire.

Ma waded into the pond with Bobbie, dipping him and raising him up like the minister did at baptisms. He screamed and cried, his arms flailing and legs kicking as he tried to run from the pain. Ma walked back to the edge of the pond and sat with Bobbie in her lap, holding him down with one arm while scooping water to pour over his cheek with the other.

Ethan was stunned. Moments ago, he'd been waiting for his mother to come outside and now Pa was dead, he guessed, burned up in that fire. He couldn't think beyond that, even though the image of Ma with the kitchen match and a smile on her face was in his mind as clear as if he'd been standing next to her. Now all he saw was her anguish.

And fire. The house was bright orange and red, flames shooting into the sky, every room and memory feeding them. The heat hurt his face. The fire burned his heart.

Slowly, the pieces assembled in his mind. Pa was gone. His chest hurt.

Ma started the fire.

Bobbie got burned.

He felt ashamed when he had the thought, Why did she wait so long? Why didn't she burn up Pa when Pa gave *him* his first shiner?

Ethan bit his lip to keep from crying. Ma was crying now, too, and he had to stay strong for her. His burn hurt, but he knew it was nothing like what Bobbie was feeling. He couldn't look at Bobbie's face. Ma couldn't look anywhere else.

Men came to them. Farmers and firemen, then the police. One of the firemen put salve on Bobbie's cheek and wrapped a white bandage around his head. An ambulance pulled up close, and they brought a stretcher for Bobbie. He was quiet now, maybe passed out, Ethan thought. One of the firemen offered to help Ma into the ambulance, but she shook her head no. Bobbie went off in the ambulance, alone, and Ma took Ethan's hand in both of hers. She told him to look in the barn, on the workbench. There was an old coffee can on the bottom shelf. There's money in it. Don't let anyone see you take it.

She told him he was a brave boy and pushed him toward the barn. She tried to smile, but it was a brittle, beaten down attempt. Two policemen stopped talking as he came close, so he veered away from them and headed toward the house. He found Teddy by the front steps, untouched by the fire. He picked up the stuffed animal, hoping nobody thought it was his. He'd bring it to Bobbie at the hospital. They'd fix Bobbie up and he'd be fine, happy to have Teddy to sleep with. Then the three of them would live somewhere else, somewhere without Pa and his drinking and fists.

In the barn, Ethan found the coffee can. There was thirty-eight dollars inside. He'd never seen that much money. He stuffed it in his pants pocket and wandered back outside, awed at the sight of men and machines as much as the destruction of his house.

A policeman asked where his mother was, and he pointed to the pond. The sun was beginning to set, and with the gray smoke drifting across the landscape it was hard to see. Vehicles and strangers flowed across their land, lit a burnished orange by the flames. They didn't have many visitors. Pa didn't get along with folks, and Ma was never allowed to waste time chatting with the other wives from the farms along their road. Ethan felt worried until he remembered Pa wasn't about to come storming out with his strap.

Ethan looked everywhere for his mother. He called to her in the dusky light, and the policemen looked his way, probably wondering themselves where she'd gotten to. He went to the water's edge and saw the bright blue gingham dress floating several yards out. He flushed red, wondering why Ma had taken off her dress with these men around. But then he saw clearly, saw it was her body floating face down, her brown hair a halo as it spread free across the coldest depths of the pond.

Chapter 10

S kitter and Shard jumped from the truck as it stopped in front of the camp warehouse. Horseface pointed to another truck, larger and filled with cases of food. Their job was to unload it and stack the cases inside.

"No stealing," Horseface said with a wagging finger. Shard spread his hands and grimaced, as if offended by the warning. Horseface laughed, a good sign.

The warehouse guards were in a good mood and waved them inside, pleased at the arrival of new food supplies. The Chinese ate better than the POWs, but that didn't mean they ate well. When supplies were short, it was usually because US aircraft had blown the trucks sky-high on their way to the camp. Not a good thing for the prisoners, since the guards became surly and angry. Beatings increased and more of the POWs' rice went to the guards, leaving millet and soybeans at best.

Shard and Skitter finished with the heavy crates and began moving sacks of rice and flour, stacking them on pallets in the warehouse, moving farther inside each time. When they couldn't be seen by the guards at the entrance, Shard dropped his sack and looked for something to steal.

"No," Skitter said. "They'll search us. You heard Horseface. It's not worth it."

"Horseface was only acting tough. He might pat us down, but he's not going to make a big deal out of it. He selected us, so it would make him look bad if we got caught." Shard took his time, casting his eye over the stores of food, looking for the right item.

He found it in the truck. Under the last of the rice sacks were heavy burlap bags filled with cabbages. As he hoisted a bag over his shoulder, he worked a finger into the thin material and pulled when he dumped it in the warehouse. Green cabbages lay exposed, and Shard held up his hand to Skitter, telling him to hold off on dropping his bag. Skitter shook his head but was powerless to stop him. Shard took off his blue cap and ripped leaves off the cabbage, stuffing them inside the hat. When he put it on, he signaled Skitter to put his bag over the ripped hole.

"How does it look?" Shard whispered, adjusting his cap.

"Like you got cabbage for brains," Skitter said. "But it looks okay. Not worth the risk though."

"We need greens," Shard said. "Cabbage has vitamins. Besides, sometimes I can't stop myself." Skitter reached up and tucked an errant cabbage leaf under Shard's cap, the kind of thing you might do to a child's unruly hair. He felt embarrassed and hustled ahead to get the next load of cabbages.

They cleared out the truck, burying the ripped burlap under a dozen other bags. Outside, they found Horseface and the other guards laughing and smoking, paying them no attention. The warehouse was behind the administrative building, away from the watchful eyes of the more zealous comrades, and Horseface was taking full advantage.

Shard and Skitter leaned against the truck, angling their faces to catch the feeble rays of the sun. Horseface told a joke, or so it seemed by the tone of his voice, and the younger guards laughed. As Horseface grinned and drew on his cigarette a look of stunned horror overcame his face. Shard saw Comrade Yuan rounding the corner, followed by two other senior comrades. They were not smoking or smiling.

Horseface dropped his butt and stepped on it. At the same time, he raised his voice at the other guards, probably berating them for smoking on duty. They stood to attention as Yuan drew closer. Horseface advanced on Shard, yelling incoherently. He swung his rifle butt against Shard, determined to show Comrade Yuan he was on top of the lazy recruits and even lazier prisoners.

"No!" Skitter yelled, blocking Horseface's swing with his arm. It was too late. The rifle butt bounced off Skitter's forearm and caught Shard on the shoulder, sending him tumbling to the ground. Horseface froze as Shard's cap flew off his head, revealing the hidden stash of bright green cabbage leaves.

January 1951
Mining Camp, North Korea

The first thing Shard thought about was that he was in a bed. Not a comfortable one, but a bed, nevertheless. A cot, he figured, from the feel of canvas and wood. It wasn't the cold bare earth, and that was all that mattered. It was the first time since Japan that he'd slept off the ground.

The second thing he thought about was the dream. Bobbie. He ran his fingers over his heart, where the scar rippled across his chest. Bobbie's cheek had lain there, seared into his flesh.

The third thought that came to him was the fire last night. Or when was that? The barracks fire. Skitter, and the list clutched in Collier's hand. He was confused, images of Bobbie and Skitter mingling in his mind, both of them curled up in the corner of a burning building, unable to move. Cries and moans forced themselves into his awareness, seeping into his consciousness as he came to.

He forced himself to open his eyes.

It was an infirmary of sorts. Rows of cots filled with sick and burned men. Agonies unabated by morphine, sulfa, or bandages. A place to die. Chinese orderlies rubbed some sort of ointment on burns, and Shard noticed it covered his arms. At the sight of his own red flesh, a spasm of pain shot through him, but not as bad as he'd expected. He calmed himself and looked at his arms again. The burns weren't too serious, not like the black and blistered skin on some of the POWs. Not like Bobbie's once soft cheek.

Shard grabbed the edges of the cot and pulled himself up. He placed his feet on the floor and stared at the salve on his arms. The pain was tolerable. Either he was numb, or it really did help. The Chinese had some strange ideas about medicine, not the least of which was not allowing POW doctors or medics to care for the sick. Chinese doctors were even rarer, but there were plenty of orderlies, or nurses, or whatever these people in dirty, blood-smeared white coats were. Once, a prisoner with an infected wound had had a chicken liver sewn inside his chest. They'd thought the Chinese were torturing him, but he got better. Luck or the chicken liver, no one could decide.

He stood, shaky on his feet, but he stayed up. An orderly rushed to him, shaking his head *no* and pointing back to the cot. Another white-coated Chinese, maybe older, maybe in charge, said something and pointed to a note on Shard's blanket. Whatever was on the paper, it calmed the younger orderly down, and he escorted Shard to the exit, pointing to a pile of clothes by the door. Shard's own uniform was falling apart, now ripped and scorched as well as worn out. He rummaged through the pile, taking layers of warmth, pulling on three pairs of pants and finding the largest field jacket to fit over shirts, sweaters, and his field jacket with its scorched back.

He threw his own ruined clothing on the pile and wondered if he should be taking so much. But then, most of the men in here wouldn't be needing clothing. He doubted that nine out of ten would make it through the next few days, never mind the coming winter. He found some decent rubber-sole sneakers and pulled them on over as many socks as he could fit on his feet. The orderlies ignored him. Usually, guards took the best clothing when a prisoner died. The orderlies must live pretty well, Shard mused, to not claim the discards of the dead and dying.

The stench assailed his nostrils as he made his way outside. The camp always stank, but the recent fires had added an aroma that could have wafted up from the gates of hell. The cloying smells of excrement, garbage, unwashed bodies, diseased men, and their unwashed clothing wrapped themselves around the odor of blackened, burned wood and charred debris to produce a scent that was palpable, clinging to his nostrils and skin. Shard remembered the smoky smell when he lost his parents, and how for days he couldn't wash it away. But that had been the least of his problems back then.

He crossed the main road, heading for his barracks, or what was left of it. He figured he'd find the others there. Guards eyed him warily, and he noticed that the other prisoners stood in groups, listening to lectures in the cold wind or marching for some unknown reason. Chinese voices boomed over microphones, chastising the imperialist demons of Wall Street, demanding that the prisoners work for peace and harmony. The Chinese insisted on giving their interminable lectures first in Chinese, then translating the speech into English. They also thought that screaming worked better than speaking, since both versions were delivered in shrill, high-pitched shrieks.

Shard walked between two barracks and encountered a group of prisoners listening to another POW read the *Shanghai Times* from his perch on the front step. As he recounted news of the successful rice harvest in southern China, a guard ran to Shard, motioning with his rifle that he should join the group. Shard rolled back his sleeve as far as he could, revealing the burns and the greasy salve covering them. The guard nodded his understanding but gave him a shove with his rifle nonetheless. The POWs listening to the news showed no interest.

Shard found his section. Comrade Wong was haranguing them from the flatbed of a small truck, no microphone necessary. Thirty or so men, survivors from the burned barracks, stood at attention facing Wong. From the looks of them, this lecture had been going on for a long time. Faces were drawn, glassy eyes vacant, mouths slack.

"Section Leader Shard!" Wong hollered. "Get in line! Stand at attention!" He motioned to a guard with a sharp snap of his hand, and Shard felt a bayonet digging into his back, moving him into place. The guard then finished with a rifle butt to his ribcage, and Shard struggled to stay upright. He caught sight of Skitter silently staring straight ahead.

"At attention!" Wong demanded. He waited for Shard to stand up straight, in the best imitation of attention he could muster. "You are a terrible section leader, Comrade Shard. You allowed criminals in your section to destroy the people's property. This is a grave crime against the peace-loving people of North Korea and against the Chinese People's Volunteer Army. We give you food and a place to sleep, a roof to protect you from the elements, and what do you do in return? You destroy it! Madness!"

Shard couldn't disagree, not that Wong would care. He was working up to their punishment, and all Shard could do was listen and take it. He wondered why Wong was still referring to him as the section leader. Couldn't he get himself fired from this job? Maybe that was his punishment—eternal section leader in a Chinese POW camp.

"In the People's Volunteer Army," Wong was saying, "if a soldier willfully destroys the people's property, his comrades know they must help him to confess and find the way to right thinking. But you Americans are cowards; you do not confess, and you harbor the criminals among you. Do not think I believe your lies that the guilty men perished in the fire. Eight of your comrades died, but I do not believe they were responsible. They are victims! Victims of your treachery, just as the Korean people are victims of your government's aggression." Wong stopped and lit a cigarette. He blew smoke toward the sky and shook his head sadly, as if commiserating with the gods at the intransigence of these Westerners.

"I will give you one last chance," Wong said, "to see the wisdom in confession. If you tell the truth, you prove you are a friend of the people. If you lie, you are an enemy of the people." He took another drag on his cigarette and tapped the ash delicately. "Tell me, Section Leader Shard. Do you know who burned the barracks?"

"No, Comrade Wong." Shard used Wong's title, hoping that this little obedience would sooth his anger.

"I believe you," Wong said. "It was brave of you to rescue your friend, Comrade Skinner. Only cowards lie." His eyes searched the ranks, looking for guilt or fear on the faces of the POWs. It wasn't easy to read their looks. Illness and grime made everyone look half-dead.

"You will all stand here, at attention, until the guilty party gives himself up or is revealed," Wong said. "No food, no water. If a man falls, he will be shot." He placed his hand on his holster for emphasis as he stared at the men, searching each row, locking onto each prisoner's eyes.

"He did it," Tiny said, his voice booming as his finger stabbed out at a POW one row up. "I heard him talking about it. He set the fire." A murmur ran through the ranks. Shard tried to discern if it was approval or condemnation.

"You!" Wong shouted. "Come forward." Guards pulled the frightened POW to the truck where Wong stood. "Did you start the fire?"

"Yes, Comrade Wong. I'm sorry. I was so cold. I couldn't take it anymore." Shard glanced at the man, recognized him as a PFC named Davis. He was hunched over, nearly bowing to Wong. He couldn't have been more than twenty, tops. Davis began to cry.

"Good, good," Wong said. "This is a good confession. Your name?"

"Davis, sir. I mean, Comrade."

"Prisoner Davis," Wong said, standing with his hands on his hips, smiling down at the boy. "Did anyone else start the fire with you?"

"No, Comrade. It was just me. They tried to talk me out of it, so I waited until they were all asleep."

"Ah," Wong said. "I see. Good. That is all I wished to hear. The truth. Now that we have this confession, you may all return to your barracks for the night. See how the truth sets you free?" He dropped his cigarette and crushed it beneath his boot.

"Which barracks, Comrade Wong?" Shard asked, risking the question even though they were supposed to be at attention. This was too easy, it had to be a trick.

"Why your barracks, the one that Prisoner Davis burned down. It will be your home until we move to another camp." Wong chuckled, pleased with the shocked look on the men's faces.

"There's hardly anything left," Shard said, remembering to add, "Comrade."

"That is not my concern," Wong said. "You are dismissed. All except for Prisoner Davis."

Davis looked at Shard expectantly, hoping for help, fear etched on his face. He never saw Wong draw his pistol, never heard the shot, never felt the bullet smash into his brain.

Chapter 11

April 18, 1953
Camp Eleven, North Korea

Shard covered his head as best he could, curled up on the ground as boots and rifle butts crashed into his ribs, back, and legs. He heard Skitter begging Horseface to stop, but all else was lost in a torrent of yells and curses. Horseface screamed his lungs out, hoping his fury would distract Comrade Yuan from what he must have glimpsed, no matter how fast Horseface ditched the butt. A prisoner could be shot for stealing food. A guard might end up in the front ranks of a human wave attack through a minefield for letting him get away with it.

Yuan's voice broke through the melee, and the blows stopped immediately. Shard didn't dare move. He stayed in the fetal position, surveying his injuries. Sore ribs, maybe broken again. His kidneys hurt, and he could expect to piss blood for a while. Otherwise, he was okay. Alive.

"Stand, Prisoner Shard," Yuan said. That wasn't good. POWs in good standing were comrades. Prisoners were war criminals. They were all prisoners, of course, but in Chinese Communist logic, comrades were considered guests of the benevolent People's Volunteer Army, guests who understood their proper role. Those who didn't understand were war criminals, prisoners, aggressive imperialists, enemies of the people.

Shard stood, holding his side, and as he looked at Yuan, he remembered how his mother stood so many times, gazing at Pa, hoping for mercy as she held her cracked ribs. Yuan, Pa, Wong, Bak, all his tormentors blazed through his mind, churning up rage and shame, hatred and desperate passion. He clenched his fists until his hands shook, trying to stay in control. He didn't want to give Yuan an excuse to end it all here and now. It was tempting, but Shard still dreamed of a life where no one held power over him, and he was desperate to live that life for at least one day.

"Yes, Comrade Yuan," Shard said, wincing as he spoke.

"You obviously have been caught stealing the people's food. I did not think you a common thief."

"Capitalism is theft, isn't that what you taught us?" Shard asked, remembering a phrase from the indoctrination classes. "I was raised a capitalist. It's a hard habit to shake."

"At least you were paying attention," Yuan said, stepping closer and studying Shard's face. Then he backed up, perhaps uncomfortable at having to stare up at the tall American. "But tell me, why steal a few cabbage leaves? Is that worth a life?"

"I'm a lousy capitalist," Shard said. "We lost the farm."

"Ah, yes, I remember," Yuan said, tapping his finger against his temple. "Your parents both died, yes? The house burned down, and you and your brother became separated."

Shard nodded. Each POW had had to write out a biography for their captors. Long and detailed, they were used to determine what class each man came from, and to exploit weaknesses where they could be found. Like the loss of a family farm.

"Comrade Yuan," Skitter said, edging sideways into the conversation. "Shard only took the leaves that fell out of one of the bags. They would have rotted away if he didn't. And they were for me. I have night blindness, and Shard thought a few extra greens would help."

"You have night blindness because your air force shoots anything that moves on the roads!" Yuan said, his words exploding in anger. "No one gets enough. My men have night blindness too. If supplies got through to us, you would have enough vegetables and vitamins. Do not make excuses. Theft is theft."

It was an excuse they'd heard before. Every shortage was due to the criminal bombing and strafing of peaceful civilian convoys carrying food and Red Cross parcels to the camps. Some of it was true, it stood to reason. But the Chinese had their own justifications for withholding food. They gave extra rations to the progressives and kept the best for themselves. Even so, guards suffered from vitamin deficiency just as POWs did. Night blindness had caused several Chinese to fire on POWs at night, not recognizing a prisoner simply going to the latrine.

"I apologize, Comrade Yuan," Shard said, hating himself for the bow he gave him. "We have been working hard, and I failed to control myself." Shard figured it was worth a try. Yuan hadn't shot him instantly. Maybe he would be in a merciful mood.

"I do not sense sincerity," Yuan said languidly. He spoke to the guards, and they grabbed Shard by the arms. "Now you will go in the pen."

January 1951
Mining Camp, North Korea

Wong made the POWs drag Davis's body back to the burned barracks. His corpse would keep them company during the night, to remind them of their lack of right thinking. Guards patrolled the perimeter of the barracks with orders to shoot anyone who left.

The barracks frame was still standing. The fire had eaten away the roof and walls, but the wood had been so old and dry it had flamed too quickly for a sustained burn. Some floorboards were still intact, and the prisoners cleared away what debris they could, making spaces for small groups to huddle together, miserable in the cold night air.

"Don't look at me like that," Tiny said as he took a spot against a blackened support beam. "You know more guys would have collapsed and been shot. Davis was too yellow to admit what he'd done, so someone had to speak up."

"And you were just the guy to rat him out," Collier said.

"Hey!" Tiny said, reaching for Collier and grabbing him by the sleeve. "Watch your mouth."

"Lay off!" Martinez cried, crawling between the two men.

"Tiny was right," Shard said. Everyone looked surprised, especially Tiny, who let go of Collier and eased back into his corner. "Davis would have gotten more guys killed. He'd already caused eight deaths, no reason to add more. But it's no one's fault. Not Davis, not Tiny. We're in an impossible situation. There are no rules, no chance for fair play. We're not going to judge Davis; he was at his breaking point and made a bad decision, that's all. Tiny did what he had to do. For all we know, he saved the life of someone in this room."

"What room?" Skitter asked, his hands held up to the ruined timbers and night sky. One, two seconds of silence were following by laughter. Howls of laughter, maniacal laughing that wouldn't stop. As soon as they calmed down, someone would say *what room*, and they'd break up again.

"Thanks," Skitter whispered to Shard after things had calmed down. "For saving my life."

"You'd do the same for me," Shard said. "Forget about it."

"I can't," Skitter said as he rolled over, hands tucked under his armpits. "And I won't."

"Yeah," Shard answered after a while. "I know."

He knew about not forgetting. No matter how far he pushed it down, memories of his house burning down always came back. It had been months since he'd dreamed about it like that, but it was always the same. The sense of foreboding, knowing he should understand what was about to happen, but always failing. Never able to stop it. He wished that just once he'd dream of staying with Bobbie, walking away from the house in flames with Ma and his brother, hand in hand. He'd left Bobbie that day, only for a minute, but it was a minute too long. It was easy for Shard not to judge other people since he was such an unforgiving judge of himself.

They'd sat him in a police car as they dragged his mother's body out of the pond. She was distraught, the policeman said. Ethan didn't know what that meant, but it sounded right, so he nodded. Later, he saw the firemen and police talking to each other. One of the firemen held an empty mason jar and gestured with it toward the house. Gray smoke was still idly rising into the night sky, the fire nearly out by then. The roof had caved in, and the front of the house was covered in black, sooty, scorched wood, marking where the fire had spread. It smelled bad. Ethan wondered how they'd get Pa out of there. He waited in the police car a long time, thinking about Pa all burned up and Ma drowned in the pond. Fire and water. It almost made sense. But Bobbie burned so bad, that made no sense.

They took him to the police station. Ethan said he wanted to go to the hospital, but the sheriff said he needed to understand what had happened, and Ethan was the only fellow around who could tell him.

Ethan didn't want to talk. The sheriff said he knew his Pa, knew he drank a lot and was likely mean most of the time. He asked about the moonshine. Ethan had seen the sheriff with the jar, so he figured it wouldn't hurt to say yeah, Pa drank the white lightning. He even told him about the Chivas Regal bottle. The sheriff liked that, but Ethan couldn't tell why. Maybe he drank Chivas Regal.

He asked Ethan about Pa hitting his mother. Ethan thought maybe people knew about that, too, so he told the sheriff that Pa hit them all. It was true, and Ethan didn't think it meant much. Didn't all kids get a whooping from their fathers?

Were you upset, the sheriff wanted to know? About your Pa beating on all of you.

Sure, Ethan told him.

You know where your Pa kept his moonshine?

Sure, Ethan said again. In the kitchen, right by the Chivas Regal bottle.

Then the sheriff asked him to empty his pockets. Ethan put the thirty-eight dollars on the table in front of him, along with his jackknife. The sheriff counted the money and whistled. Ethan began to get a bad feeling, a sick feeling in his stomach. He asked again if he could see Bobbie.

Not quite yet, the sheriff said.

That was when Ethan began to understand. The way the sheriff figured it, Ethan started the fire. He asked if he hated his father for beating up on his Ma and starting in on Bobbie, not to mention the times he'd hit Ethan. It was hard to say no to that; it would make him sound like he didn't care about his mother and kid brother. So he said yeah, I hated him. The sheriff nodded and told Ethan he was sorry how it came out, that Ma was so upset with what he'd done that she went and drowned herself. He made it all sound so sensible. Ethan nodded, thinking he might have done it if he'd only thought about it first.

The sheriff told Ethan he might have done the same, stolen his father's money and then lit the fire. After all, he was only defending his little brother and his dear, sweet mother. He wasn't old enough to understand what the consequences might be. He couldn't have foreseen what happened. It wasn't his fault, really, but confession was good for the soul, the preacher says, so why not get it all out?

Ethan thought it over. The sheriff was being nice to him, and he wasn't used to grown men treating him with kindness. He thought the sheriff might not believe him if he said Ma started the fire, that she had it all planned out. Besides, he didn't want to tell the whole world that his mother killed his father. He didn't want her remembered like that. People wouldn't understand. Yes, Ethan said. I took the money, and I lit the fire. I was going to run away.

The sheriff wrote it all out for him. All Ethan had to do was sign his name, and this would be all over, and his Ma could rest in peace. Never speak ill of the dead, she'd told him once. So he signed.

He spent that night in a jail cell. The sheriff kept saying he could see Bobbie tomorrow, if things worked out. It was late, and maybe there was no place else for him to sleep. After all, he had no home, no parents, no relatives to go to. That didn't make him feel any better, and he cried into his pillow, hoping no one heard him. He was nearly grown up, a fourteen-year-old-almost-man, and men didn't cry. Not that he'd ever seen.

In the morning, the sheriff put him in the back of his patrol car. Ethan asked if they were going to the hospital, but the sheriff didn't say much, except that they were going to Zanesville. So he stopped asking, since the sheriff wasn't being so nice today, and he didn't want to get him angry. Maybe the hospital was in Zanesville. It was a big place, the county seat, biggest town Ethan had ever been to. It took about an hour, winding along the road on the banks of the Muskingum River. Ethan enjoyed looking at the scenery and the boats gliding along the waterway.

They parked behind the county courthouse, and the sheriff led him inside, grasping his arm in a tight grip. It hurt, but Ethan was no stranger to pain, so he didn't let on it bothered him. They waited a while, then went into a room and sat at a long table while a judge and some other men talked about him. One man argued with the sheriff and tossed the piece of paper Ethan had signed back to him. It was confusing. Ethan looked to the door, and for a second hoped his mother would come get him. He almost cried, but he thought about a good thing instead, like Pa not beating him for getting in trouble. He wiped his nose on his sleeve and tried to follow what the judge was saying. Something about lack of evidence. Then, remanded until the age of majority. Ward of the state. Danger to himself and others. The Boys' Industrial School. None of it made sense, and no one mentioned Bobbie.

He was smart enough not to bother asking.

Two men put him in another car, and they headed west. The men smoked cigarettes and didn't speak to Ethan or each other, so he didn't say anything either. After about an hour, they passed a sign that read Lancaster City Limits. Then through a gate with Boys' Industrial School written in the iron latticework. They slowed to a stop in front of a big brick building, three stories high with lots of peaks and chimneys. Ethan was scared, but he kept his voice steady when he asked what kind of place this was.

Reform school, one man said. The other man said they weren't supposed to call it that anymore, and they both laughed as they got out of the car. Ethan tried to open his door, but it was locked, and he had to wait for the man with the key. He understood now where he was going.

Prison.

Shard woke up, gasping in frigid air. He'd been dreaming. Or remembering. It was never clear to him. The story of the fire, the courthouse, the reform school played itself out whenever it wanted, and he had no control over it, awake or asleep. Ever since he'd left on his eighteenth birthday—his age of majority—the onslaught of memories had stayed with him. Even here, in North Korea, in another prison without walls.

A layer of frost coated the men, despite being huddled together for what little warmth they had. The eastern sky betrayed a glimmer of dawn, and Shard recalled what Wong had said. They'd stay here until they left for another camp. How long would that be? Too long and they'd die of exposure. Snow or freezing rain could come at any time.

"Chop chop," a guard cried in the near darkness. That was camp slang for food, since the Chinese chopped up whatever they had and threw it into the mixture of rice, sorghum, or millet.

"Why so early?" Skitter asked, barely moving from his spot, burrowed in between Shard and a mound of charred debris.

"So we can get an early start on the march," Shard said. It was the only thing that made sense.

"Where to?" Skitter said.

"Does it matter?" Shard said, looking at Collier. Collier nodded and quietly tapped his pocket. The list was safe.

Chapter 12

April 18, 1953
Camp Eleven, North Korea

Shard dug in his heels, knowing it would bring more blows from the guards, but he couldn't stop his feet from resisting the progress toward the pen. Set in the open space in front of the administration building, it was a four by four hole in the ground, two feet deep and encased in a chicken wire frame that stood another two feet above ground. Not for the comfort of the prisoner, but to make it easier for guards to poke him as they walked by. Sticks, usually. Bayonets now and then. Spit and piss, every day. No food, no water, no shelter from the rain. Men released after three or four days made it out on their own. Five or six days, they couldn't stand and had to be dragged out. After a week, they were corpses.

The guards unlocked the top of the cage and threw Shard in the pen. With a clattering slam, the cage came down, pinning Shard in four feet of space. Gasping for air, he rose on all fours and watched the guards leave. Horseface wasn't among them, which was good, since he'd blame Shard for getting caught. Maybe Horseface would be punished. There was no figuring the Chinese. Yuan had shot men for nothing, but these days, with the peace talks going on at Panmunjom, the unexpected violence had lessened. Everyone was waiting, waiting for peace and the voyage home. Even the Chinese. They were no more volunteers than Shard was a Wall Street imperialist, but they all had their parts to play.

Shard gazed across the open ground, looking for Skitter. What were they doing with him right now? He cursed himself for his stupidity. This close, and he had to pull a stunt like that. Cabbage leaves. Anything not belonging to another POW and not nailed down was fair game, always had been since they first were captured. But lately, Shard had not been able to control his desire to steal. He had a talent for it, sure. But back in Japan he'd always judged the risks and acted only when it was reasonably safe, not to mention rewarding.

The cabbage leaves had been neither.

Finally, he saw Skitter, thrown down the steps of the administration building, guards following and kicking him as he rolled on the ground. Skitter got up and did what he did so well—dancing away from the guards, staying one step ahead, waving his arms as if he were explaining something obvious to them. They kept their rifles leveled at him as they approached the pen. Skitter grinned and gave Shard a thumbs-up.

The guards advanced and Shard crawled away, knowing he could never escape the reach of those bayonets, instinctually curling up into the fetal position. Laughing at his fear, the guards opened the cage and motioned for him to get up. Skitter, glancing at the guards to be sure it was okay, reached in and helped Shard out.

"What happened?" Shard said, wincing as he moved. He was stiff from the beating he took, but he shook off Skitter's assistance. He'd walk on his own.

"I made a deal," Skitter said. "I'm going to do a broadcast about germ warfare."

"You can't do that," Shard said. "There's no germ warfare, that's all Red propaganda."

"That's exactly why I can do it," Skitter said. "Everyone knows it's bullshit. Even those pilots who gave a speech about it, they said it was all crap when the Chinese weren't listening. And they were officers, for Christ's sake. So why can't I say the same thing?"

"Because it's selling out your country," Shard said, doing his best not to hobble as they made their way back to their hut.

"You want to go back in the pen?" Skitter asked.

"Can't say as I do," Shard admitted. "What the hell do you know about germ warfare anyway?"

"I loaded canisters of it on transport planes, back in Japan. Saw it with my own eyes."

"We never loaded any planes," Shard said.

"Well, we were right next to an airbase," Skitter said. "Close enough."

"It's your funeral," Shard said. "But thanks. I appreciate you getting me out."

"No problem," Skitter said. They sat on the log bench outside their hut, watching the sun set over the mountains. "But it might be the last favor I can do for a while."

"What do you mean?"

"I'm on the list for Operation Little Switch. I'm going home," Skitter said, whispering as if the opportunity might vanish if he spoke too loudly. "Yuan told me himself, said he didn't think I was sincere about refusing repatriation, but that I deserved this reward for being a leader in class."

"I thought that was only for sick and injured POWs," Shard said.

"Hey, you know how the Chinese operate," Skitter said, keeping his voice low. "They're going to sprinkle in some progressives and hope for good press. I had to promise not to renege on the germ warfare story, though."

"What's to stop you?" Shard asked. Skitter didn't answer right away.

"They'll send you to a camp in Red China if I do," he said. "For life."

February 1951
Death March, North Korea

They began the march at dawn. The Mining Camp was at the base of three mountains, which meant every route out went up. The first man was bayoneted before the sun was fully over the horizon, a guy who'd been wounded in the P-51 attack. His arm was in a sling, and he limped from an unhealed wound in his leg.

"Make it quick," was all he said as he collapsed on the mountain path. The guard didn't understand him, but it was quick, as was the kick that followed, sending his body rolling down the hillside, to be half-buried beneath the cascade of small clattering stones that followed him down.

"Gerald Winter," a POW told Collier.

"Gerald Winter," he repeated. "Gerald Winter."

"Halt!" Wong shouted. The entire column of men, over three hundred POWs, stopped. Wong began yelling at the guards, pointing to the body at the bottom of the ravine.

"I can't believe he's mad about Winter being killed," Shard said.

"Maybe he's got new orders," Martinez offered.

"It must be hell to be an optimist in North Korea," Collier said.

"No one is allowed to stop," Wong shouted, turning in every direction to be heard. "Sick prisoners must be carried. The dead must be carried." He barked orders at the guards, who in turn sent four POWs into the ravine to drag Winter's body up.

"That's crazy," Skitter said in a whisper to Shard.

"Mean as hell," Shard said. "Not crazy. Now he's got us doing his work for him. We'll talk anybody who stops into keeping on, so we won't have to haul their carcass over these mountains."

"Jesus," Skitter said. They watched the POWs stagger up the hill with Winter. They were exhausted, but stood, ready to go. Two others took the body as Wong signaled for the march to continue. The column struggled on the narrow road, nothing more than a rutted track cut along the side of the mountain. Four men could walk abreast easily. A fifth man would go over the edge if his attention drifted.

"Watch each other," Shard said, moving about his section of thirty men, gathering them together. "Don't let anyone fall behind, stay together."

"Where we going, Shard?"

"Are they gonna feed us?"

"I heard we're heading into China. That so?"

The questions flowed over him from half the guys in his section, the ones that had any energy left for talking. He told them to shut up and march.

Each step was arduous as the incline increased. Each breath became more painful as they climbed higher, the air thinner and colder, the wind whipping against their threadbare uniforms. Some men had no shoes, their boots stolen by the North Koreans or the Chinese guards, their replacement sneakers worn down to nothing. Scraps of cloth encased their feet and made for a slow, shuffling gait.

"This has got to be the top," Skitter gasped as they neared what seemed to be the crest. It wasn't. The road dipped a bit and curved into another incline, steeper than the one before. "Shit." The curses continued as men stumbled and tripped over loose rocks, sending cascades of stone tumbling behind them.

It began to snow. Thick, heavy flakes that men caught on their tongues and savored like fine wine. Then it began to really snow, Korean style. Sideways, the wind kicking up and blasting their faces. Guards, with their faces covered in scarves, yelled at them but the words were lost in the savage wind. They began pushing with their rifles, and Shard understood.

"Move away from the edge," he said, moving up and down the line. "Walk to the left or you'll go off the side!" Guards pushed their way to the mountainside, taking the safest position. The column marched on, blind, freezing, starving, exhausted.

Shard kept one hand on Skitter in front of him and Collier to his side, shouting above the howling wind to stay together, grab the man next to you, hold tight, and keep moving. There was no sense of time or space, nothing but blinding whiteness and the footprints of the man in front of you. Each step was aching, ice cold agony, the wind razor sharp against exposed skin. Visibility was under six feet. Shard made out two men being carried within his small group alone.

Shard closed in on himself, trying to leave the cold behind, but it didn't work. His arm, resting on Skitter's shoulder ahead of him, was exposed and frozen. He could no longer feel his other arm, grasping Collier on his left. He knew he shouldn't let go, but it would be so easy to walk off into the white, to leave all of this behind, to never be beaten or cold again. To sleep.

Shard shook it off. No. Stay alive, be a free man one day, he kept telling himself. No POW camp, no army. He'd find Bobbie and make things as right as they could be. But he'd never let anyone control him. Never again. When he was eighteen, the army had made sense, especially after they threatened to bring him up on charges as an adult for the fire that had killed his father. Shard knew how that would go. Better to go straight into the army and away from Ohio fast as he could.

He'd had no home, no skills, nothing but what they taught him at the Boys' Industrial School. How to work on a car engine. How to steal, fight, and survive. It wasn't a bad place, but there were bad people in it. All sorts of bad people. He should know, he'd been one of them. The kid who killed one parent and drove the other to suicide. Other kids were there because their parents were dead, run off, in prison, or crazy. Some had killed, in a fight or by accident, stupidity, or neglect. He was unique, which meant he had to prove himself against the older kids who felt threatened by the rumors surrounding Ethan Shard.

"Shard," someone said. He barely could hear. "Shard!" A hand shook him, then another.

"What?" He managed to croak.

"We're not going up anymore," Skitter said. "It's flat."

"And the wind's not so bad," Collier said. "We might be out of the worst of it."

Shard looked at them. The snow was falling straight down now, covering their shoulders and faces with thick, intricate snowflakes.

"Don't hope for too much," Shard said. "You won't be disappointed when you find out it's worse than you thought. Keep moving." He shuffled ahead, ignoring the chatter of the others, knowing this was only a respite. They should shut up and save their strength.

They left the snow behind them as the track began its descent around the curve of the mountain. Billowing dark gray clouds moved past them, the storm heading into the valley they had climbed out of. The march continued, but with a palpable sense of relief among the POWs and guards alike. A tenuous truce emerged, smiles exchanged, even a few cigarettes handed out by the younger guards. Not falling off a cliff and disappearing into a raging storm forges a bond between souls, no matter how different people are. Shard watched, knowing it wouldn't last long, letting the men enjoy it. Why not? They'd be okay unless they let their guard down, expected kindness in an hour when they became the Western imperialist devils again.

Smokes and smiles vanished as they plodded along, the gravel road dipping slightly and then rising again, repeating the process as they moved between mountains, making for a pass the guards pointed out in the distance.

"Don't take too much," Shard said to Martinez, who was scooping up a handful of snow. "Just a little, otherwise you'll freeze up inside. You can't let your body temperature get too low."

"This snow is warmer than I am," Martinez said, licking the snowball slowly. That got a little laugh.

They came to a village, if a cluster of three huts could be called a village. The guards split up, half of them herding the POWs into a field, the other half making for the huts and what warmth they offered. The field was wet with snow and mud churned up by livestock. Pigs squealed from their pen and a few scrawny cows chewed hay from a rickety wooden manger.

"Not much of a farm," Shard said, sitting on a rock and knocking snow off his sneakers.

"Not much of a country, far as I can see," Tiny chimed in, eyeing the hay the cows were eating.

"We have eight men missing," Collier said, from his perch on the largest boulder in the field. He'd been counting men, including the dead man, Winter, who was still being carried.

"You sure?" Shard asked. Collier nodded. He'd counted twice. The POWs were crowded together, huddled for warmth in the open field. No one was under any illusions about where they'd spend the night.

Two trucks trundled down the mountain road and stopped by the field. Guards streamed out of the huts, standing at attention. Comrade Wong stepped out of the lead truck, his face pinched with anger. He barked out orders and guards ran to the rear of the first truck. They pulled out seven men and a corpse.

"Damn," Shard said, standing as Wong drew his pistol. "He's going to execute them."

"I said no one was to stop," Wong announced in a loud voice, waving his pistol in the air. "No bodies were to be left behind. These men have disobeyed orders and must be punished." They were half dead already. Thin, bandaged, all with the vacant stare of a POW who had given up, the only hope left that death be quick. The Chinese forced them to their knees.

"Comrade Wong," Shard said, advancing through the exhausted prisoners. "May I speak?" Wong nodded, a short, sharp snap of his head. "The storm was a special circumstance. I'm sure no one saw this man die, and the others may have become lost. They did not try to escape, did they?"

"Of course not!" Wong said. It was a ridiculous thought. Wong stared at Shard for a full minute, then came to a decision. "Are any of these men in your section?"

"Yes, Comrade. Samms is. Jack Samms," he said, pointing to one of kneeling men.

"Other section leaders, here!" Wong shouted. Ten POWs joined Shard in front of the kneeling men. "Point out your men to me." They did. One section leader claimed the corpse. Four had one man each and one section leader claimed two as his men. Five of them had no men among those who had fallen out.

"Section Leader Thornton," Wong said. "You are the only leader to have more than one prisoner drop out. Therefore, you will be executed." Wong walked in back of Thornton, who stood up straight, nodding to his two men.

"It's not your fault, boys," Thornton said, then turned to Wong who stood behind him. "If this were the American army, a man would be entitled to a court-martial before being shot."

"This is not the American army," Wong said, turning Thornton so he faced his men before shooting him in the back of the head. "You two will carry your section leader tomorrow."

Shard shook with rage, barely able to contain himself. It would be worth it, he thought, to grab Wong and snap his neck like Kelso had taught us. It would be worth dying to do that. But the guards would slaughter the others in revenge. And Shard would never find Bobbie. So he trembled, his hands limp at his side, until Skitter pulled him back.

"Put him with his arms straight out," Skitter said to the two POWs dejectedly staring at Thornton's body lying face down in the blood-splattered snow. "He's going to freeze up tonight. He'll be easier to carry that way." Skitter always worked the angles.

The second truck contained their meal. Rice balls with millet seed. A ladleful of bean milk per man.

"Curtis Thornton," Collier said softly when he finished eating.

"Gonna be more come morning," Tiny said. "I need something to cover my hands."

"Anyone in our section dies, we give his clothes to whoever needs them the most," Shard said. "You're pretty well outfitted, Tiny."

"Yeah, and so are you," Tiny said. "They treated you real well since you saved Skitter. Gave you both new clothes."

"Our uniforms were burned off our backs, for Christ's sake," Skitter said.

"You're a progressive, just like Hawkins," Tiny said, spitting out the word like a curse.

"I think for myself," Skitter said. "Just because I don't buy every damn thing the army tells us, don't go calling me names. And Hawkins isn't so bad." Hawkins was sitting right next to Tiny, trying to not get drawn in.

"So what's the deal, Hawkins?" Shard asked. "You buy the Commie line?"

"I'm no Communist," Hawkins said. "It's not very American. But maybe if I was Chinese, I might think it was okay. They've got a lot of people to feed."

"You ain't Chinese," Collier said. "Try and remember that."

"Shut up and get some sleep," Shard said. "Everyone in tight?" All thirty of Shard's section were grouped together, lying in the snow in a large spiral. The plan was to wake every hour or so and rotate the outermost guys into the center to get warm. It wasn't much, but it was all they had. Frosted breath rose in the moonlight, the sounds of men moaning in pain and animals grunting in their pens rising to the gray and clouded sky.

In the morning, Shard was on the outer ring of the circle. His jacket was frozen to the ground, and he had to pull to loosen it from the snow and ice. He checked his section and was surprised to find no one had died during the night. Tiny blew on his fingers, looking disappointed.

A truck rolled in with a breakfast of bean milk and boiled millet seed. As the sections lined up, Shard saw two bodies left in the snow. It could have been worse.

Wong appeared from one of the huts, looking pleased with himself after a warm night. In a magnanimous gesture, he decreed that only Section Leader Thornton would have to be carried today. Winter and the two other dead could be left behind.

Winter's body had been stripped naked during the night. The guards took what they wanted from the other two and left the rest for the POWs to pick over. Tiny was up like a shot and elbowed his way into the crowd of scavengers. He pulled off two threadbare socks and pulled them over his hands. A section leader protested, but when Tiny raised his fists and told him to take the damn socks if he wanted them, he backed off.

An unspoken rule had been broken. Each section had been distributing the remnants of clothing from the dead within their own group. But Tiny was big and strong enough to break the rules, even after his time in the turnip hole. Shard eyed Tiny, knowing that in his own weakened condition after the fire and the march, he was in no shape to oppose him. Shard would need every ounce of endurance he could muster to survive the day.

The sun barely rose above the mountaintops as they marched. The road was better, wider and flat, but the temperature was frigid. Even the day of wind and snow hadn't been this cold. It was clear-blue-sky cold, like frozen steel. Below freezing, below zero, beyond enduring.

Gerald Winter, Curtis Thornton, Jack Samms, Joe Klimsey, Roy Sunsdahl. Collier repeated the names of the dead on the march. Their route took them up another mountain, negotiating a series of switchbacks before heading down the other side. Clay Christopulos and Larry

Anderson joined the list, both shot by Wong for dropping out of the column.

Collier added their names to his litany.

"They didn't care," Martinez said. He'd been farther back and saw both executions. "They knew what they were doing, and they didn't care."

"Fools," Tiny said. "Dead ain't a rest cure."

"Tiny," Shard said. "Every now and then you say something halfway intelligent."

"Go to hell," Tiny said.

"Then there's the rest of the time," Shard said, trying to grin, to get a laugh, any response except a fist from Tiny. Nothing. They walked on, into a valley so deep the sun vanished behind a mountain. The road curved around a large rock formation. Ahead, Shard and the others heard a groan of disappointment. As he drew closer, Shard couldn't keep himself from uttering the same.

They had to cross a stream.

It was wide and fast-moving, but shallow, to judge from the rocks showing above water. Knee-deep at worst, which was bad enough. A truck was waiting on the other side, but that was for the guards. It came across for half of them and brought them over. They stood with rifles at the ready, as if a POW planned to swim for it. Maybe the stream led to a river that went to the sea. Shard watched the water flow by, wondering if it would get out of North Korea before he did. Probably so.

The remaining guards prodded men along with their bayonets, into the river.

"Help the sick and wounded," Shard said. "Pass the word."

"Come on," Collier said to Martinez, and they took a shivering, near dead prisoner between them, forming a chair with their arms to keep him out of the water. Skitter pointed to a bandaged prisoner using a stick as a cane, and he and Shard did the same with him.

"Tiny," Shard yelled. "Pick up Sparks. He can't make it." Sparks had dysentery, a bad case. He was skin and bones, nothing for Tiny to toss over his shoulder. Shard was surprised when Tiny obeyed and picked up Sparks in his arms.

The first step into the stream was a shock. Ice-cold water flooded into Shard's canvas sneakers, soaking his socks and freezing his feet. His ankles went numb as he and Skitter stumbled across the streambed, gravel slipping away under their feet.

Halfway across, the water hit their knees and Skitter began to chatter, his teeth rattling against each other. He'd never been that cold before, not even ice fishing in northern Michigan. That was a spring day compared to this.

"Hang on," Shard said. "We're getting close."

"God damn!" Tiny cursed, his words followed by a splash and a terrifying scream. "That bastard crapped all over me!" Sparks was in the deep water, his head barely above the surface. Tiny had thrown Sparks down when the dysentery got the better of him. "Son of a bitch!" Tiny muttered, grabbing Sparks by the collar and dragging him through the water. Others ran through the raging stream as best they could to reach Sparks, but Tiny outpaced them, throwing Sparks down on the rocky shore. Two guards kept their rifles trained on Tiny, looking afraid that he might go on a rampage. Once he sat on a rock, wiping himself off, they laughed, pointing at Sparks, whose entire body was shivering violently.

"What the hell were you thinking?" Shard demanded, as he and Skitter climbed out of the stream.

"I said I'd carry the bastard," Tiny said. "I never said I'd let him shit on me."

"He's got dysentery, for Christ's sake," Shard said as he put his hands on Sparks' face. It was ice cold, his eyes unfocused. "He can't help it."

"That's his problem," Tiny said. "You don't like it, we can have a talk about it any time you want." With that, Tiny leaned back against the rock and closed his eyes, at peace with himself.

Sparks died.

Wong ordered Shard's section to carry Sparks, since they should have taken better care of him alive. Two men went forward to pick up the body.

"Tiny," Shard said. "You take him to start."

"No."

"Come on, Tiny," Skitter pleaded. "The river washed him clean. No big deal for a guy like you to take some extra weight."

"Now listen, all of you," Tiny said, turning and facing the rest of his section. "There's nothing washed clean here. There's nothing good here. There's only me and anyone who gets in my way. That's my world. You think the river washes you clean? Then you're a fool. And no fool tells me what to do."

Shard carried Sparks, fireman style, across his shoulders. He blamed himself for giving Tiny a chance to do something responsible. It wasn't possible, not if it inconvenienced Tiny one bit. He should have seen it coming, prevented it. Story of his life.

Gerald Winter, Curtis Thornton, Jack Samms, Joe Klimsey, Roy Sunsdahl, Clay Christopulos, Larry Anderson, Don Sparks.

Collier chanted names, his voice hoarse. Skitter stayed by Shard, uncertain of what to say. Ice formed on their feet and pants. The sky darkened.

They slept in caves that night, the low ceilings coated in ice. Frozen rice balls and millet seed. A bucket of water, ice an inch thick on top, for each section.

"Don't sleep with wet feet," Shard said. "You'll get trench foot in no time."

"What choice do we have?" Martinez said.

"Body heat," Shard said. "Take your socks off and put them next to your skin, under your shirt."

"They're ice cold," Skitter whined.

"It'll take your breath away," Shard said. "But your body heat will dry them out. Trust me, a guy who fought in the last war told me about this trick. Said it worked in the Ardennes."

"Where the hell is that?" Tiny asked.

"Where they fought the Battle of the Bulge," Collier said. "France or Germany, I ain't sure. It makes sense, but now we got nothing on our feet."

"You're probably not going to like this part," Shard said, and proceeded to show them. He and Skitter lay opposite each other. Shard took Skitter's bare feet and guided them under his shirts and jacket, up under his armpits. Between Skitter's feet and his socks on his chest, he began to shiver. But once Skitter did the same, he felt the warmth build in his own feet, and was able to stop his own convulsions.

"It ain't pretty," Collier said, "but I'm game."

"Diekman, get over here," Tiny ordered.

"Remember, it works both ways, Tiny," Shard said, aware that it was hard to sound authoritative with your feet stuck in another man's armpits.

"Yeah, yeah," Tiny said, jamming his big feet under Diekman's jacket. "This better work."

Most guys paired up and followed suit. Everyone was surprised in the morning when their feet and socks were dry and warm. Especially Shard, who wasn't sure if the janitor at the Boys' Industrial School had been pulling his leg or not.

Wind scoured the mountainside where they'd taken shelter. It was soaked corn in buckets for breakfast, about the worst thing for being on the march. They drank the frigid water and put the corn in their pockets, knowing not to each too much at once. The air was dry and cold, the sun nothing but a useless orb that would give meager light for a few hours before vanishing behind another peak.

Everyone had come out of the caves, ready to go. Wong eyed the ranks from the running board of his truck, looking disappointed as he signaled the column to start.

"What do you think their game is?" Skitter asked, chewing a handful of corn.

"Maybe they don't have a plan," Shard said. "Maybe this is all they know. Marching, killing. They were fighting a civil war before the Second World War. They've been at this business for a long time."

"Yeah, I get it," Skitter said. "So why not just kill us all? Look at this place, it's god-forsaken and desolate." He gestured around them. Pale, brown mountains. Rocky slopes with little or no vegetation. No houses or farms, nothing green or beautiful.

"They've killed plenty," Collier said.

"Yeah, but not all of us," Skitter said. "Everyone's not going to make it to where we're going, that's a fact. But the question is, what do they want from us?"

"They want our souls," Shard said. "Shut up and keep walking."

Everyone wanted something from Ethan Shard. Obedience, confession, reformation. He'd been down that road before. He'd confessed, played the part of the repentant, wayward youth. He'd reformed. And after all that, they still hid his brother from him. Dangerous. That was the verdict on young Ethan Shard at age seventeen, as he readied himself to go out into the world. All because of a few fights with the oldest boys, the bullies, the Tinys of Lancaster, Ohio. Fights he won. And one punch to a teacher, who'd deserved it.

Hours faded into days. The road was the same road. The cold and the mountains were the same, the fields and caves in which they slept were the same. The deaths were the same. Collier kept reciting the names, now in a singsong melody to help himself remember. He still had the list, hidden away. But he no longer had a pencil, only his memory, memory numbed by cold and hunger, thirst and deprivation.

Some said they'd marched for eight days, some said ten. It didn't matter. What mattered was that they had arrived. This was their new home, someone said, but Shard barely heard, just kept on walking into the camp with the remains of his section behind him. Prisoners from the camp crowded around them, as gaunt and half-dead as they were. Words were spoken to him, but he heard nothing. Skitter led him to a firepit. A POW was melting snow in a beat-up, dented pan, feeding the fire with bits of wood, cornstalks, and corncobs. Steam swirled above the water. Warmth.

"Not much in the way of welcome, boys, but it's all I've got," the POW said, offering a chipped cup of water to Shard. Shard waved it off and gestured for the other men to go first. Skitter stood by him as they surveyed the camp. Dozens of huts scattered across the landscape. Maybe once it had been a village, a real community. No wire. There were fenced enclosures at each end of the camp. A couple of barracks-style buildings, probably for the Chinese, whose red banner flew high above their new home, snapping in the cold wind.

Finally, it was Shard's turn for the warm drink. It was the best thing he'd ever tasted. The warmth glowed inside him, giving him a euphoric sense of hope, which left as quickly as it came, sadness replacing that brief moment of joy. He wished he'd never tasted it.

"What is this place?" Shard asked, once he could get his voice to work.

"Camp Eleven," the POW said. "I'm Father James, by the way. Chaplain. Most days I have another name for this place. Hell on Earth."

Chapter 13

April 18, 1953
Camp Eleven, North Korea

" So you're going through with it?" Shard asked. Again. He tensed with each breath, his bruised ribs sending sharp shivers of pain throughout his torso as they watched the western sky from the log outside their hut. The skies turned hues of red and yellow as the sun began its descent into sunset.

"I have to, now," Skitter said. "Unless you want to go back into the pen. And Yuan would not be happy with me reneging."

"The army isn't going to be happy about your germ warfare yarn," Shard said, turning his body to look at Skitter. It hurt too much to turn his head.

"Screw the army," Skitter said. "They haven't done anything but stick us out on that damn hill with no support and then spend two years dickering with the Chinese over ending this war. Remember, we could have been home two years ago if it wasn't for the army arguing with the Chinese about non-repatriation."

"That was the government, not the army," Shard said. Everyone had been excited back in '51 when the peace talks started. But they stalled over the American insistence that Chinese and North Korean POWs held by the UN forces be allowed to choose whether they wanted to be returned home or to Taiwan or South Korea. The Communists knew that thousands would never go back to Red China or the north, so the war dragged on as both sides sat across the negotiating table repeating the same thing over and over again.

"It's all the same," Skitter said. "They hung us out to dry. I don't give a good goddamn where any gook ends up. I want to go home."

"Hard to argue with that," Shard said. "What if they court-martial you?"

"Listen, Shard," Skitter said, laying his hand on Shard's arm. "As soon as I hear you're free, I'll tell them what the deal was. I'll renounce everything. But until then, I'll stick to my story."

"Tell them on the QT," Shard said. "Maybe they'll go easy on you once they know why you did it."

"Yeah, right," Skitter said, his disgust with that notion clear. "You trust the army, Shard? You trust them to keep quiet about the Chinese blackmailing me with a threat to keep you in a prison camp for life? It's a propaganda goldmine for them. They'd run with that story and demand your immediate release. There'd be a bullet in your brain within the hour. You know I'm right."

"Yep, I do." Skitter was dead right. They were pawns at this point in the game, pawns to be sacrificed for the greater good at a moment's notice. The Chinese greater good or the American greater good, it made little difference when the trigger was pulled.

Four guards marching double time, rifles at the ready, came from the administration building. Shard watched their approach carefully, calculating at a certain point that they were not coming for him.

"What's going on?" Collier asked as he emerged from the hut.

"Don't know," Shard said. "They look like they mean business." The guards passed their hut and kept going, heading toward the officers' enclosure. "I wonder what they're up to."

It didn't take long to find out.

They returned with Lieutenant John Cooper, two of the guards prodding him with bayonets toward the now empty pen. He looked at Shard as they passed, an accusation of betrayal in his eyes.

March 1951
Camp Eleven, North Korea

More prisoners poured into Camp Eleven in the weeks that followed. Frozen wraiths greeted by Father James and his steaming pot of water. All of them as half-dead and stunned as Shard and the others had been at what they had endured, as well as the fact of their survival. What small joy there was in the end of the journey was quickly tempered by the reality of life at Camp Eleven.

Mornings began with a 5:30 bugle call for assembly. No matter the weather, all prisoners had to fall out by sections to be counted. Anyone who died during the night was brought out for the count as well. Death was no excuse for missing roll call. Then exercises. As soon as the men worked up a decent sweat, the Chinese started in on their speeches. A speech might be two minutes one day and two hours the next, first delivered in Chinese and then in English. By the time the speeches were over, men were shivering in their damp clothes.

Then the morning meal was distributed. Barley with turnips became the standard fare, with potatoes or rice every fourth or fifth day. Today was a potato day, and with the extra food came extra duties. Shard and his section were assigned to work on the recreation hall. The flooring and frame were already in place, and the POWs carried wood planks from the warehouse, nailing them to the studs. Their task was to finish two sides of the building before evening roll call.

"Hurry, hurry," Comrade Wong shouted at the men. "The sooner you are done the sooner you can warm yourselves and study Marxist-Leninism and the works of Chairman Mao." Wong's harangues came without the slightest hint of irony or humor.

"That's one small stove for such a big room," Martinez said, as soon as Wong's attention went elsewhere. The hall was large, big enough to seat a hundred men. One small cast iron stove sat in a corner, its chimney spewing smoke as guards fed it scraps from the lumber pile. They turned their backs on the POWs and warmed their hands. Long silk banners hung from the ceiling joists, twisting sinuously in the wind, bright red like a flickering fire with a yellow star at its heart.

"Be a lot of hot air in here," Collier said as he hammered a plank into place. The tool fell from his grip, and he blew on his bare hands to try and warm them. It was impossible to work with no gloves in this freezing cold without warming your hands constantly. But Comrade Wong did not like excuses or a POW standing still with both hands under his armpits and had ordered prisoners beaten for any halt in their labors.

"Better in here than another movie night," Shard said, picking up the hammer. "You and Martinez go to the warehouse and get some more planks. We're almost ready for them." The guard in charge of the warehouse was an older guy, not a bad sort. He kept a fire going in an old fuel drum and didn't begrudge the POWs a quick warm-up when they came in for supplies.

Collier nodded his thanks and headed off with Martinez. The movie night had been surreal, even by POW camp standards. It was blowing snow and well below zero when the POWs had been rousted out of their huts. The Chinese had nailed a sheet up on the wooden beams of the recreation hall and were showing a Russian film without subtitles or translation. It was about building a hydroelectric dam, far as anyone could figure. The soundtrack was full of grand-sounding speeches and martial music, which might have been bearable in a warm room, but the epic was an hour long, and the prisoners had to stand at attention to show respect for the great Marxist achievements of the Soviet Union.

When the film ended, the prisoners responded with great applause, prompted by bayonets closing in on all sides. The only unenthusiastic POWs were two men dead from exposure.

No one understood the reason behind the midnight showing, but it spurred the POWs on to finish the recreation hall as fast as they could, fearing a repeat performance. Which, Shard thought, was probably the very purpose Wong had in mind. He was deputy camp commander now, in charge of political indoctrination. Commander Peng was Wong's boss, but he seemed to leave things to his subordinates. Peng was an older soldier who walked with a limp and didn't engage in the kind of political ranting and raving Wong enjoyed.

"You are working diligently," Wong said, appearing silently behind Shard.

"As best I can," Comrade Wong," Shard said, nails held between his teeth.

"I am sending Comrade Skinner with something to help you," Wong said, lighting a cigarette, cupping the match in his hands against the biting wind.

"Thank you," Shard said cautiously, wondering what it could be, but not wanting to speak with Wong any more than he had to. It could only be dangerous. Wong smiled and blew his smoke skyward as he walked away. Ten minutes later Skitter showed up, his arms cradling rolls of paper.

"What the hell is that?" Shard said. "Wong said you were bringing something to help us."

"He should have said inspire you," Skitter said, unrolling a dozen large posters. The one on top showed two Chinese soldiers, rifles held high, chasing a caricature of MacArthur across a battlefield strewn with burning American tanks. The next portrayed MacArthur in an oversized gold braid cap wielding a bloody knife over a Korean mother and her dead child.

"Jesus Christ!" Shard said. "They gotta be kidding."

"I think they made MacArthur's hat a little small," Skitter said, grinning. "I got to get these up before the paste freezes."

Skitter mounted the posters along the wall of planks they'd just nailed up. Heroic Chinese and Korean soldiers standing shoulder to shoulder against the imperialist aggressors. Or so Shard guessed since the writing was all Chinese characters. One poster showed a chunky Chinese woman holding a lamb, obviously touting the achievements of Communist farming techniques. She attracted a number of whistles and catcalls, at which the guards took offense. This naturally resulted in more whistles, but from a safer distance. POWs wandered over to look at the posters, laughing and shaking their heads. Skitter wasn't the only one to make a joke about MacArthur and his cap. The general liked his gold braid, everyone knew that.

"They do add some color to the camp," Collier said on the way back for evening roll call.

"Yeah, more red. Exactly what we need," Martinez said. "But I do like Comrade Bo Peep. Think you can get one of her for our hut, Skitter?"

"You been a POW too long, Martinez," Skitter answered. The banter went back and forth, and Shard listened, enjoying what he heard. He imagined it was a bunch of guys walking home from work, making fun of the boss, ready to stop in a neighborhood bar for a quick one. He enjoyed the daydream, thinking of the day when he'd walk into some joint and ask for a cold draft beer. Whatever Wong had intended with the posters, they had given the prisoners a break from the harsh routine of the camp. Something to laugh at, a rare commodity.

The laughter stopped and the men went quiet as they neared the graveyard.

POWs died every day at Camp Eleven. Most died in the night, found frozen stiff in the morning. There was nowhere to bury the bodies, no tools to break the frozen ground. The Chinese had designated an area as the graveyard, which was quickly filled with the first layer of corpses. Stacked like cordwood covered by layers of snow, bodies stretched in a line thirty yards long, four feet high. Bare feet stuck out, the ones at the bottom rotting and black, the newest at the top ice white, crystals forming on faces in the frigid air. Blood and feces stained the corpses, testimony to their final agonies.

There was a camp hospital, nothing more than a holding area for the graveyard. No medicine, no beds, simply a hut with a dirt floor where the sick were taken to die. No one came out cured, only feet first.

"Father James," Shard called out as they neared the end of the pile. The chaplain was kneeling by the bodies, praying.

"Hello, fellows," Father James said, rising and dusting the snow from his knees. He was young for a chaplain, maybe twenty-five. Blond fuzz stood out on his cheeks, and his light hair blew in the wind.

"Where's your hat, Father?" Shard asked. "You shouldn't be out here without it."

"Oh, I gave it to some poor fellow who came in today. He was in terrible shape, needed it more than I did. Unfortunately, the Lord will provide," he said, gesturing to the dead.

"Let's go get some of that delicious coffee, Father," Martinez said. "Warm you right up."

"Best offer I've had today," Father James said. It was barley water, not coffee, but they called it that since it was brown and warm. The brew was served after evening roll call, which was at 4:30 in the afternoon, taking advantage of the last light of the day. "I'll be holding Easter services, boys, in case any of you want to attend."

"When's Easter?" Skitter asked.

"Sunday, April 3rd," Father James said. "Which by my calculations is in two days."

"The Chinese going to allow that?" Shard asked.

"Oh no," Father James said. "All religious services are still banned. But I'll find a way, even if I have to go hut to hut."

"You can use ours, Father," Shard said. "You could get twenty or more guys in there no problem."

"You sure?" Father James said. "There could be trouble."

"I'll never forget you being there with the warm water when we stumbled into this dump," Collier said. "So you got my vote, and I'll be at there."

"Anyone have a problem with that?" Shard asked, looking at his group as they assembled for roll call. He stared at Tiny who shrugged his shoulders and looked away, as close as Tiny got to agreeing to anything. No one spoke up.

"Let us know when, Father," Shard said and lined up to be counted.

Chapter 14

April 18, 1953
Camp Eleven, North Korea

"Christ," Shard swore. "He has to think I betrayed him. Why else would I get out so quick?"

"It had to be Horseface," Skitter said as they watched the guards throw Cooper into the pen. "Cooper'll figure it out. If you had admitted talking to him, you'd both be in the pen together. Maybe he doesn't even know you were in."

"News travels fast," Shard said, standing and groaning in pain. Skitter was right about that. With nothing much to occupy their minds, POWs became adept at passing information, spreading facts and rumors faster than old gossips on a party line. The story of Shard and his cabbage leaves probably reached both ends of the camp before he'd reached the pen.

"Let's tell him then," Skitter said. "Listen, Horseface got into trouble over you stealing right under his nose. Stands to reason he wouldn't admit that he took a bribe to let you and Cooper talk."

"Yeah, could be," Shard admitted. "But he might report that Cooper tried to bribe him, to get back in Yuan's good graces."

"Makes sense," Skitter said. "That would have been a good move for him, if he were willing to take a risk." The two of them stood about twenty yards from the pen, waiting for the guards to leave. They had amused themselves by banging on the pen with their rifle butts and throwing small stones at Cooper, yelling with glee when one got through the chicken wire and scored a hit. They finally left, kicking dirt through the wire as they did.

Skitter and Shard walked around the pen, waiting until no Chinese remained in the vicinity. It was forbidden to give prisoners in the pen food or water, and the guards would routinely chase off any POWs who even got close. Sometimes it cost a beating, depending on the mood of the guard. Skitter moved off to keep himself between the pen and the administration building, so he could warn Shard of any threat from that direction. Shard stood ten feet away, close enough to speak, far enough so no one would accuse him of helping Cooper.

"What happened, Lieutenant?" Shard asked.

"You tell me," Cooper said. "They came in and grabbed me."

"It wasn't me," Shard said. Cooper had a black eye and a ripening bruise on his cheek.

"I heard you were in and out of here in minutes," Cooper said. "How'd you manage it?"

"That had nothing to do with you," Shard said. "I got caught stealing cabbage. Skitter made a deal with them, promised them something about germ warfare. They ate it up."

"You must be worth your weight in gold to Skitter," Cooper said. "He's taking a hell of a chance."

"He thinks it might help him get out early. You heard of Operation Little Switch?"

"No," Cooper said. Shard filled him in. "So we assume there's a Big Switch coming soon?"

"Yeah," Shard said. "Must have been a breakthrough at the peace talks."

"I hope they don't forget me in here," Cooper said. "See if your pal can put in a good word for me. He seems to have Yuan's ear."

"Yeah," Shard said, edging away as two guards came by on patrol. "He does."

Easter Sunday, 1951
Camp Eleven, North Korea

Father James made his way to Shard's hut, cloaked by darkness and a low rolling cloud cover that obscured the heavens, obscuring the crystal clear starlight and dulling the new moon. He stopped, dropping to all fours behind a woodpile, listening for the telltale footsteps of a guard detail. The penalty for being out before the morning bugle call was death.

The padre moved closer to Shard's hut, trusting that at this early morning hour the guards were content to stay warm indoors. All they really guarded against was POWs raiding the warehouse and kitchen for food. Other than that, there wasn't much the prisoners could do except die of exposure. He ran toward the rice paper door and slammed against it, misjudging the distance in the murky gloom. The door slid open, arms grabbed him and pulled him in, as the door was quietly closed.

"Jesus, Padre, could you make any more noise?" Diekman said as the chaplain fell over him. "Sorry, I didn't mean to curse like that."

"And I didn't mean to make such a racket. All is forgiven," Father James said. "My night vision is getting worse by the day." Silence. "That was a joke, boys."

"Good one, Padre," Martinez said to the low, polite laughter. "You sure no one saw you?"

"Half the guards suffer from night blindness as well," Father James said. "I didn't see anyone far as I could tell, but that doesn't mean much. As a matter of fact, I can't see your faces."

"Take your time, Father," Shard said. It was dark in the hut, but gradually faces and shapes would take form.

"Let us begin the service," Father James said, moving away from the thin rice-paper door behind him. He took out a candle stub, about two inches high, and huddled over a match, struck it, and lit the candle. "Tiny, could you move in front of the door? To hide the reflection?" Tiny shoved the guy next to him and sat by the door, not even a grudging grunt escaping his lips.

In the glow of the candle, Shard watched Father James look at the men surrounding him. Unshaven, cold, emaciated, they still radiated hope. Perhaps it was the softening light of the candle. Or something else.

"If we were in church," Father James began, "everyone would light their candle from the Paschal Candle as we sang hymns of praise. But here we can't lift our voices or spread the light. All we have is this single flame, hidden in the night. Still, the light is as strong as a thousand candles in the greatest cathedral, because it brings us together this Easter morning. It symbolizes the resurrection of Our Lord from the grave, and the light of salvation and hope God brought into the world. It illuminates the triumph of the light of God's grace and salvation over the darkness of death and sin. As you men have triumphed by your presence here."

Shard listened, moved by the words, but he wondered if he was more impressed with Father James than God Himself. Father James took risks, put himself out there, all for the men. But where was God? He watched the padre go through the service, bowed his head in prayer when asked, but still he wondered. Where was the God of Father James?

Maybe it didn't matter. All that mattered was comfort, and the soft light and angelic words were comforting. Even Tiny couldn't look mean here. Skitter had his hands folded in prayer, his head bowed. Martinez crossed himself, and Shard wondered how many denominations were represented in this cramped and cold hut. He didn't know what Father James was. Protestant, he thought.

"One final prayer, boys, and then I have to move on."

"Better put out your candle now, Padre," Skitter suggested. "Let your eyes get used to the dark."

"Yes, good idea," Father James said, blowing on the candle as he held his hand behind it. The room descended into darkness. No more the soft, glowing, flickering light, only a calm silence, waiting.

"Christ is Risen," Father James prayed. "The world below lies desolate." The POWs joined him, whispering the call and response.

Christ is Risen: The spirits of evil are fallen.
Christ is Risen: The angels of God are rejoicing.
Christ is Risen: The tombs of the dead are empty.

As the last words faded into silence, the door was torn open, flashlights blazed, and bayonets were thrust into the room. The POWs covered their heads and squirmed over each other to get away from the guards as they advanced into the hut, yelling in a fury at the prisoners.

Father James sat still, facing the harsh lights that blinded him.

"This is forbidden," Wong barked, his pistol at the ready. The guards ceased their screams and withdrew from his path. "Chairman Mao tells us that religion is poison. You shall soon find out how poisonous it can be." Wong had to stoop down until he reached the center of the hut, where he kicked at POWs until they made room for him so he could stand up straight. Beams from the flashlights played around the interior as prisoners raised their hands against the blinding light.

"This was my doing," Father James said. "These men are innocent of any disobedience."

"Yes, you would like that," Wong said. "To become a martyr. But it is not so easy to eradicate poison. Your irrational Western religion causes these deluded individuals to look to you as a leader. But all you can do is rain down suffering upon them." Wong spoke to his guards and pointed to Diekman and Martinez, gesturing savagely with his pistol, then pressing the barrel to each of their foreheads.

"No!" Father James said, holding out his hands in protest. "Please, take me instead."

"It will not be that easy, Prisoner James," Wong spat. He holstered his pistol and nodded to the guards, who dragged Martinez and Diekman out of the hut. "You say the tombs of the dead are empty. We shall see."

Father James stared through the smashed doorway as Wong left, the play of flashlights providing glimpses of Martinez and Diekman holding their arms up, warding off fists and rifle butts as they were hurried along to the administration building.

After roll call, exercises, and a long speech about religion as a tool of foreign colonialism and feudalism, it was announced that there would be no morning meal served. Wong stepped up to the podium and surveyed the ranks, waiting for the disgruntled murmurs to die down.

"If you are hungry," Wong said, "ask Prisoner James to bring food from heaven for you." Father James stood in the ranks, miserable. Shard wondered if anything could save Diekman and Martinez. Probably nothing. Wong was enjoying this, denying punishment to the padre and visiting it upon his followers instead. Smart, Shard had to admit. Wong turned to one of his men and pointed to Father James. The guard trotted over to the padre and produced a small loaf of bread from inside his quilted uniform jacket.

"Take it, Prisoner James," Wong said. "You can make many loaves, yes? Do it with the bread, and I will give you a fish as well." He translated for the enjoyment of the guards, who dutifully laughed.

"I cannot perform miracles," Father James said.

"Ask your god to do so," Wong said.

"It doesn't work that way," Father James said, his voice low and sad. It was evident he wished it did.

"You are right. It does not work," Wong said. "Your religion is a folk tale, nothing more. You are dismissed."

Wong strode from the platform, leaving Father James clutching the single small loaf of bread in the midst of hundreds of hungry men. It was a sublime torture.

"I've got that, Father," Shard said, taking the loaf from his hands. Shard could see how pained the padre was, grasping the only food the entire camp would see before the evening meal.

"Give it to the sick," Father James said distantly, his eyes unfocused.

"Sure," Shard said. That was most of the camp, but he knew of some guys who needed it the most. There were others to whom it would be a comfort, but they'd be dead by tomorrow anyway. Shard took Skitter with him, visiting three huts housing POWs who suffered from severe dysentery. He gave out pieces of bread to each sick man, hoping the solid, plain food would stay with them. It was damn little, and the POWs who were well—a relative state in Camp Eleven— looked on enviously as their hutmates chewed their precious portions.

Returning to their hut, Shard and Skitter watched Collier repairing the rice-paper door. It was a cold, gray morning, but the wind was calm, so a door didn't make much difference one way or the other. The Chinese didn't allow heat in the huts. Instead, men huddled together, pooling body heat, each night a misery of frosted breath and killing cold, the days not much better. Shard paused, catching sight of Father James. He was where they had left him after roll call, on his knees, his hands folded in prayer.

A forbidden activity.

Guards passed him by, as if he were invisible.

Shard couldn't take it anymore. He knew what Wong was playing at, and Father James was falling right into his trap. He strode over, grabbed the padre by the lapels and dragged him to the hut over surprised and shocked protests. "Shut up, Father," was all Shard said.

"What the hell are you doing?" Collier asked as he slid the door open. Skitter followed Shard, a confused look on his face as Shard pushed Father James in. A murmur of protest arose from the men inside, even Tiny looking shocked at how Shard was manhandling a chaplain.

"Listen," said Shard as they all gathered around. His eyes bore in on Father James. "Did you ever wonder why the Reds let you stay in the enlisted men's camp? You're a lieutenant, after all."

"I think because they don't see me as a real officer," Father James said. "I don't fit into their notion of an officer or an enlisted man. They don't have noncombatants in their army. Now let me go." He moved to get up, but Shard pushed him down.

"No," Shard said. "They think of you as a political officer, like a Soviet commissar. If they left you in with the other officers, you might encourage them to show some leadership. That's what a commissar does. But in here, there are so many more men, it's overwhelming. You have a huge flock to tend to, and keeping them alive is all you can manage to do. When you go against the Party and hold a sacred service, they get scared."

"They didn't look scared," Father James said.

"But they were. Why do you think they took Martinez and Diekman? To make everyone afraid of being seen with you.

They're too afraid of you to go against you. Wong was right; they don't want a martyr. That's why they're ignoring you out there, to show they think your power is meaningless."

"Do you think it's meaningless, Shard?" Father James asked.

Damn him, Shard thought. "Not to the men in here," he said.

"How about Diekman and Martinez?" Father James asked. "What can I do about them?"

"That's out of our hands, Father," Shard said. "My guess is that they're working on them to say you're a counterrevolutionary or war criminal or whatever else they dream up."

"You mean torturing them, so they can say it was my own people who betrayed me," Father James said, nodding his head as he began to grasp Shard's meaning. Judas.

"Yeah," Shard agreed. "Old story, huh?"

"Maybe I can do something," Skitter said. His eyes were downcast, not meeting Shard's. "Since they call me a progressive, I might as well see what it gets me."

"What are you going to say?" Shard asked him.

"Whatever I need to," Skitter said, moving quickly out the door.

"Do you think he can do it?" Father James asked.

"He has a talent for staying in their good graces," Collier said. "But the Chinese aren't much on give and take."

"Yeah, they are," Shard said. "You give and then they take more. But I think I've figured something out."

"What?" Collier asked.

"When we were on the march, Skitter and I talked about what the Reds wanted us for, why they didn't kill all of us in those mountains."

"I've wondered the same thing," Father James said. "They let so many die but gave us enough to let some survive."

"We're like hot iron on an anvil being forged," Shard said. "Everything good is being melted away. Once they get us to the point of no hope, no chance, no one to turn to, then they'll shape us into what they want."

"Another way of sayin' we're getting' the shit beat out of us," Tiny put in.

"Yep," Shard said. "And when they're done, we'll see what they want from those of us left."

"It's not a pleasant picture, is it?" Father James asked. "The way you put it, the more overt acts of resistance, the harder they'll crack down, until we break."

"So what are you saying, Shard?" Collier asked.

"I don't know," Shard said. "I haven't figured it out that far."

Skitter came back a few hours later, holding his side, a grimace on his face. "No good," he gasped. "Wong wouldn't even see me. The guards let me wait and then tossed me out with a few kicks."

"Did you hear from Martinez and Diekman?" Shard asked.

"I heard them," was all Skitter said.

It took two days.

Shard was summoned along with Father James to Wong's office. Diekman was there, being held upright by two guards. He was stripped to the waist, his face bloodied, one eye swollen shut. His skin was pale blue, and he was shaking so violently the guards could barely hold him. His torso was wet and ice crystals hung from his hair and beard. His bare feet were black and swollen with frostbite.

"Section Leader Shard, you are here since this violation occurred in your hut," Wong said, staring at Shard as if they were the only two in the room, indifferent to the suffering of Diekman.

"I understand, Comrade Wong," Shard said, wondering if he had a single card to play other than groveling obedience. "May I ask, where is Martinez?"

"Prisoner Diekman, speak," Wong said, ignoring the question while holding Shard's gaze. "Do you recognize this prisoner?" He pointed to Father James.

"Yesssss," Diekman said, his teeth chattering with cold. "He's an officer, one of the ruling class. He works to create discontent within the enlisted men." Diekman looked toward the ceiling with his one good eye, as if the words he'd memorized were inscribed there.

"What else?" Wong barked.

"He spreads his disobedient attitude throughout the ranks. He urges us to resist the lenient treatment policy of the People's Volunteer Army." His arms quivered uncontrollably, the guards struggling to hold onto him.

"Is that all?" Wong asked, as if that wasn't so bad. Diekman shook, his mouth working, trying to overcome the pain coursing through his savaged body.

"You shouldn't have gone through this," Father James said to Diekman. "I am so sorry. Please forgive me." Tears stained the padre's dirty cheeks.

"He is a reactionary. He is against the people," Diekman said, meeting the padre's eyes with a nodded apology, an understanding, perhaps a benediction. A violent tremor overcame him as he spoke, and he passed out, his head lurching back. The guards let him drop.

"Very well," Wong said. "We cannot allow reactionaries to cause trouble in Camp Eleven. It is a threat to the other prisoners who appreciate our benevolent treatment. Prisoner James, you will be transferred to the camp at Pukchin, which you richly deserve. You have brought this on yourself, as shown by the testimony of this man."

"The man half-dead on the floor," Shard pointed out.

"That is immaterial. You are dismissed, Section Leader Shard." Shard took a step back, bowing his head, but not leaving.

"Pukchin," Father James said. "The Caves?"

"I believe that is what the reactionaries call it," Wong said, smiling.

"I wish he'd denounced me sooner," Father James said to Shard, knowing that any further talk with Wong was useless.

"I'll do my best to help him," Shard said. Wong spoke angrily to the guards, tiring of listening. They grabbed Father James and rushed him from the room, Wong shuffling through papers on his desk.

"May I see Martinez?" Shard asked, taking a deep breath before speaking, working to stay calm. He'd heard of the Caves. The last stop for the most resistant of POWs. A death sentence. Wong gestured to the window at the side of the room as he lit a cigarette, moving on to the next piece of paper.

Two stakes in the ground. Buckets of freezing water. Tied at one stake was the frozen body of Martinez, his head hanging limp. Blood-streaked ice encased his lower naked body. He hadn't given in. At least Father James hadn't had to see this.

Shard turned away from the window, staring down at Wong, who calmly drew smoke into his lungs, a faint smile on his face. Shard couldn't look away, felt his lips form into a sneer of distaste, his fists involuntarily clench. The two of them were alone in the office, except for the unconscious Diekman. The look of distain faded from Wong, a sense of panic flitting across his features before he regained control.

Watching Shard, Wong yelled for a guard, his hand moving to his holster. There was no immediate response. Wong unsnapped the holster. Shard considered what it would take. His chances were good. One step, then twist the neck like Kelso had taught them. Quicker than Wong could draw his pistol. Wong knew it, sensed his mistake.

Shard's sneer turned to a smile as he stepped away, his eyes fixed on Wong. Hurried footsteps sounded and the guard burst in, looking for signs of trouble. Shard bent to pick up Diekman, draping the limp POW's arm across his shoulder, giving Wong a final glance.

You're not worth dying for. That was the message he'd given him. Wong had looked stunned at the ferocity of Shard's gaze, the animal intensity that filled the room. Fear had surged through Wong as he waited for the guard to appear. He might take his revenge one day. Or keep the secret of his fright deep within and ignore Shard as if he were of no consequence.

Wong pushed aside the papers in front of him, lit another cigarette, and sighed.

Chapter 15

April 18, 1953
Camp Eleven, North Korea

Shard edged away from the pen as two guards approached. They were talking energetically, rifles slung over their shoulders and gesturing with their hands. Scuttlebutt about Horseface maybe? They ignored Shard, stopping for a smoke close by. He saw Skitter moving fast, making a circuit around the administration building, head down, and hands bunched in his pockets. Sometimes it was as if he were invisible, a shadow of a guy darting from one dark corner to another.

Shard watched the guards as they ambled off, one of them laughing, no others in sight. From his vantage point he could see the kitchen. No guards at the door. Maybe the commotion today had disrupted things. Maybe it was Horseface's duty to oversee the evening meal preparation, and he was busy being questioned by Yuan. Worth a look.

Shard checked his pockets. Two cigarettes stashed away. He took the long way around, observing both sides of the long kitchen building. He could hear the Korean workers inside talking, clattering pots and pans, the usual sound of chop chop being cooked. He stuck one cigarette behind his ear and walked slowly along the side of the building. Officially, no POWs were allowed inside. The kitchen was locked between mealtimes, the penalty for breaking and entering, death.

But the door was open, inviting. No guards in sight. He took a step inside, ready to retreat, bribe, grovel, do whatever he had to do. The lure of food was too great to resist. The theft of food, Shard had to admit to himself. A successful steal was as nourishing as the food itself; a silent symbol of his spirit, something that the North Koreans or the Red Chinese could not break. Through the door, he stood in the hallway which led into the main cooking area. Stoves were lit, tables arranged with turnips, leafy vegetables, sacks of rice and potatoes. Workers in white shirts busied themselves at the far end of the room, unaware of Shard's presence.

Another step closer, and he was even with a pantry door on his right. No one was looking his way, all the cooks busy, intent on their tasks. He laid his hand on the latch and pressed, quietly and slowly, holding it tight as he slowly pushed the door open. He froze in place.

Horseface was on the floor, straddled by a chunky Korean girl, her back to Shard. She was naked from the waist down, Horseface's pants down around his ankles. She moved languidly, her long black hair caressing Horseface. They moved in undulating silence. As the girl arched her head, Shard edged back, carefully pulling the door shut as his left hand reached out for a can of fish, mackerel by the picture on the label. He shut the door and let the latch fall into place without a sound, standing still for a moment before moving, listening for any sign he'd been heard. Then he moved off, the mackerel in his pocket, and the image of the girl's buttocks burned into his mind.

June 1951
Camp Eleven, North Korea

Comrade Wong was no more. Promoted, probably, for his excellent work at Camp Eleven. The stack of bodies had grown to five feet high before the spring thaw, the prisoners too weak to heave even the most emaciated corpse to the top. He'd done what he'd been sent for. The prisoners were broken.

Comrade Yuan took over. Yuan could be pleasant, and he had the appearance of an educated man. His English was perfect, with only the slightest trace of a British accent, perhaps from schooling in the Hong Kong territories, Shard thought. Yuan saw to it that the bodies were removed and buried in a mass grave, not far from camp. No ceremonies, no recognition of their suffering, but it was better than the smell of rotting corpses as spring arrived.

"It is time for your political education to begin," Yuan intoned from his perch on the riser at the front of the recreation hall. He looked out over the gathered POWs, Shard's section. Thirty men, half of them new. The ones they replaced were either weathered bones on mountain roadsides or lay in the mass grave. "We will start with a review of the origins of this conflict."

It was the usual Party line, except that it was the first time they'd heard it in a small group and without the usual repetition in Chinese and English. Plus, they were comfortable, the wood stove providing a pleasant warmth against the morning chill. And they were seated.

Shard listened as Yuan explained how President Truman had rammed the United Nations resolution on the war through the Security Council without the Soviet Union being there to veto it. He left out the fact that the Soviet Union was voluntarily boycotting the council, but Shard didn't correct him. They weren't here for the truth; they were here to be reeducated.

Yuan described the American-led invasion of North Korea, ignoring that it was in response to the North's invasion of the South. He covered the Chinese intervention, how the Chinese Volunteer People's Army came to protect their Korean comrades and to keep the UN forces out of China. Shard had to admit Yuan had a point. If the newspapers they'd been given were only half true, MacArthur had been ready to go into Red China.

"You have been told you are fighting for freedom," Yuan continued, "but of course that is not true. When your planes bomb our convoys as they pass through villages, many innocent civilians are killed. That is not freedom. And the right-wing clique that rules South Korea, they do not allow freedom. That is why the South Korean forces fought so poorly, leaving many of you exposed on the battlefield."

Shard had to hand it to Yuan. He combined one crazy idea with one solid one, so they both ended up making sense. He knew the South Korean president Syngman Rhee was a repressive and corrupt strongman. He looked around and saw heads bobbing in agreement, Skitter's among them.

Yuan continued in the same vein for twenty minutes, telling the prisoners that as enlisted men, they were tools of the imperialist ruling class. They were not to be blamed for their unwitting behavior in helping the forces of Wall Street try to conquer the people of North Korea and to make war on the people of China.

"Unless, of course, you fail to properly understand the role you have played," Yuan said. "Then you make common cause with the reactionary regime of the criminal Syngman Rhee. Then, you would be war criminals." Yuan let that sink in, his eyes roving across the seated men, as if searching for an argument.

What he said made sense, or at least Shard was sure it made sense to Yuan. He seemed sincere, not vicious the way Wong had been. Yuan was a new angle to be worked, and Shard intended to study him carefully, which meant taking everything he said seriously. If he could understand what Yuan believed, he could work out something—a way to stay alive until the war was over. How much longer could it be?

"You have been patient with this first session," Yuan said, walking near the men. "We will spend much time together here. You must pay attention and diligently study what I say, as you have today. As a reward, each man will receive a millet cake. We will have a ten-minute break now." Yuan clapped his hands, and a guard appeared at the door carrying a box of millet cakes. Shard told the men to come forward by rows, waiting until everyone had received a cake before taking his.

"Very good, Prisoner Shard," Yuan said. "You practice true democracy within your section. The leader has no special place among his men, no formalities that place him above the average soldier."

"I wasn't elected, Comrade Yuan," Shard said, breaking off a small bit of the millet cake.

"There is no need for elections when the people share a common goal," Yuan said. "Here, your goal is to remain alive and return home. The more you work together and cooperate with our lenient policy, the closer you get. Why bother with a vote? Who would not wish to see peace and freedom?"

"I see your point," Shard said. "But tell me Comrade Yuan, what is your goal?"

"Peace," Yuan said, pushing back a strand of thick black hair that had fallen over his forehead. "I work for peace, and I hope you will not resist our plans. That would be a tragedy." He held Shard's eyes for a moment, then turned away and signaled for the session to resume.

"Now we begin to review the basics of Marxist-Leninist thought," Yuan announced. "You will come to understand that Communism is at once a complete system of proletarian ideology and a new social order. It is different from any other ideological and social system, and it is the most complete, progressive, revolutionary, and rational system in human history."

He spoke for three hours, finishing with the inherent wisdom of the masses.

"Chairman Mao has taught us that if we attempt to go on the offensive when the masses are not yet awakened, that would be adventurism. If we push the masses to do anything against their will, we would certainly fail and be guilty of the crime of commandism. If we do not advance when the masses demand advance, that would be right opportunism and we will also fail. Adventurism, commandism, right opportunism—these are all crimes against the people."

Shard could barely keep his eyes open. He rose with a heavy sigh, telling himself the millet cake was worth it. "I can't believe we have to sit through this every day," he said to Skitter as they walked to the assembly area for afternoon roll call.

"I wish I knew what he was after," Skitter said. "I can't figure it out."

"I asked him," Shard said. "He was spouting something to me about our goal being survival, so I asked him what his was."

"Jesus, Shard," Skitter said. "Wong would have pistol-whipped you for that. What did Yuan say?"

"Peace," Shard said. "And that it would be a tragedy if I resisted."

"Hey, who doesn't want peace?" Skitter said, a nervous laugh escaping his lips.

"There's all sorts of peace," Shard said, stuffing his hands in his pockets. "Anyway, I don't think he cares much what we say when we get back home. Here, it's a different story."

At roll call, Hawkins and Collier held up Diekman. He still had trouble standing, and his ribs hurt whenever he lay down. Everyone was amazed he'd survived the water torture and beatings and gave him gentle pats on the back as he made his way to the formation. Two new men joined Shard's section, GIs from the 2nd Division, captured north of the 38th parallel.

"I'm Bell, this is McCormick," one of the new guys said. Their uniforms were clean, hair cut short, and barely a decent stubble showing on their faces. Shard and the others from his original group hadn't had a haircut or a shave since they were captured. Their clothes were tattered, and their bodies stank. Layers of shirts, sweaters, and jackets fused into a single filthy mass, home to lice, sweat, and decay.

"Jeez, I forget what the hell we've turned into," Collier said, taking in the newcomers' relative cleanliness. "Sorry, boys, but this is what you've got to look forward to here at our little rest camp."

Bell and McCormick looked at each other, their noses crinkled in disgust.

"Yeah, we haven't had a bath in a while," Shard said as roll call ended. "We're supposed to get oil drums and fuel for heating water soon. Then we can wash our clothes and get cleaned up. Helps get rid of the lice eggs too."

"When's that happening?" Bell asked, looking like it couldn't be soon enough.

"When the Reds feel like it," Collier said. "Best not to worry about stuff like that. If it happens, fine. If not, you haven't lost any sleep over it."

"What happened to him?" McCormick asked, pointing to Diekman as they headed back to the hut.

"He held out," Skitter said. "Didn't want to rat out our chaplain."

"Somebody had already ratted him out," Collier said. "The Reds wanted confessions about Father James. They wanted us to sign his death sentence. It's how they work. Use us against each other."

"But he didn't confess?" Bell asked.

"Oh, Diekman confessed," Collier said. "He held out as long as he could, but finally he gave in. No one blames him for it either. I know I couldn't have managed it. Now my buddy Martinez, he was real religious. He didn't want to betray the padre. He died half frozen, tied to a stake."

"What did your chaplain do, for Christ's sake?" McCormick asked, oblivious to the answer within his question.

"He prayed, held Easter services," Shard said. "Got caught doing it. Someone told the Reds what he was up to."

"What happened to your chaplain?" Bell said.

"They sent him to the Caves," Shard said. "Nobody comes back from the Caves."

By the light filtering in through the rice-paper door, Shard oversaw the distribution of the evening meal. The usual barley and turnips. They'd recently been given wooden bowls and spoons, which made mealtime an almost gracious affair.

"This is it?" McCormick asked, looking at the glob of food in his bowl.

"Hell no, McCormick," Skitter said. "There's water too. Probably give you the trots until you get used to it."

"Sorry," McCormick said. "It takes some getting used to. And call me Mac, everyone does."

"Don't worry, Mac, you'll get used to the food, if only from pure repetition," Diekman said, from the corner where he sat against the wall.

"Yeah," Mac said, glancing at Diekman, unable to keep his eyes on him. Bearded, dirty, nearly crippled, he wasn't anything a new guy wanted to think about.

They talked past dark, mostly pumping Mac and Bell for news about the war. They'd been captured during a major UN offensive. Pyongyang had been taken. MacArthur had been fired by Truman, which the POWs had heard about from the Chinese. Bell said most GIs liked their new commander, General Matthew Ridgway, better than MacArthur. He didn't spend every night in Tokyo, as MacArthur was famous for doing. Soon the conversation faded, and the men curled into themselves on their sleeping mats, escaping into slumber.

"Wake up!" The door was thrust open, and Yuan appeared with a flashlight, working his way into the center of the room. A guard stood at the door, cold air blowing in. "Wake now!"

"Comrade Yuan," Skitter said, recovering his wits as Diekman screamed, covering his face with his hands. Bell and Mac looked at each other in disbelief, as if this might be a nightmare.

"You!" Yuan bellowed, the beam of his flashlight hitting Tiny full in the face. "What did we discuss today? Speak!"

"What? The war, you told us about the war, didn't you?" Tiny held up his hand against the glare.

"What about the war? You! Tell me." The flashlight moved to Hawkins.

"About Truman, and how he got the UN to declare war," Hawkins said, looking to Shard for an explanation or to make some sense of this sudden onslaught.

"On who?" Yuan demanded of Collier, stamping his foot in impatient anger.

"North Korea," Collier said, the answer so obvious that it worried him.

"No! On the people," Yuan said, his voice a shrill scream. "North Korea is a place. The people, the masses, that is who your corrupt government makes war on! First the people of Korea and now the people of China. Did you not listen? We fed you and put you in a warm, comfortable room. The People's Volunteer Army shared food with you, and you could not thank us for leniency and kindness by even listening!"

"We're sorry, Comrade Yuan," Shard said. "We weren't expecting this, in the middle of the night."

"That is a pitiful excuse, Section Leader Shard," Yuan said. "Tell me now, what are the three crimes against the masses we discussed? Can anyone tell me?" Silence. The flashlight moved around the room until it came to rest on Skitter, his hand held up like a shy schoolboy's.

"Adventurism, commandism, right opportunism," Skitter said. He'd been listening to Yuan as he studied him, looking for his angle to work. Perhaps he'd found it.

"Only one prisoner shows promise, Section Leader Shard," Yuan said, smiling at Skitter. "This must change." Yuan clicked off his flashlight and left, leaving stunned silence and frosted air in his wake.

"Does that happen every night?" Bell said. "What was he talking about?"

"Indoctrination classes began today," Shard said. "I guess he wants us to pay attention. Nice going, Skitter."

"Yuan wasn't flapping his gums for the hell of it," Skitter said. "I knew he had an angle, and that I'd better figure out what it was. So I listened and remembered. That's my angle, and it sure as hell got us out of hot water tonight."

Skitter was right, but it only went so far. The next morning, after roll call, Shard's section was told to report directly to the recreation hall. Thirty-two men watched as the morning meal was delivered in enamel buckets to the other huts as they trooped into the hall. Comrade Yuan did not look pleased as he mounted the dais.

"More comrades have arrived to teach the other sections," Yuan began. "As deputy camp commander, I can only teach one section. Yours. This means you must excel in your understanding of right thinking. Just as I must be an example to my men, so must you be to the other prisoners."

Shard raised his hand.

"No complaints," Yuan said, staring at Shard. "No useless questions. You lost your morning meal privilege because you were inattentive. You did not take yesterday's lesson seriously, did you?"

"No," Shard said. "We failed yesterday. I have a suggestion, not a complaint or question."

"Very well," Yuan said, nodding curtly for him to continue.

"If we could take notes, it would help us remember," Shard said. "So much of this is new, the words and ideas are strange to us. It would help if we could review things after the class."

"I will consider it," Yuan said flatly. "Now, we will review the initiation of this war by the United States and the three crimes against the masses." Yuan delivered the same lecture, this time to rapt attention. He led the group in reciting the three crimes against the masses and then announced a break. "Yesterday the people provided you with additional food. All but one of you was ungrateful for that gift, therefore today, only that one will receive it."

Yuan walked to Skitter, seated next to Shard in the front row. He withdrew a millet cake from his pocket, offering it to him.

"I can't," Skitter said, looking at the men around him. "It wouldn't be fair." He broke out into a sweat under Yuan's glare and the stirring of prisoners near him.

"You must eat," Yuan said. "It is exactly fair. You recalled the lesson. Therefore, you eat. Tomorrow, others may eat as well if they do the same."

"No," Skitter said, his eyes avoiding the cake Yuan held inches from his face.

"You are a backslider, Prisoner Skinner," Yuan said, shaking his head sadly. "I had hoped this section would show progress. Perhaps I have shown too much leniency."

"Eat it," Shard said. Murmurs arose from the seats. Not everyone agreed. Skitter looked to Shard, who nodded. Yuan, holding the millet cake, watched them both. Skitter took it and broke off a piece, chewing it slowly. He let his hand drop, holding the cake cupped in his palm.

"All of it," Yuan said.

Skitter bit into the cake, its dryness reminding him of his first communion, eating the wafer, the entire congregation watching him. He never liked being singled out, hated all eyes on him, judging him, seeing his faults. But he ate every piece of the cake.

"Very good," Yuan said softly, as if giving the benediction.

After the evening meal, Skitter led a review of what Yuan had covered. He defined adventurism, commandism, and right opportunism in the simplest terms. Truman was the aggressor, bringing the United States into the war through an illegal action of the United Nations Security Council. China sent a volunteer army to help the Korean people. MacArthur was replaced because his war crimes were too much even for Wall Street to bear.

That night, when Yuan and the guards burst in with bright lights and shouted questions, all the answers were prompt and correct. Yuan asked Tiny what adventurism was, and Tiny clearly stated that it meant going on the offensive when the masses were not yet ready. Yuan smiled, a look of pleasure crossing his face. He shined his flashlight on Skitter and nodded, a slight bow of the head, showing respect for his progressive attitude.

"Section Leader Shard," Yuan said, not looking away from Skitter, who was looking sheepishly proud. "You have a fine assistant. Your political officer, one might say." Skitter's face clouded over, uncertain of what that meant for him, but sure that Yuan said it for a reason. Yuan said something to the guards as he ushered them out. They laughed, one of them glancing back at Skitter. The departing guards left the door open, and a chill breeze wafted over the prisoners as they sat in silence.

"It never pays to stand out," Shard said. "Believe me."

"What did he mean?" Skitter asked. He thought he'd done well by everyone, but Yuan's remark and the laughter of the guards worried him.

"He meant to throw you off balance," Collier said. "Calling you a Commie political officer is only going to get you in trouble, here and after the war. There's no pleasing these people. Give them what they want, and you're in deeper, and they only want more."

"What should I have done?" Skitter asked no one in particular. "Let us miss another meal?"

"There's no right answer," Shard said. "Just like there's no surefire way to survive this. You helped everybody get through tonight's drill. Now you're paying the price. Everyone here knows you acted in their best interest. But keep a low profile for a while."

The next day they had their morning meal. Barley and turnips, again, but no one complained. As they walked to the recreation hall for class, an old Korean farmer awaited them, a pair of shears in his hand. "Stand in line," Yuan ordered the men. "I cannot stand to look at your dirty beards all day. This man will cut your hair."

The Korean was expressionless. He wore baggy pants and a black jacket and stood on a wooden crate to more easily reach the taller Americans. His sparse hair was gray, and his dark eyes set close together. The shears looked in better shape than the old man. No one wanted to go first.

Yuan yelled at the men to hurry, so Shard stepped up, taking the one cigarette he had been saving to trade for food and giving it to the farmer. No reaction, except for the swift clipping of Shard's beard, which fell away from his face in clumps. The old man was good, cutting swaths of greasy long hair from Shard's head. It probably wasn't pretty, but Shard appreciated the feel of his scalp after so long.

The men gave the farmer what they could spare. A few more cigarettes, hard candies, matchbooks, the treasured bits and pieces of a POW's life. It wasn't pity that drove them, rather a desire to leave the encounter with a decent trim and two intact ears. An hour and a half later, he was done. He stepped off the crate and gave a small bow to his audience. No expression crossed his face as he walked through the crowd of prisoners and made for the road out of the camp.

Inside the classroom was another surprise. Small notebooks, like the exam booklets Shard remembered from school. Pencils. He and Collier exchanged a quick glance, each man understanding immediately. The list. They had talked about another copy, transcribing the names from the multiple scraps of paper onto a single list. That way there'd be a backup in case the Reds found one of them. Shard looked away from Collier, afraid triumph might reveal itself on his face. There weren't many good days in Camp Eleven, but this was shaping up as one of them.

"Now you see how learning is rewarded," Yuan said. "I do not have to look at your ugly hair, and you have pencil and paper." He smiled, and it took everyone a moment to decide that Yuan indeed had made a joke, one that demanded to be rewarded with a suitable ripple of laughter. Skitter held back, but then joined in when he saw everyone, even Tiny, laughing.

"The topic for today is dialectical materialism," Yuan began, his face set in stern lines. The laughter ended as the prisoners grasped their pencils. "Dialectical materialism tells us that every economic order evolves to a state of maximum efficiency, even as internal contradictions and weakness contribute to its ultimate decay. Simply put, nothing is an accident. No single event can be understood without seeing it in connection with its surroundings. We live in a state of movement and change, where all things move to a central purpose, some rising, others falling. Now it is the masses who are rising, and Western society that is falling."

Skitter's pencil flew across the page. It made sense to him, at least the parts he understood. Especially the part about rising and falling. He'd seen that played out around him all his life: in Michigan, in the army, in Korea. It was always a choice between rising and falling, and it was usually guys like him who took the fall. Now he understood. It was the march of history, and if he didn't get on the rising side, he'd be a loser again. He'd grabbed his chance in Tokyo, and it had worked for him. First time in his life.

Shard wrote as well, small, cramped notes, leaving blank pages to be filled in another time. He couldn't resist a smile and a glance at Collier. Thinking of the list cheered him up. It was something to live for, a measure of revenge upon his captors, to bring the truth of what had happened to them back home.

Chapter 16

April 18, 1953
Camp Eleven, North Korea

They sat inside the hut in silence. The rice-paper door was open, and Shard positioned himself so he could watch Lieutenant Cooper in the pen. Anger seethed within him, his stomach in a knot. He ate, knowing he had to. Every scrap of food was precious. Life.

Shard had been freed from the pen, but he worried Cooper had been sacrificed for him. Skitter had come back claiming he'd seen Horseface getting a tongue-lashing from Yuan. But Shard had seen Horseface, and it wasn't Yuan who'd been lashing him. He'd kept quiet about Horseface and the Korean girl. Seeing them together had upset him more than he'd wanted to admit, reminding him of everything he'd been missing. The pleasures of the flesh, his and a woman's.

It wasn't only Cooper. The truth had come at him hard, but Shard had accepted it even though it had ripped into his heart and soul. Men had died on the altar of Skitter's survival. His as well. It had to be set right, but he hated the idea. It would be easy to tell himself it wasn't true, he was halfway around the bend, wire-happy, except there was no wire. That made it even crazier. Shard laughed. A sharp, bitter hack that made Skitter jump.

No one spoke. Shard pushed around the rice and vegetables in his bowl, spooning up the last remaining morsel. Eat. Live. It was all that remained.

July 1951
Camp Eleven, North Korea

"What's the total?" Shard asked Collier.

"Four hundred and fifty-two," Collier said. "Dates and places for most of them." They were alone in the hut, the others gathering firewood to heat water for washing. Collier had carefully copied names from the first list onto three pages of notebook paper, in the smallest print he could manage. The original list was a wad of scrap papers, everything from a cigarette pack to pieces of wallpaper. Most of the prisoners from the original group knew about the list, but only a few knew where it was hidden. Skitter, Diekman, and Tiny, the only men left from the early days, knew where it was tucked behind a loose stone in the wall.

But Shard had told Collier to keep the copy a secret. Only the two of them knew of its existence, and if the original was discovered, it was their ace in the hole. Literally. Shard used a sharp stick to gouge a hole in the dirt floor while Collier folded the transcribed list and placed it in a small tin he'd scrounged from the dump. He wrapped the tin in cloth before placing it in the small cavity.

"Feels like a funeral," Shard said as he tamped down the dirt and erased any trace of his digging.

It was Sunday, their day of rest. Classes were held every other day of the week, and the nightly cognitions, as Yuan called them, continued. The POWs were made to write out their biographies, detailing how living in a capitalist society had made life hard for them. Everything was a lesson to Yuan; everything had to fit into his view of the world.

Food had improved slightly, and the Chinese provided the steel drums they'd been promising for washing. The drums were placed on rocks and firewood stacked underneath. It was a warm day, and as the water boiled the men stripped down and tossed in their greasy clothes, stirring them until the lice were killed off and the water was slick with dirt. The garments were hung on lines, and the process repeated for the next batch as men cleaned themselves and sat in the sun to dry. A table was set up with razors, one per hut, for the men to shave. Pots of water were carried out by Korean workers from the kitchen.

"Almost like a day at the beach," Skitter said, pouring water over his head.

"Cold beer and hot dogs would make it perfect," Hawkins said, splashing cool water on his face after he shaved.

"What about women?" Bell threw in.

"Hell, I've been in here too long," Diekman said. "Beer and hot dogs are tops on my list. What about you, Shard?"

"I haven't dreamed about a woman in quite a while," Shard said. "But thoughts of a cold bottle of beer will keep me awake all night." The new guys, Bell and Mac, were the only ones still talking about sex. Everyone else debated the finer points of beach picnics. Cold chicken versus a cookout. Tuna sandwiches, deviled eggs, ham on rye with mustard. It went on until roll call, when the evening meal of potatoes, turnips, and cabbage ended the fantasy.

The holiday spirit didn't last long. The next morning after roll call, Yuan announced that there would be a special event today; no classes were to be held.

"I wondered why they let us get cleaned up," Shard whispered to Skitter.

"Visitors, maybe?" Skitter said. The prisoners buzzed with anticipation as rumors blossomed and spread. The war was over, the Red Cross was coming, the Chinese were going to take pictures and release the names of the POWs. Shard thought the last was the most logical. As far as anyone knew, the Reds still had not exchanged lists of POWs with the United Nations. It had to happen sooner or later, and it would explain the cleanliness routine.

"Commander Deng will now address you," Yuan said, stepping away from the microphone. Deng limped his way forward and began a long-winded speech in Chinese. There was a lot of finger-pointing, harsh words, and a few scattered smiles bestowed upon the prisoners. When Deng's speech ended and he stepped back, Yuan sprang to his feet, applauding, as did the other Chinese. The POWs dutifully followed suit.

"Whatever it is," Collier said, "they like it a lot."

"Commander Deng hopes you have enjoyed the labors which the People's Volunteer Army has undertaken to improve cleanliness within the camp. This is a reward for the diligent work studying the tenets of Marx and our great leader, Mao Tse-tung. He salutes your progress!" Yuan paused here, an evident signal for more applause, which quickly followed. Deng lit a cigarette, smiled, and nodded to Yuan.

"Now we must make the theoretical practical," Yuan said, a serious tone creeping into his voice. "The Chinese people wish you to join them in signing an appeal for peace. We seek peace and freedom for all people, and in order to bring peace to Korea, we are asking you to voluntarily sign our petition for peace." Yuan halted his speech and looked out over the thousand-plus men arrayed in ranks before him, letting the notion settle in.

"Who doesn't want peace?" Skitter said. Shard remained silent, listening to the same sentiment rippling through the ranks.

"The petition states that since the Soviet Union was absent from the United Nations Security Council," Yuan continued, "the subsequent actions of the United Nations and the United States were illegal, and that the UN should withdraw from the Korean peninsula. This will bring peace and freedom for all, including prisoners such as yourselves." This drew a scattering of applause from the POWs. Skitter raised his hands to join in, but Shard grabbed one hand and forced it down.

"The petitions will be delivered to the UN Security Council following a presentation to the International Peace Conference in Stockholm, Sweden," Yuan said. "Discuss this appeal with your section leaders. At noon we will assemble again. Those who agree to sign the petition will line up to my left," Yuan said with a wave of his hand. "Those who do not wish to sign stand on my right. Any of you who are undecided will form ranks in the center. Please have a free and open discussion while you eat your meal."

It was all very courteous. The chop chop was special, too, rice with onion and garlic along with the usual turnip. Shard's section sat seated around him outside their hut.

"So what's the problem?" Skitter asked, running his finger inside the wood bowl to eat every last kernel of rice. "It is true that Russia wasn't at the Security Council meeting."

"Skitter," Shard said, shaking his head as if he were talking with a backward child. "You can't sign a petition calling for the US to withdraw from Korea. You're in the army, for god's sake!"

"Yeah," Diekman said. "You notice Yuan didn't mention China withdrawing at the same time."

"It's only a piece of paper," Skitter said. "No one's going to listen to us anyway. If it makes Yuan happy, then we all benefit. He looks good to his brass, and we get rewarded. Clean clothes, better food. What's wrong with that?"

"I'll sign anything to get more food," Tiny said. "The army taught me how to shoot, but they never taught me what to do in a POW camp. I figure it's every man for himself, or they'd have said otherwise." It was a long speech for Tiny. Skitter and Hawkins nodded in agreement.

"What about you guys?" Shard said to Bell and Mac. "Did they mention anything in training about what to do in a POW camp?"

"Give your name, rank and serial number is all," Mac said. "Except they haven't asked for any of that."

"Right," Skitter said. "This is a whole new world, and we're left to figure it out best we can. I say sign now and tell the army we were forced to."

"Not far from the truth," Tiny said. "We have another winter like the last one, there won't be anyone left."

"Show of hands," Shard said. "How many are ready to sign?" More than half.

"Undecided?" Ten hands tentatively rose.

"Not signing?" Shard, Collier, Diekman, Mac, and Bell. "Okay. Form up the way Yuan said, but remember, this could come back to haunt you."

"So could dying," Skitter said.

It was about the same ratio for the entire camp. More than half the POWs stood for signing the peace petition. A smaller group stood in the middle, undecided. An even smaller group was for not signing. Yuan stood at the podium, looking out over the divided prisoners, chatting with Deng.

"What do you think they'll do about us?" Collier asked.

"They'll probably pressure the undecided first," Shard said. "Then work on us."

"We have a special guest to speak to you today," Yuan began. "As you know, we have kept the officer class separate from you in order to defeat their attempts to coerce you into serving their interests. Noncommissioned officers are kept in their own area as well, since they are well-known running dogs for the ruling class. But the chance for peace is so important that we have brought you one of your sergeants to report to you on how they, and the officers, have responded to the peace petition. Prisoner Kelso, please come forward."

"Kelso?" Shard gasped as his old sergeant stepped onto the stage. Maybe Skitter had been right. Could Kelso had given up Coop and gone over? It was hard to believe.

"Men," Kelso began, standing rigid with his arms clasped behind his back. The prisoners went silent. "I am here to encourage you to voluntarily sign the peace petition. The officers and the sergeants have already done so. Unanimously." Kelso paused, letting that sink in. "I urge you to follow our example. You should sign, and don't worry about the army. I will take full responsibility for the enlisted men who sign, which I hope will be every one of you. It is the best way for all of us to get back home."

"Thank you, Prisoner Kelso," Yuan said, moving him away from the microphone and addressing the POWs. "In light of the actions of the officers and sergeants, I will give you one minute to reconsider your opposition to the peace appeal and join those who wisely have already agreed to sign."

"So voluntary means unanimous or else," Shard said to Collier and Diekman.

"I think Kelso was giving us a message," Collier said. "The best way for us to get back home. Meaning if you don't sign, you don't go home."

"Ever," Diekman said. "Sorry boys, but I'm signing. I can't take another round of beating."

"No problem," Shard said. "You've done more than your fair share. Don't worry about it." Diekman joined the steady stream of prisoners joining the ranks of the signers. All of the undecideds went over, along with most of those against signing. Finally, it was only Shard, Collier, and half a dozen others.

"One of us should sign," Shard said to Collier. "The list is the most important thing."

"Maybe we should both sign," Collier said.

"The minute is up," Yuan announced. "Prisoner Kelso will be allowed one last chance to talk with the remaining reactionaries who stand against the peace process." Yuan gestured for Kelso to descend the steps.

"Shard," Kelso said, giving a quick nod as he approached the group of eight holdouts. "Here's the deal, boys. The Reds want this to be a unanimous thing. We went through the same thing, so did the officers. It's also another way to get our names out to the rest of the world. Bottom line is, if you don't sign, you will be transferred to a special camp for reactionaries. Immediately."

"The Caves?" Shard asked.

"No," Kelso said. "Anybody who goes to this special camp never goes home. It's a life sentence."

"You all really signed?" Collier asked.

"You bet. Once Yuan explained things. The senior officer, Colonel McLaughlin, he took responsibility. I'm the senior noncom here, and so do I. It's extreme duress, worse than torture or beatings. Life in a Commie prison camp, probably deep inside China. You'd never see home again."

"Okay," Shard said. He looked at the others, wishing there was another choice. "I'll sign." That was all it took. The seven others followed Shard as he made it unanimous. Voluntarily, of course.

Kelso was taken away, his usefulness over. Tables were brought out and lines formed at each. Prisoners signed their name, rank, and serial number, the Chinese showing interest in that information for the first time. Each POW was given a piece of hard candy after signing. Cameramen in green jackets with red stars on the collars roamed the crowd, taking pictures of smiling POWs. The entire process took about an hour, after which the announcement came to assemble once again.

"Congratulations," Yuan's voice boomed. "You are no longer war criminals. You are now liberated soldiers,

campaigning for peace!" He paused, the now clear signal
for applause. The POWs complied, some with genuine
enthusiasm. The cameras rolled as the Americans clapped,
lingering on those who grinned and kept it up. Skitter was
one, rolling the candy around in his mouth, clapping, and
glancing at the men around him, making sure he wasn't the
most vocal of the bunch. Or the least.

"Now that you have joined the peace camp," Yuan
declared, his arms spread wide in an inclusive gesture, "it is
time to match deeds to words. Your unanimous participation
will be news throughout the world. We will march in
celebration, common soldiers standing together under the
banner of peace."

"What the hell is he talking about?" Collier said.

"Look," Shard said, pointing to signs and banners being
unfurled by their guards. "He meant it literally." The red
banners were inscribed with "Peace" and "Long Live Mao
Tse-tung." Cameramen filmed as the guards blended in with
the POW ranks, making it look like they were holding the
banners aloft. Guards herded the prisoners toward the road
as cameramen recorded the spontaneous parade.

"Where are we going?" Skitter asked, eyeing the guards
who kept on the flanks of the march. No rifles, that wouldn't
look good on the newsreels.

"Maybe the war's over," Hawkins said. "Maybe we're
going home." It was a good rumor, but their destination
wasn't the Golden Gate Bridge. It was a ramshackle Korean
village two miles outside of camp. Koreans lined the street,
looking sullen and gaunt. Two guards at the head of the march
blew on bugles, a shrill, piercing tune that was evidently
the signal to cheer. The Koreans cheered and clapped. The

POWs waved and smiled beneath their red silken banners. The cameras rolled. Flashbulbs popped. Shard played along, knowing that any deviation from the desired script might reap a terrible punishment. The thought of nothing more than life as a POW chilled him deeper than a North Korean winter. It was a clever threat. Instant death might be seen as welcome after all the suffering they'd endured. Honorable even. But life in a Chinese prison camp? A horror. So Shard marched in the parade, waving to the Korean villagers. They shouted and clapped loudly, but their eyes were blank, staring at something far beyond the strange Americans, seeing nothing, understanding everything. A photographer stepped close, took a picture of Shard and Skitter shoulder to shoulder, the banner heralding Mao behind them.

"They'll call us traitors," Shard said, smiling for the camera. Jubilation drowned him out.

Chapter 17

April 18, 1953
Camp Eleven, North Korea

"We should do something about Cooper," Shard said. It was dusk, a full moon rising at one end of the camp, the sun setting at the other. The air was cooling. It would get damn cold in the pen tonight.

"Like what?" Skitter said. He sat near Shard on a log outside the hut. Collier was stretched out on the ground, his back against the hut wall.

"I don't know," Shard said. "What do the Chinese want?"

"Propaganda," Collier said.

"We gave them everything they asked for," Shard said. "What more could we do?"

"Trade something. Make a deal. Did Shard tell you about Operation Little Switch?" Skitter said to Collier. Skitter filled him in on the planned exchange of some sick and wounded prisoners.

"How's that help Cooper?" Collier wanted to know.

"I'm on the list. They're letting a few progressives out at the same time. I could maybe make a deal with Yuan, promise to say something to the newspapers about their lenient treatment."

"Think he'll go for it?" Shard asked.

"He might," Collier said. "If we're that close to a prisoner exchange, any propaganda he can squeeze out of us is worth more than punishing a single POW. Thing is, will he trust Skitter to keep his side of the bargain?"

"He can always throw Cooper back in the pen," Shard said. "Or us."

"So, Skitter," Collier said, turning to look him in the eyes. "I guess the question is, can we trust you?"

"Sure you can," Skitter said. "We've been together since the start, haven't we?"

"Every step of the way," Shard said. "You want to give it a try?"

"Why not?" Skitter answered. "Yuan can only say no. I'll go now while he's still in his office." Skitter took off, moving with ease across the parade ground and jogging up the hill to the administrative headquarters.

"Think it'll work?" Collier said.

"Hard to say," Shard said, after some thought. "But Skitter's good at making deals." Better than you can imagine, he thought.

September 1951
Camp Eleven, North Korea

"What did Yuan want?" Shard asked. Yuan had told Skitter to stay after the morning class. Skitter had shrugged when Shard gave him a questioning look. Shard had waited, hanging around the kitchen, looking for food to filch. He had one cigarette in his pocket, but it was a Pall Mall, long and nearly twice the size of a Lucky. It was enough for the guard to allow a walk through, during which Shard grabbed an onion, a bulb of garlic, and a small tin of sardines. His movements were perfect. Eyes straight ahead, a confident brisk pace, arm movements kept to a minimum as he took only those things he could reach without altering his forward motion.

It was a good haul, he thought, as he waited for Skitter. He'd been nervous while Skitter was inside, and he took more risks when he was nervous. It calmed him. The Korean cooks turned a blind eye to him; anyway, if the guards had let him in, they had little to say about it. As long as he didn't start carrying out sacks of potatoes, they would simply ignore him, turning away with their passive faces.

"He wants more," Skitter said, falling in beside Shard as they walked to the hut. "I pay attention in class, so now he wants me to get everyone else to."

"The guys do pretty well in class," Shard said. "No one wants the midnight cognitions to start again." Yuan had ceased the nightly flashlight inquisitions soon after the peace parade.

"Yeah, but now he insists on enthusiasm," Skitter said. "Says we don't understand our proper role in the vanguard of the working class."

"Christ," Shard said. "I'm sick of listening to this crap."

"Hey, sorry," Skitter said. "Don't shoot the messenger. What's that in your pocket?" He tapped against the onion protruding from Shard's field jacket.

"Onion. Got some garlic and sardines too."

"Shard, you're a one-man grocery store," Skitter said, laughing. "Flavor and protein, two things in short supply around here." Their food had improved recently, eggs and the occasional fish head appearing in their meals. The Chinese had agreed to exchange lists of POWs with the United Nations and now had to at least try to keep their prisoners alive.

Shard hid the food in the hut. He used the heating ducts leading from the stove in the tiny kitchen. They'd add the garlic and onion to their evening meal and save the sardines for later. Diekman was the only other POW in the hut. His legs still pained him, and he spent more and more of each day lying down.

"Nice going, Shard," Diekman said as he watched him stash the food. "I might even put some weight on the way things are going."

"The name exchange was the best thing that ever happened to us," Shard said, squatting next to Diekman and checking his bone-thin arms and twisted legs. "No one is going to believe the Reds about their lenient treatment if they send back a bunch of skeletons. Hang in there, okay?"

"I will," Diekman said. "They haven't killed me yet. You could use some fattening up yourself."

"Yeah," Shard said, aware of how thin he'd become. His legs, once muscular, were lean at best. His threadbare pants hung from his waist in baggy clumps. He was glad there were no mirrors in Camp Eleven.

"Guess I'm lucky," Skitter said. "I was born skinny."

"Anybody born skinny wouldn't have lasted the winter," Diekman said. "You're more wiry than skinny. You're lucky you haven't wasted away to nothing by now."

"Must be my metabolism," Skitter said with a grin. "My mom always said I had more energy than sense."

The sound of engines in the distance pulled Shard to the door as he was about to comment on Skitter's health. He was in decent shape, the best shape of anyone in the hut. He wished he had Skitter's metabolism, if that's what did it.

"What's happening?" Diekman asked from his mat.

"Six trucks coming into camp," Shard said. They helped Diekman stand and joined the throngs of POWs watching the trucks. The trucks drove past the administrative building, which drew even more attention. Something was coming in or prisoners were going out. Either was a major event.

The convoy halted past the recreation hall, then turned and backed up, gears grinding and exhaust belching as they slowly rolled toward the gathering prisoners. The crowd moved back, uncertain what the trucks held in store.

"Line up by sections at each truck," Yuan announced over the loudspeaker. Shard jumped at the sound, his attention so fixed on the vehicles he hadn't noticed Yuan approach the microphone. The trucks halted as Chinese soldiers let the tailgates fall open, the loud clanking sound sending the POWs scurrying back even further. Shard felt a tremor of fear as he imagined machine guns firing on the mass of prisoners.

"The People's Volunteer Army has provided for your clothing needs," Yuan declared. "Every man will be outfitted for the coming winter. You must discard your old clothing, for health reasons."

"I wonder if we're going home," Collier said as he joined his pals. "They'd want us spruced up and out of these lice-ridden uniforms."

"Sounds good to me," Diekman said. "For whatever reason."

"It could be," Skitter said. "They released our names last month, didn't they?"

Lines formed at each truck. Guards instructed the POWs to strip naked and toss their clothes in a pile as they received their bundles. It was a cloudy day with a biting wind, but no one minded. The pile of filthy clothing, crawling with lice and worn down to nearly nothing, looked as pitiful as the pale, scrawny bodies of the POWs. Shard felt ashamed of his body—not the nakedness, but the body itself, what it had become. Weak, like a child's. What was a man but what he showed the world?

Skitter tossed his clothes onto the pile, with joyful enthusiasm. He rubbed his hands together, generating warmth as well as glee. Skitter of the good metabolism. Wiry Skitter with muscle still left on his bones.

Each man received two bundles, one large and one small. Skitter and Shard carried theirs back to the hut, hurrying inside like kids, laughing and pushing each other. Collier and Diekman were already there, opening the parcels like it were Christmas morning.

"Look!" Skitter exclaimed, slapping a fur-lined cap with ear flaps on his head. "And gloves too!"

New rubber sole shoes, cotton-padded blue trousers and jacket, shirt, underwear, socks. Sizes were pretty much hit or miss, so the men traded as others came inside and dressed. The small bundles contained a towel, a bar of soap, toothbrush, and tooth powder.

"Who's got a large size cap and shoes?" Tiny bellowed out, holding up a pair of sneakers that would have been small for a Korean. No one replied. He strode through the crowded hut, searching for the larger items until he saw a pair of shoes in Bell's hand that looked right.

"No," Bell said as Tiny grabbed for them. He pulled back but Tiny moved fast, grabbing Bell's cap and tossing him the smaller one he'd gotten.

"Stop it!" Shard yelled. Tiny ignored him, kicking at Mac who fell over as Tiny took his shoes, tossing the smaller pair at Mac's head.

"You go to hell, Shard," Tiny said, retreating to his sleeping mat. "I can't wear that small stuff." He shouldered his way past Diekman, sending him reeling. He put on his jacket and the guys nearest him breathed a sigh of relief when it fit.

"How can he do that?" Bell asked.

"He's the biggest guy in camp," Skitter said. "He does pretty much what he wants."

Tiny didn't keep spirits down for long. At the evening meal, Shard brought out the onion and garlic. Lacking a knife, Collier went to work with his spoon, mashing the garlic and cutting the onion as best he could. Tears flowed down his cheeks as the guys laughed and joked.

"Hey, Collier, that's enough salt in mine!"

"Don't be so sad, Collier, you look good in blue!"

Everyone laughed, even when the catcalls weren't funny. It wasn't often that good things happened in Camp Eleven, so they made the most of what they had.

In the morning, things got worse. No one was surprised.

"You will remain in ranks," Yuan ordered over the loudspeakers. Roll call had been completed, and everyone expected the normal routine. "Your huts will be searched for contraband material. This means anything unauthorized, including uniforms which were to be turned in. Remember, you are now in the peace camp, and you may not wear the uniform of the imperialist aggressor!"

"Is this for real?" Shard said as a buzz rose from the assembled POWs.

"We've heard crazier," Skitter answered.

"Who would want to keep those dirty old clothes anyway?" Mac said. "We've only been here a few months, and ours were ripe as all get out."

"It doesn't make sense," Shard said. "But then, what does in Camp Eleven?"

"Silence!" Yuan yelled. "No talking until dismissed."

Guards, with bayonets leveled, stood at the perimeter as their comrades ran to the huts and burst inside. Sleeping mats and what little personal gear the POWs had were tossed outside. Wooden bowls, fur caps, socks, all ended on a heap in front of each hut.

Shard glanced at Collier, who looked pale. The list.

Would they search the loose stones in the masonry wall? Doubtful, Shard thought. The sardines. If they had half a brain, they'd look in the heating ducts of the gudeul system for contraband. That was an obvious hiding place. There would be a punishment for sure, a harsh one. He could say they bartered with a guard, but what would they have had to trade? Nothing. Theft was the obvious conclusion.

Were they really looking for the remnants of American uniforms? Why? So returning POWs couldn't show how worn out their original clothing was? Which didn't make sense if the Chinese were sending them home in these snazzy blue outfits. What could they possibly find that was of value?

The list. It was the most precious thing in the entire camp. But they couldn't know about it. Who would have squealed? Even if someone had talked, Yuan could have walked right in and taken it. So why the big act?

I'm overthinking it, Shard told himself. Nothing makes sense because this place has no sense to it. We're playing by rules we don't understand, rules that we can't grasp even when Yuan spells them out for us. I understand the rules I live my life by. Tiny knows his rules, not many people are as clear as he is. But what about everybody else?

Shouting came from behind them. Guards ran to the stage, jabbering at Yuan. He turned his back on the POWs and conversed with the guards, then pocketed what they handed over.

"All sections are dismissed," Yuan said. "Except for Section Leader Shard's."

Yuan came down from the podium and circled the section. Thirty-two men stood at attention, some with no idea what was happening, others all too certain. Yuan spoke to a guard who removed sixteen men, those who lived in the hut next to Shard's. Then Mac and Bell were let go, too new to have anything to do with the list.

"What is this?" Yuan shouted, his hand grasping bits of paper. The original list, from the hiding place in the wall. "Who is responsible?"

"I am," Shard said. Yuan spoke to a guard who pulled Shard out of line and forced him to the ground. Yuan drew his pistol and aimed it at Shard's head.

"I do not believe Section Leader Shard," Yuan said to the assembled men. "He is too attached to his men to speak the truth. But that makes him a war criminal and enemy of the people, for which he can be executed."

"I wrote the list," Collier said. Yuan swung his pistol around and aimed at Collier.

"Is that true?" Yuan demanded.

"It's true," Tiny said. "The two of them wrote those names, but none of us knew where they hid it."

"Of course not," Yuan said calmly. "Who can support this assertion?"

"Me," Hawkins said, raising his hand like a schoolboy afraid he had the wrong answer. "I heard about it, but never saw it. I wasn't sure if it even existed."

"There are many names," Yuan said, holstering his pistol and thumbing through the papers. "Prisoner Collier, step forward." Not a good sign. They'd been comrades since the peace parade.

"Yes sir," Collier said, standing before Yuan.

"Why did you make this propaganda for your government?" Yuan asked, looking at the wallpaper pattern on some of the papers.

"It's not propaganda," Collier said. "It's for the families. After the war."

"But we are still at war," Yuan said. He nodded to a guard who stepped forward and struck Collier on the side of his head with his rifle butt. Collier went down, and two other guards joined in, hitting his back and ribs as Collier covered his head with his hands and rolled into a ball. Shard got up only to have a guard slam him in the chest and send him reeling, gasping for air.

"Stop!" Diekman shouted. He broke ranks, running at the guards who continued to beat Collier, grimacing from the pain in his legs as he drove forward. A guard thrust his rifle, the bayonet catching Diekman in the chest, pushing him back as blood sprayed from his mouth. Diekman fell, lifeless. The guard placed his foot on his chest and withdrew the bayonet.

The beating stopped, even the hardened guards shocked at the sudden attack from normally docile prisoners.

"You will remain at attention," Yuan said to the eleven men who were left standing. He walked away, pocketing the list. The guards exchanged looks and kept their bayonets leveled at the group. Shard rose and stood ramrod straight in front of Collier. His chest hurt with every breath, but he was in better shape than Collier. Or Diekman.

They stood for two hours. Shard watched Collier, hoping he was playing possum and not unconscious. He could tell he was alive; his chest rose and fell, and his leg twitched a few times. A soldier came trotting down from Yuan's office and spoke to the other guards. They simply turned away, leaving Shard and his remaining men standing over Diekman's body.

"Are they gone?" Collier asked, rolling over and grasping his midsection. His face was bruised and bloodied, one eye swollen shut.

"Yeah," Shard said, signaling for Skitter to help. "Can you walk?"

"I think so," Collier said, gasping in pain. "They busted up my ribs." He wiped blood from his eye and stared at Diekman. "Why?"

"Why did he do it?" Shard said. "Or why did they kill him?"

"Just why?" Collier said, leaning on Shard.

"Hawkins, Tiny," Shard said. "Take Diekman to the graveyard. It's the least you can do after you ratted out Collier."

"I didn't rat anybody out," Hawkins said, his voice shrill with denial.

"I ain't dragging his corpse all the way over there," Tiny said, and walked away, hands stuffed in his pockets.

"I'll help," Skitter said. "Sorry about the list, Collier." He and Hawkins lifted Diekman's body. Even though he was nothing but skin and bones, they had a hard time carrying him away. Hawkins stumbled under the weight, but Skitter stayed upright, shouldering most of the load all the way to the graveyard, which was nothing more than an open pit near the garbage dump. When a body was laid in it, the pit was extended a couple of feet as dirt from the new section covered the body. An endless grave.

Nobody else spoke to Collier about the list. Those who had known about it understood what its loss meant to him. It had been his personal memorial to those who had died by the wayside during that horrible winter. Men were shocked it had been discovered; that over four hundred names were gone. Only Shard and Collier knew differently. The second list was safe, still hidden away from the Chinese. Perhaps even safer now that the original had been found.

Shard eased Collier down onto his sleeping mat. He cleaned his face with water and wiped away the dried blood with his towel. He asked where Diekman's towel was, since his was already caked in blood. No one answered. Shard looked at Tiny, sitting against the wall, Diekman's towel, fur cap, gloves, and extra socks in his lap.

"They're mine now, Shard," Tiny said. "You try to take my stuff, and you'll end up worse than Collier. The damn fool could've gotten us all killed."

"You'll pay one day," Shard said, his teeth gritted in anger. "There'll be an accounting, Tiny, for the deaths you've caused, the food you took from the sick, everything."

"We'll all have our stories to tell, Shard," Tiny said. "Like how you managed to stay Section Leader after the list was found. Makes a guy wonder who snitched."

Shard sprang at Tiny, launching himself from a crouch, a low growl coming from his snarling lips. All the rage that had been tamped down since he was captured, all the anger at being forced into this role, it all came out straight at Tiny. Then he was on him, pummeling him with his fists, but it only lasted a few seconds. Tiny was too strong, too powerful. He tossed him off his chest like Shard was nothing but a rag doll.

"Stay away from me, Shard, I'm warning you," Tiny said, wiping blood off his lip. "I'm not going to fight you, not when you have Yuan in your corner. After we get out of here, anytime. But not with your Red pals protecting you."

"What's going on?" Skitter said as he entered the hut. Shard sucked in air as he got up, his bruised chest aching.

"He's stealing . . . Diekman's stuff," Shard managed as he gasped for breath. He didn't mention Tiny's accusation. It rang too true. At times it did seem like Yuan favored him. Any other section leader found with contraband in his hut would have been severely punished. Beaten. Thrown in the pen.

"How's Collier?" Skitter asked, casting a nervous glance in Tiny's direction.

"Ribs are busted," Shard said. "Time will tell how bad." He went and sat next to Collier, checking him for other injuries. His face was swollen, but there were no obvious wounds to worry about. Collier opened his one good eye and beckoned Shard closer.

"Diekman," Collier whispered. "Lester Diekman."

"Lester Diekman," Shard repeated in a low voice. They clasped hands, Shard smiling at the pleasure it gave him to know Collier was still game. One way or the other, the list was getting out.

A few minutes later, Shard went into the cooking area, saying he was getting water for Collier. He slipped his hand into the heating duct and was surprised to find the tin of sardines where he'd left it. Why did the guards overlook such a predictable hiding place, yet discover the list inside the wall?

That night, Shard fed Collier half the sardines, then passed around one per man, even Tiny. He drizzled the oil on their rice and turnip chop chop and wondered why again. Why hadn't a guard simply pocketed the sardines for himself? Why did Yuan choose that moment for a search? Why was he still a section leader?

Why all of it? Why everything? Why did his father beat them? Why didn't his mother say something before she lit the fire? Why had they taken Bobbie away?

Why? It was too hard of a question. The answers were even harder.

Chapter 18

April 18, 1953
Camp Eleven, North Korea

"It's no good," Skitter said. "Yuan wouldn't see me, and the guards kicked me around until they got bored." He sat next to Shard on the log outside their hut. A full moon hung in the clear night sky, bright enough to read by.

"You're a progressive, Skitter," Shard said. "Why won't your comrade see you?"

"I don't know," Skitter said. "I said I wanted to ask about Cooper. Maybe he's in no mood to talk."

"Glad you tried, anyway."

"Yeah. Poor Cooper."

"That would make two Coopers lost in Korea," Shard said. "A sergeant and a lieutenant, both killed in POW camps. There ought to be some justice for that, don't you think?"

"Sure," Skitter agreed. "But that's not going to happen. It's not like the last war, where we won and put people on trial."

"No. Probably the only ones put on trial will be guys like us," Shard said, gazing at the starry night. "Guys who signed petitions and gave aid and comfort to the enemy."

"Hell, we were forced to," Skitter said.

"Maybe. Maybe we shouldn't have given in so quickly."

"Diekman didn't give in," Skitter said. "And he's dead. There's a lesson there, pal."

Shard didn't reply. He inhaled deeply, drawing the cool night air into his lungs. The faint aroma of fried fish rose in his nostrils.

March 1952
Camp Eleven, North Korea

Shard walked alone past the sergeants' compound. He sighted Kelso and slowed as he approached the wire. "Hey, Shirt," he said in greeting.

"Shard," Kelso nodded in return, flapping his arms to keep warm. It was way below zero, icy cold with a Siberian wind that hadn't stopped blowing since January. Unlike last winter, the Chinese allowed wood gathering and fires for warmth. They even distributed blankets. But in this severe cold, men still died in their sleep, frozen stiff by morning.

"Is it true?" Shard asked, trudging through the knee-deep snow parallel to the fence.

"Yep," Kelso said. "Yuan came in himself. Told us to end the strike, that there'd be no more mandatory indoctrination classes."

"Damn," Shard said. "So all you did was refuse to attend?"

"Timing, Shard. It was all timing. The army has our names, so the Chinese need to return a reasonable number of us when this thing is over. Last year, we would have been shot. Anyway, Yuan's probably happy to stay in his warm office instead of trying to teach us the finer points of Marxism. Said we were hopeless, reactionary running dogs."

"I'd take that as a compliment. I wish some of my guys were as hopeless."

"He said there'd be voluntary classes for the enlisted men. Think he'll have many takers?"

"I could name a few," Shard said, moving away as he came to the corner of the wire. "See you later." Shard continued down the road, slick with the icy footprints of POWs who had searched this area for firewood. He kept to the road, which had been denuded of wood long ago. The snow was too deep to go cross-country. The rubber sole Chinese sneakers weren't much use either. They were better than nothing on hardpack, but out here the snow went over the tops, soaking his two pairs of socks, and freezing his feet.

Skitter had traded for boots. The Koreans and Chinese had stripped most guys of their combat boots, but a few of the newer POWs arrived with most of their clothing intact. But none of them would trade; good boots were the most valuable commodity in camp, and they tended to stay on the owner's feet. Skitter had traded most of the stuff in the one and only Red Cross parcel they'd received last Christmas and made a series of good deals. He'd swapped food for a pocketknife a POW named Schuman had been able to keep hidden. Then the pocketknife went to a crooked guard, who probably stole another guard's American boots for the trade. The Camp Eleven economy was a case study in capitalism.

And cruelty. Schuman had been sent to the turnip hole, probably for his part in the trade. And he was still in it. He froze to death one night and the guards ordered his hutmates to fill in the hole. None of his pals had any idea why he'd been thrown in. As far as Shard could tell, they knew nothing about a trade. Only Skitter was in on the deal, and he came out with a good pair of boots while Schuman got a raw turnip six feet under. Skitter had come up smelling like a rose, or as close to a rose as Camp Eleven had ever seen, too many times. Was he lucky? No. A guy who got himself captured wasn't lucky by definition.

So what *was* Skitter?

For that matter, what was Shard? Comrade Yuan's favorite section leader. A dubious distinction. There were rumors about him, he knew. One was that he'd betrayed the list and gotten Diekman killed. Guys from the early days with Bak had talked about Collier getting beaten for collecting the first set of names and had questioned how Shard managed to keep his post.

Shard stopped, a plume of frosted breath his only company. Off in the woods, he spotted a downed branch. It looked like deadwood, worth going into the heavy snow for. He climbed down into an icy drainage ditch, then struggled into the woods, shuffling through the snow cover. Fluffy, at least. The wind bit at his back, whistling through the branches, broken twigs littering the whiteness. Shard's foot caught on a log, or a rock buried beneath the snow, sending him reeling forward. His head hit something hard, and stars swirled in a dizzy pattern above his head. He rolled over, tried to get up, and saw drops of deep red blood in the snow. He touched his forehead, his fingers coming away sticky. He pressed snow to his head, cleaning himself up as best he could, icing the bruise, conscientiously keeping the blood off his gloves. Gloves were precious, almost life itself out in this sub-zero cold.

Shard squatted on his knees, applying snow to the wound until he saw only traces of pink. He wished he had brought

Skitter along. Skitter watched out for him, was always there when he needed help. Skitter had saved his life, for god's sake, back in the Mining Camp when dysentery nearly killed him. Soup. Sick rations for the whole group. And on that first march, when he'd all but given up, he'd been fed soup by Father Cadars; soup that Skitter had finagled.

Shard sat in the snow, staring at his gloved hands, realizing he was arguing with himself.

Shard finally rose, his legs shaky and his stomach in knots. He tried to break the deadwood, but only managed a few pieces before he vomited. Acidic bile ate at his throat as he doubled over and retched again. The argument was over.

Chapter 19

"We need to talk," Shard said to Skitter. "Where no one can listen."

"What's wrong with right here?" Skitter said. They were back sitting on the log outside their hut. The wood was shiny and cold, worn down by months of sitting, watching, and waiting. Moonlight cast long shadows across the camp. It loomed huge in the night sky, surrounded by a blaze of stars.

"No. I don't want someone coming out and hearing us. Come with me," Shard said, standing and waiting for Skitter.

"Jeez, Shard, I've been following you around camp all day," Skitter said. "I'm tired of it."

"Let's go," Shard said. "It's important."

"Okay," Skitter sighed as he got up. "Where?"

"The recreation hall," Shard said, and began walking.

"We're not supposed to go in there alone," Skitter said, jogging to stay with Shard. "You know that."

"Hey, I'm a section leader, and you're one of Yuan's prize progressives," Shard said. "That ought to buy us something."

"Yeah, well I didn't spend all that time listening to Yuan to blow it at the last minute," Skitter said, checking the area for guards. "They're saying Little Switch could start any day now."

"Any idea who else is getting out?" Shard asked as they approached the door to the rec hall. He laid his hand on the latch, waiting for Skitter.

"Ferguson is," Skitter said in a whisper, glancing around to be sure they hadn't been spotted. Ferguson was in the hospital, running a high fever. The Chinese would be glad to get him off their hands. "Me and Richards, that's all from this camp." Richards was another progressive, and in good health, as most of them were.

"I thought Operation Little Switch was for the sick," Shard said. There were other sick POWs the Reds could have chosen. Shard knew two guys, one with beriberi and the other wasting away from an undiagnosed illness. Neither would last without medical treatment.

"Hey, this is only one camp. They're probably sending more sick guys from the other camps. We going inside or what?" Skitter hugged himself against the cold, his legs jittering in place as he waited. Shard took his time answering.

"Yeah," Shard said. "We're going in." He opened the door.

"What's so hush-hush?" Skitter asked.

Shard walked to a table near the window and sat. He motioned for Skitter to take the chair across from him. "Sit down," he said, hard, between clenched teeth.

"Shard, I'm getting fed up with this," Skitter said, taking a step back. His eyes took in the darkened room, searching for a reason as to why they were there. The red silk banners hanging from the rafters rippled in the breeze from the doorway.

"Sit," Shard said, tapping his finger on the table. Moonlight streamed through the window, his hand silvery in the night's radiance.

"What?" Skitter said, sliding into the chair, his weight only half on it, ready to bolt at any second. His voice was sharp, irritated. He wasn't often that way with Shard, but tonight he was worried, maybe even scared.

"I know," Shard said, the words like a sigh from deep within him.

"You know what?" Skitter said, leaning forward, his voice low even though it was only the two of them.

"I know it all, Skitter. I know what you've done." Images of betrayals flashed across his mind, the beatings and the deaths, all revisited on the long walk around the camp that began this morning.

"What?" Skitter spread his arms and laughed. "What have I done?" His eyes darted back and forth, and Shard felt a childhood memory wash over him, the fear as fresh as it had been to the six-year-old Ethan. When he was accused by Pa of some misdeed, he played it the same way. Buying time, trying to figure out what Pa knew and what he didn't, his mind racing to make sure he didn't reveal anything Pa hadn't found out about.

But this was North Korea, not an Ohio farm. It wasn't broken windows or skipped chores.

"You kept yourself alive," Shard said. "At any cost."

"Yeah?" Skitter said, sarcasm edging out the fear in his voice. "You're alive too, Shard."

"I know," Shard said, nodding his head solemnly. "But you had your reasons, didn't you? You needed me to watch out for you, to make sure you were protected."

"Shard, this is your buddy Skitter you're talking to. What's come over you, pal?"

"We aren't buddies, Skitter," Shard said, slamming his palm down on the table. "We aren't pals. We're criminals. We stole from the army and made a lot of money selling to gangsters. We both brought our talents to the table and made a lot of dough. I was a damned fool."

"I thought we *were* pals," Skitter said, sitting back in his chair. "We're not? I saved your goddamn life, Shard, you remember that?"

"Yeah, I remember. I remember the soup you got from Major Bak on the march. For both of us."

"Right. You were half dead, but I convinced Bak that he needed you. And that I was the guy to look after you."

"I've thought about that soup a lot," Shard said. "It's amazing that you talked a bastard like Bak into doling out soup to a couple of POWs."

"It saved your life, Shard, let's leave it at that."

"The next day, Bak went after Collier and found the list he'd started. Remember the mock execution? How do you think Bak knew about the list?"

"I don't know." Skitter's voice was soft, his eyes downcast.

"Remember Miller and Lefkowicz, the two tankers? I wondered for years who'd informed on them. I should have checked back then and found out who else they told about the new Pershings. Far as I know, it was just you and me."

"Is that why you brought them up today with those other tankers? What is this, an inquisition?"

"No," Shard said, "more of a trial. I've been watching you all day, Skitter. You're a nervous guy in general. Lots of energy to burn, always ready to go. But you were real jittery whenever we talked about what happened to those tankers."

"I'm not nervous now," Skitter said, folding his arms across his chest. He leaned back, his leg vibrating as he tapped his heel.

"Kelso and Cooper," Shard said. "Your big catch. You told Wong about Kelso in the Mining Camp. Then you saw Coop was there, too, and turned him in. Did you know they were going to kill him?"

"Shard," Skitter said. "How can you believe that?"

"Sick rations for the whole group," Shard said. "You'd smartened up by then. Took the focus off you. All that bullshit about Bak, then Wong, and now Yuan wanting me as a section leader. It wasn't them. It was you. You wanted me in charge, so I'd watch your back. Like today. You didn't want me in the pen, so you squealed on Lieutenant Cooper. Made a nice deal with Yuan, then pretended to intervene with him."

"Yuan wouldn't see me," Skitter said, a touch of panic entering his voice. "I told you."

"You came back smelling of fried fish," Shard said, leaning forward and sniffing the air, letting Skitter know he had the goods on him. "All those times you went alone to see the Reds, you were informing and getting fed for it. That's why you kept weight on. It wasn't your metabolism. If anything, a high-strung guy like you needs more food, not less. And you found a way to get it."

"I didn't do any of those things," Skitter said, his eyes wide with disbelief, unable to take in his best friend turning on him. "I saved your life at the Mining Camp. Dysentery would have killed you. You needed those extra rations, you needed to live!"

"Yes," Shard said. "Yes. God forgive me, I wanted to live. I can still taste that soup, feel it filling my belly with warmth. I didn't ask questions. I didn't want to." They sat, facing each other across the moonlit table, neither man moving. "But a part of me always knew." Shard felt his heart ache. For how much it hurt him to understand what Skitter had done, as well as the hurt of being used, of being an unwitting pawn.

"Shard, we're a team," Skitter said, his voice almost breaking.

"What about Schuman? You told Yuan about the jackknife, didn't you? For a pair of boots. What did that have to do with us being a team?"

"I gave you a pair of socks," Skitter whispered, his head bowed down. Shard had to gulp to hold back tears of pity. Skitter was acting like a child, his voice sweet and low, as if socks answered all questions. Shard could see Bobbie in that pose, head hanging low and on the verge of crying. But he didn't offer comfort.

"Did you know they were going to kill Coop?" Shard said, bringing the conversation back to the Mining Camp, reminding himself that men had died for Skitter's deeds.

"I didn't know anything," Skitter said. "I just got soup for you."

"Maybe you didn't. Maybe you didn't see Coop right away. When you told Wong that Kelso was really a sergeant, you saw them take him away, a little beat up, but alive. Then you saw Coop, so you figured Wong would reward you for another sergeant. What could it hurt, right? But things didn't go as planned. They pulled Coop out of there and shot him dead."

"You needed soup," Skitter said, rubbing his eyes, his fingers coming away moist.

"You didn't mean for Coop to be killed, I believe that much," Shard said.

"No," Skitter said, tears flowing down his cheeks as he choked back a sob. "It was for us, so we could make it. We're a team, remember?"

"I remember," Shard said, feeling like he'd been kicked in the gut. Even though he'd been sure about Skitter for some time, it was a shock to hear it from his own lips. Part of him had wished Skitter would explain it all away, convince him he was wrong, that it was one big misunderstanding. He wished Skitter had argued, become angry, struck out at him, any of the things an innocent man might do. Instead, he had wept.

So it was true. Skitter had blood on his hands.

"But why betray the list again? The first time, I get it. We might have died on that march, and it was only a few names. But why the last time? You could have gotten Collier killed."

"It was Yuan," Skitter said, his voice nearly a wail. "He told me I was the one who'd end up in a prison camp back in China for the rest of my life if I didn't cooperate. He's always known about the first list, and he's been pressuring me ever since the name exchange to make sure there wasn't another one."

"Skitter, those names. Over four hundred of our guys. How could you?"

"They're dead, goddammit!" Skitter hissed, gripping the edge of the table, his body trembling. "I don't care about them. I want to go home. Alive."

"So the list was your ticket out."

"Yeah," Skitter exhaled. "Yuan told me to be sure there wasn't another copy. That's why I've been asking."

"There isn't," Shard said, his voice soothing and calm, drawing Skitter out. "What did you tell him?"

"Same thing," Skitter answered. Shard leaned forward and stared into his eyes. "Really."

"Coop and Schuman dead," Shard said. "Miller and Lefty probably dead after interrogation. Coop's cousin in the pen, probably until he dies. The list betrayed. What else, Skitter? What else have you done?"

"You can't tell anyone, Shard, please," Skitter said, folding his hands as if in prayer. "They'll kill me if they find out." He hadn't answered the question, which meant there had to be more. Shard decided he didn't need to know. Didn't want to know. But how many others had Skitter informed on? What other deaths had he caused? How many men had gone in the turnip hole, beheld Doctor Bayonet, or died a lonely death in the pen?

"I haven't told anyone, Skitter." That seemed to calm him. Skitter looked at Shard, his eyes gleaming with tears.

"I've been so afraid, Shard," Skitter said, the words tumbling out. "Yuan hounds me every day, and I worry about the guys finding out. I'm dead either way if I screw up."

"That's what happens when you make a deal with the devil," Shard said. "What did you expect?"

"I only wanted to stay alive," Skitter moaned. "What are you going to do? You're not going to rat me out to the guys, are you?"

Shard sat silently, hands in his lap. They twisted and turned, fingers grasping at each other as if struggling to see which hand came out on top. Other than his mother and his kid brother, he'd never been as close to anyone as Skitter. But Skitter was more like Pa than he ever thought. Not outright mean like Pa, but he caused as much hurt.

More. And Shard had watched the fire consume Pa and never missed him for a second.

"No," Shard said, shaking his head. Skitter begging not to be ratted out sickened him, but he kept his voice calm. It was time. "But there's something you have to do. You have to refuse repatriation."

"What?"

"You're a progressive, you'll do well. It won't be a prison camp; they'll treat you like royalty."

"No, I'm due to be released any day now," Skitter said, holding up his hand, like Shard didn't get it.

"If you don't agree, I tell the whole camp what you've done." Shard laid his hands on the table. The fight was over. He wished Skitter had taken a different path, but he hadn't, and this is where it had led them both.

"No. No," Skitter cried. "They'll tear me to pieces."

"Exactly." The hardness was back in Shard's voice.

"I don't believe it, Shard. I can't go to Red China. What would my folks think? They're decent people, nothing like me. It would kill them. Please tell me you don't mean it."

"I do mean it."

"This is a joke, right? You want me to understand what I've done wrong," Skitter said, brightening now that he thought he'd figured the angle. "I do, Shard, I really do. I'm sorry."

"I'm not your big brother, Skitter," Shard said. "And I'm not the chaplain. It's no joke. This is what you have to do."

"Why me? Why not you? You took the soup, didn't you? You knew!" Skitter stood, his body quivering, his mouth twisted and eyes wide.

"I figured things out," Shard said. "Too late. But it was you who set everything in motion. There's a line, Skitter. I don't pretend to know where it is, but I know you crossed it. And you used me."

"I kept us both alive," Skitter said.

"I'll remember the price other men paid for the rest of my life," Shard said. They sat in silence, alone in the moonlight, memories both good and terrible drifting through their minds.

Shard rose and walked to a desk, bringing back a sheet of paper and a pencil. "If you want to write to your folks, go ahead. I'll deliver it to them myself. Go on. Write their address out, and I'll hand deliver it." He set the paper and pencil in front of Skitter and placed a hand on his shoulder. Gave a reassuring squeeze.

"You won't say anything about the other stuff?" He wiped his sleeve against his nose, cleaning away tears and snot. Shard knew Skitter well. He was quick to agree, but he'd try and find a way out later. A way to skitter out of trouble.

Not this time.

"I promise, not a word to anyone," Shard said. That much he owed him.

"Okay." Skitter wrote out his parents' names and address in Lewiston, Michigan, then stopped, his hand hovering over the page. "I don't know what to say to them."

"Tell them you're sorry," Shard whispered, his hand resting on Skitter's shoulder. "How very sorry you are."

Skitter craned his neck back and smiled at Shard. "Good idea." He took a deep breath and began to write, lead scratching against coarse paper.

Shard watched from behind, the slanting rays of moonlight casting his long shadow over the table. Skitter bent to the task, a schoolchild facing a tough assignment. As he wrote, Shard murmured *good, good*, nodding his head in rhythm to the soothing words, patting him on the shoulder. *Good, good.*

He lifted his hand from Skitter's shoulder and swung it across his throat, hitting Skitter's Adam's apple hard. He dug his right elbow into Skitter's shoulder and pushed against the back of his head with his right palm. Then grabbing his right arm with his left hand, like Kelso had taught them back in Japan, with one sharp push of the hand, Skitter's neck broke.

The pencil still in his hand.

Shard watched himself kill Skitter, as if someone else were in the room doing what had to be done. When it was over, he gently rested Skitter's head on the table and patted his hair, just as he had done for Bobbie so many times when the yelling and tears were done, and they were alone. But this was different. There would be no tomorrow for Skitter, no bright morning sun to cleanse the nighttime fears. All that remained was some measure of justice for Skitter's victims. For Shard, who had felt the betrayal like a knife in the ribs.

He took the sheet of paper and carefully folded and refolded it until he could tear off the address and salutation in a neat straight line. He pocketed it and left the rest on the table.

I am so sorry.

Hoisting Skitter's body onto the table and climbing up, he grabbed the nearest hanging banner. He twisted the silk fabric until it was tight, then knotted it in several places. He tied it around Skitter's neck, holding the body as high as he could.

He let go. Skitter's feet, still in the boots he had traded Schuman's life for, rested on the tabletop. Shard moved the table away, leaving Skitter dangling two feet above the floor.

I am so sorry.

Chapter 20

August 11, 1953
Freedom Village, Munsan-ni, South Korea

The big Russian-made Molotov truck rumbled up to the triple-arched Freedom Gate and screeched to a halt. Shard pushed back the gray canvas flap, released the tailgate, and jumped down to help Collier out. North Korean guards stood by, rifles shouldered. Yards beyond them was the gate. The big prisoner exchange was on, and after days of waiting, it was their turn.

Bell gave Shard a hand with Collier. His ribs hadn't healed right, and the jump would have left him gasping. Tiny hit the ground in a long leap and pushed ahead of the others, indifferent to those who needed a hand. He walked straight to the gate and the waiting American soldiers.

"I can't believe it," Collier said, placing his arm around Shard's shoulder, out of joy as much as support.

"I know," Shard said. "I thought it might be a trick." Some POWs whooped for joy, others cried, still others stood in stunned silence. Shard urged them to move through the gates. They weren't on safe ground yet. Shard and Collier waited until everyone from the truck had gone through, then followed. Shard threw his blue cap in the air, leaving it behind.

Inside the gate, an army general shook their hands. Shard thought it a nice gesture but didn't give a hoot who it was. Rows of tents were ready for them, and an army band played as they formed a line for a quick medical check. Anyone needing immediate treatment was separated out. For everyone else, it was hot showers.

They tossed their blue jackets and trousers in a pile, stripped down, and headed into the showers. It was the first steam many of them had felt in three years. Collier carried a burlap bag with him and hung it on a hook as he stepped into the shower.

Shard held the soap in his hand as if it were magical, maybe even dangerous. The smell was overpowering. The smell of clean. More towels. Dopp kits for all. Collier removed a box of tooth powder from his burlap bag and tossed the bag aside.

"Hey, bud," a corporal said. "You don't need to keep that crap, we got real toothpaste, everything you need."

"It's a souvenir," Collier said as he and Shard exchanged knowing glances. The list had made it out.

They were given slippers, soft robes, haircuts, dental and physical exams. A lounge held chairs, magazines, newspapers, snacks, and ice cream. Shard pocketed the snacks, but soon quit. He didn't have pockets deep enough. New fatigues were issued, with tailors on hand to take in even the smaller sizes to fit POW frames. Ex-POWs.

Mail was issued, some guys leaving with a bundle of letters and parcels. There was nothing for Shard, not that he expected any. He sat in a chair, listening to soft music over the loudspeaker, drinking a Coke. He looked at his hands. Clean. Then he remembered Skitter. His suicide had surprised everyone. No one thought he was the type. He had to agree.

He didn't regret what he'd done. He only wished he had woken up to it sooner. He'd turned a blind eye to the truth, but all that had done was make things worse for everyone and delay the inevitable. And made it more painful to live with. Never again, he vowed to himself.

Tiny sat across from him.

"They're already asking things," Tiny said. "Like who worked with the Reds, that sort of stuff."

"So?" Shard said.

"Best if you keep your mouth shut about any differences we had. Otherwise, I'm going to remember lots of ways you and your progressive pal Skitter cozied up to the Commies. Maybe the newspapers would like to hear about all the guys he ratted out. You, too, for that matter. You two were so close you had to be in on it. I could make things real hard for you. Collier, too."

"Differences?" Shard said, still amazed at the term, hinting of a slight disagreement. "Like when you killed Sparks by throwing him in the river?"

"Yeah," Tiny said, standing and looming over Shard. "Stuff like that."

Chapter 21

August 13, 1953
Inchon, South Korea

Following repatriation at Freedom Village, the former POWs were taken to Inchon to await the voyage home. They were housed in barracks near the docks where they signed more paperwork and received additional medical care. Collier and Shard discussed what they should do with the list and decided to wait for the chance to give it to a more senior officer rather than the fresh-faced second lieutenants they'd been paraded in front of.

After morning chow, they were told to pack their duffle bags and be ready for departure. The USS General Brewster was about to ship out to the states carrying over three hundred freed POWs.

Shard and Collier stood in line, their duffle bags thrown over their shoulders. It was a warm, sunny day, the smell of oil and rotting fish ripe in the August air. The rising tide slapped against the docks as gulls sliced through the air.

"I hear we're going to be debriefed on board," Collier said. "Maybe we can find the right guy to give the list to."

"CIC, I heard," Shard said. The Counter Intelligence Corps. Army intelligence would want to know how the Red

Chinese operated the camps. "They seem to think we've all been brainwashed."

"Whatever that's supposed to mean," Collier laughed. They'd heard the term thrown around ever since Freedom Village, but no one could tell them exactly what it meant. The line shuffled along, moving closer to the gangplank. Ahead of them were a table and a gaggle of officers.

"Has Tiny talked to you?" Shard asked as they got closer to the table.

"You mean has he threatened me?" Collier said. "Yeah. Told me to keep my mouth shut if I knew what was good for me."

"Same thing here. I'd hate to see him get away with everything he's done," Shard said.

"He told me what he'd say," Collier whispered. "That you cooperated with the Reds as a section leader. Said he'd get you court-martialed and tell the world how Skitter killed himself." When Skitter had been found that morning, the POWs had decided to report he'd died of illness, to spare his family a more terrible grief. "He also said he'd accuse me of being a collaborator, that I did it to save the list. Can you believe that shit?"

"Tiny only looks out for Tiny," Shard said.

"It's not right," Collier said. "If he accuses me, the army might not believe the list is real."

"There's gotta be a way," Shard said, half to himself. It was their turn at the table.

"Here you go, Private," a second lieutenant said, handing Shard a form. "Sign on the dotted line and get on board."

"What am I signing?" Shard said, reading through the formal language of army security.

"It's your promise not to reveal any information concerning the terms of your imprisonment," the lieutenant stated. "Under penalty of imprisonment and fine."

"What the hell . . . sir? Doesn't the army want the world to know what went on in those camps?"

"Soldier, if you have a problem with this, step out of line. We have a team of investigators who will be glad to address your concerns. When we are satisfied with your answers, you can await the next ship." The lieutenant leaned back and lit a cigarette.

"Sign or stay in Korea and be interrogated until hell freezes over?" Shard said.

"Basically," the lieutenant said. Shard signed on the dotted line and set the paper down on top of a Hershey bar that might have been the second louie's lunch. It went into his pocket in one smooth move. He climbed the gangplank, recalling that a couple of days ago he'd vowed never again to turn away from the truth.

Goodbye Korea.

Chapter 22

August 15, 1953
Aboard the USS Brewster, North Pacific Ocean

The sound of carpentry greeted them when they boarded. Along the main deck, a series of six-foot by six-foot cubicles were being built. As the ship pulled out of Inchon harbor a group of officers came on deck to watch the work. Majors and captains, all with the Counter Intelligence insignia on their khaki uniforms.

"What the hell is all this for?" Collier asked.

"Looks like we're not through with interrogations quite yet," Shard said.

By the second day at sea the cubicles were finished. Each had two chairs, a table, and a CIC officer waiting inside. Shard and Collier stood together in the early morning, waiting for their turn. Collier pulled the list from his fatigue jacket pocket. He smoothed out the creases, reading through the names that had become part of him over the last thirty-six months.

"You did it, Collier," Shard said. "There's a measure of comfort there for a lot of families."

"We did it," Collier said, and put the list away. They were beckoned forward; their turn had come.

"Private Ethan Shard," the CIC major said, reviewing a folder. "You were in a long time, captured the first month of the war."

"Yes, sir," Shard said, uncertain what the expected response was.

"We've been hearing a lot about progressives, reactionaries, brainwashing, that sort of thing. Were those terms used in your camp?"

"I never heard of brainwashing until I got out. The Chinese called some guys progressives, others, reactionaries. Depending on how well they paid attention to their classes."

"Did you pay attention?"

"Everyone had to pay attention, Major. What you were called depended on your level of enthusiasm."

"Tell me about the more enthusiastic POWs."

"You mean rat out my fellow soldiers," Shard said.

"Says here you were a section leader," the major said. "You must have been a progressive yourself to get that post."

"No, sir. I was told to be a section leader. There was no choice."

"Tell me about the men in your section. The sooner you cooperate, the sooner you can be cleared," the major said.

"Cleared of what exactly?"

"Suspicion, Private. Suspicion of colluding with the enemy. Of being brainwashed. So start by telling me about the men in your section, if that's the right Marxist terminology."

"You know, I met a guy like you in camp. His name was Yuan."

"Perhaps you are confused about which side is which, Private Shard. Now tell me about the other men. Who were the progressives?"

It went like that all day. Shard told him about the death marches, the turnip hole, the fire at the Mining Camp, the pen, all the brutalities, and injustices. He didn't mention Tiny. He needed to figure that one out. The response was always the same.

"Who cooperated? Who were the progressives?"

The day ended with threats of further sessions and a possible court-martial. The CIC major was good, never got angry, never missed a beat. Shard's biggest disappointment was that there wasn't anything to eat or steal in the little cubicle.

He wandered over to the fantail. The rear deck of the ship had been set aside exclusively for the former POWs to use. Some guys sunned themselves, others slept in the shade. Shard found Collier leaning against the rail, staring out to sea.

"How'd it go?" Shard asked.

"We played name the progressive all day," Collier said. "It's all he cared about. Brainwashing and who worked with the Reds. They don't give a crap what we went through. And now the world will never know unless we want to do time in Leavenworth." Everyone had signed away their right to talk about what had gone on in the camps. No one wanted to stay in Korea one minute longer.

"Same thing with my guy," Shard said, leaning on the rail. "Funny that I didn't want to give him names of progressives I would have spit on in camp."

"Yeah," laughed Collier. "Not quite how I imagined it."

"But you gave him the list," Shard said.

"I tried," Collier said. He pulled the list from his pocket, letting it flutter in the brisk Pacific breeze. "Know what he said? He didn't have time for all those names. Told me to put it away."

They both watched the edges of the flapping papers, trying to work their way out of Collier's grip. Finally, he put them back in his pocket. "Aw, hell," he muttered, and walked away.

It was past midnight, and Shard couldn't sleep. Nothing made sense. They had struggled to keep the list safe, chanted the names of the dead, all for nothing. Or did he have it the wrong way around? Maybe the list had kept them alive. Maybe the army and the government didn't deserve the list. So who did? Thoughts swirled through his mind until he felt he'd explode.

He got out of his bunk and walked out to the fantail in his socks and skivvies, needing fresh air and the sound of something else besides snoring and his own blood pounding in his head. The ship's running lights were on, but it was still dark. No moon, but plenty of stars. He walked out onto the empty deck, trying to make sense of how things had ended up. He didn't have much luck.

Ahead, at the end of the fantail, just above the propellers, he spied the glow of a cigarette. The form of a man took shape as he drew closer, a big man in fatigues and boots. Tiny.

He pulled on the cigarette, and the glow lit the side of his face. Tiny for sure. Shard stopped, not certain he wanted to be on this deserted deck with someone so unpredictable, big, and violent. Then he decided to try talking to Tiny, man-to-man, even though he knew it was next to useless. He moved forward, the wind whistling through the railings and wires. Would he let Tiny get away with his crimes? Would he let him ruin Collier after all he'd done to keep the list safe? Would he let Tiny tell Skitter's parents their son committed suicide?

The answer kept coming up *no*.

He was five feet away when Shard realized that Tiny hadn't heard him, hadn't sensed his approach.

He had one second to decide.

He saw the answer in Tiny's strength, the broad shoulders, the very weight of the man resting his elbows on the ship's rail, gazing into the darkness.

Tiny, who had taken from the weak. Stolen from and betrayed his fellow prisoners. Murdered them, like when he threw Sparks into the freezing water.

Tiny, whose threats still hung over them, the living and the dead.

Tiny flicked the cigarette away, the bright glow vanishing in the gloom.

Shard took two steps and grabbed Tiny by the ankles, lifted him, and heaved his weight over the rail. Tiny's bootheels vanished in the dark, falling into the churning wake. Without even a cry or a splash.

Shard took a deep breath and gripped the rail, waiting a few seconds.

"Man overboard," he said into the wind. And walked away.

Chapter 23

October 1953
The Skinner residence
Lewiston, Michigan

Shard had been interrogated several more times on the Brewster, but nothing had come of it. Tough talk from an army cop who'd never seen real action or spent a single night on the wrong side of the bars, but nothing more. The army had nothing on him.

Collier had given Shard his address in Connecticut and said to drop by one day. He promised he'd keep the list close to him, as he always had, until he figured out what to do with it. Shard told Collier he'd stay in touch, then they'd shaken hands one last time, and Collier had turned away. Shard crumpled the paper and stuffed it in his pocket. Some memories are best faded like an old snapshot, a blurry reminder of a bond when it was at its strongest.

After a few days in San Diego, the army mustered Shard out with a wad of back pay, boots and shoes, his Class A uniform and fatigues. He took the bus into town, gave the uniforms to a thrift shop, and bought some civilian clothes. He kept the boots. They'd come in handy where he was headed.

He walked to the nearest used car lot he could find and bought a blue 1950 Chevy truck. It had less than 22,000 miles on it, and Shard liked the idea that it had been new when he was captured. It was like time had stood still, except for those thousands of miles. Sort of like him. Still humming along, lots of roads left to explore, and abandoned by former owners. It was perfect.

He had no idea what the truck was worth but made a counteroffer to not look like a rube. The salesman agreed so quickly, Shard knew he should have lowballed it. While Shard was signing paperwork in his office, the salesman stepped out to talk to a customer. Shard swiped an orange from his desk.

The price didn't matter. He was on the road in a 1950 truck, a free man, with one obligation ahead of him. He took his time getting to Lewiston.

The trees were huge, and they were everywhere. Big pines that hid the sun and shaded the back roads that wound through dark and foreboding forests. There wasn't much traffic except for the big rigs with massive logs strapped to their truck beds thundering by, leaving a slipstream in their wake that needed both hands on the wheel to steer through.

He timed it to arrive on a Saturday. Good chance of finding both Mr. and Mrs. Skinner at home, and better than a Sunday since they might be at church or have family over. He found Wolf Lake Road and slowed until he came to the right number. Pulling into the driveway, he spotted a gray-haired man in a red checkered coat raking the leaves. There was something familiar in the angularity of the man, the way he moved, the crook of his head as he watched Shard park the truck. He got out, stretched, and walked over to where the fellow waited, leaning on his rake.

"Mr. Skinner?"

"Yep. What brings you all the way from California, young man?" Shard heard a tremble in his voice that told him Skitter's father might have put two and two together. A lean guy his own son's age, coming from the West Coast. Smart man. Read the angles like his boy.

"I knew your son, Mr. Skinner. We were pals in the POW camp." Shard knew he was breaking his vow about the truth, once again, but lies were so much kinder. He'd have to think about a new vow.

"Martha," the old man said, his voice hardly raised. "We have a visitor."

"What was it like?" Martha asked, once the coffee pot was on. "I mean, for Elliott, at the end?"

"Are you sure you want to know?" Fred Skinner asked, an eyebrow raised in Shard's direction. Meaning, don't tell her the truth.

"Skitter—Elliott—and I were together in Tokyo and got captured at the same time. We helped each other and our buddies as best we could. I won't lie and say it was easy. There were times we were real hungry. But we came through it okay by looking out for each other. It was close to the end when Elliott took sick. No one knew what it was. At first, we thought the flu or something. But one morning he was gone. It was peaceful, in his sleep."

"How terrible," Martha said. "But it's a comfort to know he didn't suffer. Elliott—we know he loved his nickname, don't worry about that—he wanted to see the world. At least he saw something of it. His letters were full of so much about life in Japan, he found it so interesting."

"He taught me a lot about Tokyo, sort of took me under his wing. We became close during those months, and I promised if anything happened that I'd come visit and give you his love. He spoke about you often." Had he ever? That last night, he did speak of his folks. Before then it had been nothing except for silence and curses about the backwoods life in northern Michigan.

"Thank you, Ethan," Martha Skinner said, reaching her hand across the kitchen table. "I'm sure Elliott would have done the same for you."

"Yes ma'am, I'm sure."

They drank coffee and ate homemade oatmeal raisin cookies. They asked Shard to stay the night, but he begged off, making up a friend in Flint he wanted to reach by dark. Martha began to cry and, looking embarrassed, excused herself.

"It's been hard on her," Fred Skinner said once they were alone in the kitchen. "All those months of not knowing, then hearing our boy was a prisoner, and later that he died. It took a toll, I'll tell you."

"I'm sorry you had to go through that," Shard said, sorry that he'd broken their hearts, wishing there had been some other way. But how else would there be justice for the dead?

"I'm sorry about what you boys had to go through," Fred said. "I know you sugarcoated that for Martha, and I'm glad you did. There's nothing to be accomplished by knowing too much about something you can't do a damn thing about."

"I agree completely," Shard said, standing to leave. More than you know. "Please give my regards to Mrs. Skinner."

"I will," Fred said. "Probably best to leave her be for a bit. Say, if you're looking for work after you see your friend, the sawmill outside of town is hiring. I know the foreman."

"Thanks, but no," Shard said, feeling unexpectedly emotional at the man's offer. The work would have been welcome, but the prospect of facing Skitter's father again was too much to bear. "I appreciate it, sir, but I have someplace to go."

"Where, Ethan?"

"Ohio," Shard said, pulling on his jacket. His arm went into the sleeve and reached behind Fred's back, snagging a can of tuna fish that sat on the counter. It went into his pocket in a flash as he stared into the older man's eyes. The intensity was a trick, a sleight of hand to distract Fred from the snatch.

"You have family there?" Fred said, stepping aside to let Shard pass.

"I hope so. I'm going to look for my brother."

∽∽∽

The End.

Author's Note

Of the 7,190 American servicemen captured during the Korean War, approximately 3,000 died in captivity. This mortality rate of 43% far exceeded the highest recorded death rate of American soldiers—34%—held in Japanese prisoner of war camps during World War II. Until Korea, capture by the Japanese was considered to have been the most horrendous of POW experiences. While official numbers and estimates vary, to be an Allied prisoner in North Korea was a terrible fate. The Korean War was the first conflict in which the opposing powers desired to convert the thinking of American POWs, not simply incarcerate them for the duration.

All descriptions of the brutality, terror, and physical and emotional tortures inflicted upon POWs in the Korean and Chinese camps have been drawn from historical records. While the story is fiction, the events within the narrative depicting life and death in the camps are real. This horror story is true.

After the war, the army brought court-martial charges against fourteen men for collaboration with the enemy and other crimes. Three were acquitted, the others convicted on varying charges, some for making the same speeches and signing the same documents as hundreds of others had done. The most serious charge—murder—was brought against

Private First-Class Rothwell Floyd, upon whom the character of Tiny was modeled. Acquitted of that charge, he served ten years for striking a superior officer and mistreatment of fellow POWs.

POWs were interrogated on their voyage home by the US Army to confirm the names of collaborators, as fear of Chinese "brainwashing" spread. The army required all POWs to sign documents promising not to disclose any information about their experiences during imprisonment by Communist forces, apparently to maintain secrecy concerning the degree of collaboration.

There was a list.

Private First-Class Wayne A. "Johnnie" Johnson kept a list, as Collier did in this book, eventually smuggling out 496 names of the dead inside a tube of toothpaste. While his interrogator did note the existence of the list in his debriefing file, he did not wish to accept it or act upon its existence. His reasons are unknown. It was not until 1995 that a Defense Prisoner of War/Missing Personnel Office (DPMO) analyst learned about Johnson's list while attending a POW reunion in Sacramento, California. After forty years, the army acted upon the information and published the list, kept safe all those decades by Johnnie Johnson. In 1996, he was awarded the Silver Star for valor. He died in 2011.